Stitches and

Sparks

Built to Last: Book One

E.A. Brady

Sandgate East Publishing

Contents

Dedication

To the friends who've said:
"We're proud of you. We love you. Let us support you in this!"
This one is for you.
I love you too.

A Note from the Author

Hello Friend,

Thank you for joining me on this romantic adventure. As an indie author, I recognize that your time is valuable, and I am deeply grateful that you've chosen to explore the pages of a world into which I've poured my heart and soul.

Want to know a secret? Storytelling is magic. It's the alchemy that transforms ink into dreams, and readers into fellow travelers. Together, we cross landscapes of desire, heartache, and hope.

Always hope.

And that's why I love what I do.

But here's the secret: **you** are the heartbeat of this journey. Your curiosity fuels my creativity. As an indie author, I don't have a corporate marketing machine behind me—I have *you*.

Thank you.

Can I be honest? I'm not a huge lover of social media. It's a whirlwind of posts, hashtags, and fleeting attention spans. Amidst the chaos of these digital currents, I want to extend an invitation to join me in a more intimate space—the ***Whispers and Works in Progress*** newsletter.

(Print readers – link can be found at eabradyauthor.com).

Here, you'll find exclusive sneak peeks, behind-the-scenes glimpses, and perhaps a few musings on life, love, and the writer's craft. No algorithms, no noise—just a direct line from my heart to yours.

Will you take this journey with me? Join me **here**!

(eabradyauthor.com).

With heartfelt gratitude,

E.A. Brady
xoxo

Indie Author & Fellow Dreamer

Welcome to Oak Harbor

Oak Harbor is a fictionalized mash up of a few of my favorite places in Maine. It showed up one day, fully formed, in my mind and I had no choice but to bring it to life.

This series will look a little bit different than a romance series usually does. Rather than follow members of the same family (brothers, sisters, cousins, etc.), the stories in this series are based around a family-owned construction company and will follow some family members and some employees.

Approaching the stories this way kept it fun for me to write and I hope it will be fun for you to read.

These stories do contain swearing (but that varies from character to character and book to book) and on-the-page sex scenes.

I tend to write low-stakes stories, which means there aren't really any trigger warnings. These characters have their own backstories, but generally nothing too tragic. I love to read and write escapist romantic fantasy stories.

Turn the page to get started with Jesse and Mia, the first couple you'll meet from this small New England town. Though it's the shortest of the books in this series, I hope you'll love them and their story as much as I do.

Jesse

TWO HOURS.

That's how long the doc told him the lidocaine *could* last.

Thirty-four minutes.

That's how long the lidocaine *did* last.

Pain thrummed through Jesse Murphy's right cheek. Again and again, he raised his fingers to feel the stitches that zigzagged down his jaw from just below his right ear.

Afraid of agitating the wound and potentially popping a stitch, he clutched the packets of non-stick bandages inside his hoodie pocket. *"Put on a little Vaseline to keep the skin soft. Then put this on before you go to bed,"* the doctor had said, as she handed him the bandages on his way out of the examining room. *"And don't get it wet for twenty-four hours."*

Thank God he'd already taken his post-fight shower.

The early spring day had been bitterly cold, as he and everyone else waited for the warmer weather to arrive. Now, as night fell, the chill seemed to settle deep into his bones, calling attention to all the places he'd taken hits. "I can't believe I didn't block that fucking elbow," he muttered, navigating through the crowds of pedestrians on Spring

Hills' main street. Making his way from the clinic to the bus stop, the cold sharpened his discomfort with each step.

The bus route from Spring Hills to Oak Harbor was still operational. He cursed himself with every stride for declining his cousin Danny's offer of a lift. Earlier, the thrill of victory had fueled him, but now, after a shower, an X-ray, and fifteen stitches in his face, the adrenaline had faded along right with the lidocaine.

All he craved was the comfort of home: a steak on his plate, cozy sweats on his body, and the familiar glow of the television to lull him to sleep.

"Dude, you all right?" A young man stopped in front of him, halting his group of friends mid-stride. Their expressions were a mix of concern and fear. One woman looked at Jesse the way people often did after a fight, a little bit of fear combined with barely concealed revulsion.

A swollen and freshly bruised face, complete with a line of fifteen stitches down the jaw had that effect on some people.

"I'm fine, man. Thanks," Jesse assured him, fingers wrapped around the bandage packet in his pocket. "I won by submission. It just took a little while to get there." He managed a pained smile, hoping to dispel their worries of him collapsing right there on the sidewalk.

A few nervous chuckles rippled through the group, but the young man nodded, accepting Jesse's word. "Alright then. Take care," he said, wishing Jesse a good night.

The group resumed their journey, likely heading to one of the eateries lining Spring Hill's main street, their large glass facades offering a view of the bustling scenes inside. The tantalizing aromas wafting through the frigid evening air had Jesse's stomach growling in jealousy as he passed by.

With each step, hunger gnawed at him, as did the lingering soreness from the fight. He trudged on, the bus stop only a couple of blocks away. Looking the way he did, most likely nobody would stop to help him if he just crashed on the sidewalk, so he pressed on. The bus would carry him the rest of the way home—he just had to reach it.

It was a Saturday night in early April, and Jesse had anticipated a crowd at the bus stop. Yet, he found himself alone, the sole passenger bound for Oak Harbor. The shelter, a three-walled plexiglass haven with a transparent roof, tempted him to sit on the wooden bench along the back wall. But Jesse knew better; giving in to the allure of the bench meant the potential to fall asleep and miss his ride home. So, he opted to lean against the wall of the enclosure, letting it bear his weight as he waited.

As he watched the bustling nightlife of couples and groups, Jesse's thoughts drifted to the stark changes in his life and in his body. Victory nights used to mean going out with the other fighters and a bunch of friends to get dinner and drinks, often finding someone to bring back to his place, but now, his body rebelled in silent protest, aching more and healing slower.

And while winning this fight was amazing, it didn't feel quite as amazing as it had when he first started.

In short, he was getting too old to keep doing this. The training was one thing—he could do that all day, every day. But the fighting? The actual sport of climbing into the ring and going toe-to-toe in full combat had lost its shine.

Jesus, how did thirty-two years old suddenly feel like a hundred and thirty-two?

His brothers had always been destined for the family construction business, while Jesse had carved a niche in mixed martial arts. The future used to be some far off time, not even a speck on a distant horizon. It didn't feel quite so far anymore as he stood under that plexiglass enclosure, worrying about what the hell to do next.

Perhaps it was time to accept his father's standing offer to join the family business. The thought of trading punches for blueprints had never appealed to him, yet now, it was starting to look as if the future had finally come knocking and Jesse was struggling to see another path forward.

Sunday dinner at his parents' house promised to be interesting this week, with his potential career shift about to become family lore.

Reaching into his pants pocket, he found the trinkets his nieces had given him as good luck charms for his fight. Chloe, the oldest, had given him an index card with her drawing of him standing over his defeated opponent. Her younger sister, Ava, had given him a stick, just in case he was up against a better fighter, and he might need it to poke the guy with. Rylee, their cousin, had given him a dime. She said it was lucky because she found it, therefore it would be lucky for him to carry it.

Thinking at how apt the gifts were to each of their personalities, Jesse couldn't help but smile. When a hard wind blew around him, he shoved his hands into the front pocket of his hoodie and stepped further back inside the shelter.

As the bus turned the corner, Jesse waited with relief for his diesel chariot to take him home.

Blowing out a hard breath, he looked up as the bus approached, and noticed dark brown eyes staring down at him. Immediately, the eyes snapped away, as their owner, a woman with what appeared to be a very pretty face, pretended she hadn't been looking at him.

Normally, it would have bothered him, but right then and there, he just didn't have it in him to care.

Mia

WHEN THE BUS DRIVER accelerated around the corner, Mia Reed's attention had been elsewhere. The jolt sent her head crashing against the window, adding insult to the injury of an already crappy night. "Son of a..." she muttered, massaging the tender spot that had quickly formed.

The first aid kit stuffed at the bottom of her bag was out of ibuprofen so she would have to wait until she got home to take anything to stop the budding headache.

Normally a solid way to relax, the book in her hand had been unable to keep her focus for more than two seconds. The attempted reconciliation between Mia and her sister earlier that night had been a dismal failure and it seemed it might never come to pass.

Why she thought they'd be able to reconcile, Mia didn't know. What Lauren had done was unforgivable as far as she was concerned, even if it had been almost a full year. So much for time healing all wounds.

Mia had been in Oak Harbor for the past eight months. The bridge to her past had burned after what her sister had done. The coastal town was her sanctuary, a place of new beginnings and establishing roots.

On her own. She didn't need her sister and she didn't need Brandon. They could have each other.

Embracing her new home meant it was time to establish some stability. First up: finding a permanent job for when her current contract ended. Next: finding a place she could call her own for the long haul.

Living by herself was fine if she had to, but what she really wanted was a dog. Dogs loved you just the way you were. Dogs didn't have ulterior motives. Dogs didn't fall in love with someone else all the while "working extended hours" and claiming everything was "fine."

With a huff, Mia slammed the book shut and crammed it into her overstuffed backpack. The zipper protested, barely able to contain the contents. It was past time to buy a bigger bag, or finally join the twenty-first century and keep as much as she could digitally and lighten the burden on her favorite backpack.

Riding the bus wasn't her favorite way to travel but it did the job. Since her car wouldn't be back from the shop for a couple days, it beat the hell out of walking. It had also been a long, shitty day.

And now she had a headache.

She was still rubbing the sore spot as the bus pulled to a stop in front of the next shelter. A man in jeans and a dark hoodie stood with his hands shoved into the front pocket of his sweatshirt, his face mostly obscured by the hood. Their eyes met briefly as the bus approached, prompting Mia to quickly avert her gaze.

As the door swung open and the man boarded, she instinctively shifted in her seat and tossed her backpack onto the open seat next to her. It was a tactic she'd seen among schoolchildren, one she absolutely detested, yet here she was, pulling the same childish maneuver.

She didn't watch him, but the hesitation in his step was palpable. Turning away, she pretended to be engrossed in the view out the front of the bus, while he swung into the seat across the aisle, effectively cornering an older woman by the window.

The guilt she felt at her actions stood in stark contrast to the defensive walls she had erected around her seat.

Mia's gaze was fixed on the man as he removed his hood, revealing a stark collection of injuries all over his face. The bruises and cuts were evident, with a particularly dark swelling under his eye and a trail of stitches sewn into red, inflamed skin from ear to chin, right along his solid jawline.

"Sister Mary Ellen," he greeted the woman beside him, his tone friendly yet tired. "How's your night going?"

Mia leaned forward, her curiosity piqued. Sister Mary Ellen was a nun, apparently. She caught a glimpse of the sister, who didn't look like any nun she'd ever seen. Had she ever seen a nun before that wasn't on television?

The man turned and caught Mia's eye, offering a fleeting smile. She whipped her head around and sat back in her seat, staring straight ahead, her cheeks warming with a rush of embarrassment.

"Jesse Murphy, what trouble have you gotten yourself into tonight?" Sister Mary Ellen's voice carried a mix of concern and familiarity.

Mia couldn't help but watch their exchange, an unexpected scene if ever there was one. *An old nun chatting with her friend the fighter on the bus* was not on Mia's Saturday night bingo card.

"Look at you," Sister Mary Ellen said, lifting her wrinkled hands to Jesse's battered face and gently turning it from side to side.

He laughed quietly but didn't move out of her grasp. "A man's got to earn a living, Sister. This is just how I earn mine."

Sister Mary Ellen examined Jesse's face with a tenderness that spoke of a deep bond between the pair. "You always say that, Jesse, but you can't tell me there's not another way." The old woman released his face and smiled before she patted his leg.

Mia studied Jesse's features, noting the freshness of his wounds. It seemed they both had a pretty terrible night. Without knowing it, his misery held up a mirror to Mia's own. But, while his physical scars would heal with time, her heart had taken an unseen beating. Who knew how long that would take to heal.

"I've told you, Sister, there's no other work that I'm qualified for," Jesse said, his smile brief and strained.

Their conversation continued in between long stretches of silence as the bus rumbled out of Spring Hill, across the city line into Oak Harbor.

Eventually, the bus slowed and pulled to a stop in front of the senior housing complex nestled a few blocks back from Oak Harbor's bustling waterfront.

Sister Mary Ellen retrieved her purse from the floor as she stood to leave. She patted Jesse's shoulder. "Well, there must be something you can learn to do that doesn't leave you looking like this. You're a smart boy, Jesse. Maybe it's time to start using your head for something other than a target, hmm?"

Jesse rose, allowing Sister Mary Ellen space to exit. Her hand brushed his uninjured cheek—a gesture of grandmotherly affection—before she descended the steps and disappeared from view.

Mia wondered if Jesse would say anything when he sat back down. Would he presume to sit right next to her now that Sister Mary Ellen was gone, and he had nobody else to talk to? To her relief, he chose to sit back down in his same seat.

With no pressure to engage with him, she pulled the book from her backpack and flipped to the page where she'd left her bookmark, ignoring the dull thump of her headache.

Casual glances in Jesse's direction revealed him to be absorbed in the world outside the bus window, oblivious to her. Two more times she did the same, with the same result.

She couldn't explain why she wanted Jesse to look at her, but each time she looked, and he didn't look back, those oh-so-familiar feelings of rejection roared back to the surface.

The sting of his perceived rejection was irrational, she chided herself. He wasn't rejecting her... because they didn't know each other. They were literal strangers to one another. He was just a guy on the bus trying to get home. The same way she was.

In a huff she snapped her book shut and shoved it back into her bag. Unable to stop herself, she snuck another glance at Jesse.

A stream of scarlet ran down his face and neck. Running on pure instinct, she yanked her bag open and ripped into it to get her first aid kit.

"Your stitches are bleeding," she said as she slid across the seats to help him. Sitting on the edge of the seat with her legs in the aisle, she looked at his injuries to see where the blood was coming from.

Jesse's hand flew to his cheek, and he pulled it away, blood running down his fingers. "Shit."

"What happened?" She unzipped the kit and pulled out a pair of blue latex gloves.

"I scratched it, and I must've popped a stitch." He held his blood-covered hand in the air, unsure what to do with it. "Dammit."

"You're not allergic to latex, are you?" she asked, pausing with her fingers halfway into one of the gloves.

He shook his head. After pulling both gloves on, Mia took an alcohol wipe from her kit, ripped it open and handed it to him. "Clean your hands," she said, taking complete control of the situation. Then she opened a clean cotton gauze pad and held it gently against the line of stitches.

"Convenient for me you travel with a first aid kit," Jesse joked, angling his eyes to see her without moving his head.

"Habit of the job I'm afraid." She smiled at him and carefully wiped away the blood that had dripped onto his neck, some of which had already been absorbed into the collar of his hoodie. "You'll want to soak your sweatshirt in cold water when you get home, otherwise it'll stain."

"Noted." He nodded, silent as she worked. She held the gauze firmly enough to stop the bleeding but hopefully not hard enough to cause him any more pain than he probably felt already. "What's your job that has you traveling with a first aid kit?" he asked.

"ER nurse for part of my career. School nurse at the moment," she said. "When you're around kids all the time, it's just easier to be ready for anything. All the time."

Completely comfortable speaking with him when she was the one in control of the situation, Mia slid right into her former role of Emergency Room nurse.

"Everything OK back there?" the bus driver yelled. "Need me to stop the bus?"

"No," Mia yelled back. "I'm a nurse. He'll be patched up in no time."

"Good enough for me." The bus never slowed down.

Having stemmed the blood flow, she applied several butterfly bandages across the cut. "This will hold until you can get to the doctor to have the stitches redone."

She stuffed the used gauze into the discarded wrapper then rolled the gloves off and tossed the whole thing into the trash can at the front of the bus. "And try to sleep with your head elevated a little higher tonight. It should help alleviate some of the swelling."

"Thanks," Jesse said, his gaze softening as he met her eyes.

She was disarmed by the soft look in his expression. It was in direct contrast with the hardness of his body. Not that she consciously noticed that kind of thing, but when she was so close, taking care of his injury, it was simply something her mind took note of.

"I'm just doing my job," she said, regaining her composure. "But you're welcome."

With her task complete, Mia's usual nerves returned in full force. She hastily packed away her first aid kit and retreated to the safety of her seat.

"I'm Jesse." He introduced himself, starting to offer his hand, then pausing as he noticed the dried blood between his fingers. "I'd shake your hand, but..."

"No worries," she said with a soft laugh. "I'm Mia."

"Nurse Mia," Jesse said, his smile genuine. "Nice to meet you. And, for real, I can't thank you enough for this."

As the bus neared her stop, Mia gathered her things, offering Jesse a final smile before descending the steps. She fought the impulse to glance back at him as the bus pulled away.

Curling into the collar of her coat, she tightened it against the cold, damp, blustery ocean wind that whipped up as she neared the front door of her building.

Less than an hour ago, she had no idea that Jesse Murphy existed. So, how could she explain that fleeting connection they'd shared? Was she the only one to feel it? And why the twinge of sadness at the thought that he might have already forgotten about her as the bus disappeared down the street?

Jesse

T HE BUS RUMBLED AWAY from Mia's stop and Jesse relaxed in his seat. The bus driver caught his eye in the rear-view mirror. "You doing all right back there?" he asked.

Had the driver asked him that question when he stepped onto the bus, Jesse's answer would have been a resounding no. But after his sweet conversation with Sister Mary Ellen and then the impromptu stitch repair from the woman across the aisle, his answer was a truthful, "Yeah, man, I'm good."

Jesse mused over the irony of his situation. On fight nights, he never took his own car. Serious injury was always a very real possibility. The worry of having to drive himself home with a broken arm, or worse, was taken off the table when he caught a ride with someone else. Someone who would not be fighting.

He had cursed himself for turning down Danny's offer for a ride home earlier. But as the bus rumbled on toward his stop, he found himself reflecting on the kindness of the people around him rather than the shitshow of pain that was his body.

Obviously, Sister Mary Ellen was on his ass about fighting. She'd been after him for the past few years to find a new gig. But it was the other woman, Mia, Nurse Mia, who'd turned his whole night around.

Was that weird? It sure felt weird.

He'd won his fight and been on top of the world for a brief moment. Before the reality of how bad his body fucking hurt reminded him he wasn't a kid anymore. And fighting was nothing, if not a young person's sport.

But then, like a ray of sunshine, the woman who'd looked at him like she was afraid of getting mugged, jumped in to patch him up. Without being asked. Without the slightest hesitation.

It was another five minutes before the bus pulled up near his place, a mile further inland from where Mia lived. It was too bad he didn't take the bus more regularly. Maybe there would have been a chance of running into her again.

Now his brain was really stretching things. Randomly riding the bus in hopes of seeing a pretty girl was not his style. More importantly, he wasn't in a place in life where he was necessarily in the market for a relationship. His history with women was a testament to that. Most of the girlfriends he'd had since high school lasted six months or less, so it's not like he was all that good at them to begin with.

No, it was for the best that he wouldn't be on the bus again any time soon. He had enough to focus on without trying to fit Nurse Mia into his suddenly upended life. Best to let her stay a pleasant memory.

As the bus doors creaked open, Jesse rose to his feet. A glint of something out of place caught his eye beneath the seat Mia had occupied. With a swift motion, he retrieved the item, tucking it securely into his pocket before stepping down onto the sidewalk. The bus rumbled off, leaving him alone with an object that hinted at unfinished business.

The walk from the bus stop back to his place was spent deciding how the rest of his night would go. The thought of Mia, possibly frantic over her lost possession, quickened his steps. There was no way he could relax with a late dinner and get any sleep knowing she could be going nuts looking for it. He needed to return it, but first he needed to go inside and wash the blood off his hands and change into something that didn't have blood drips all over the collar.

Over the years, he'd had roommates come and go, but over time they'd each ended up going their own ways, leaving Jesse as the sole tenant in a two-bedroom apartment on the main floor of a two-family house. It wasn't huge but the rent was affordable, the distance to the gym was less than a mile, and the upstairs neighbors worked all day and slept all night.

Stepping inside, Jesse looked over his apartment through fresh eyes, imagining how it might appear to Mia. The space, once a hub of good times and wild living, now lay stark and exposed in its emptiness. The living room was a spartan arrangement of basics—a couch, its fabric worn from years of use, and a solitary chair that had seen better days. They faced a television that was too small for the room, perched atop a stand that doubled as a catch-all for mail and miscellaneous crap.

The kitchen, a functional space devoid of any sense of hospitality, boasted a card table that bore the scars of one too many drinking games and late-night poker matches. Lawn chairs, brought inside to replace the wood ones as they broke, now served as permanent fixtures around the table. The yellow overhead light cast soft shadows over the worn linoleum floor that, despite everything, was strikingly clean.

A sense of vulnerability crept in as he considered his apartment. The bachelor pad that once felt like freedom now seemed neglected, a mirrored reflection of his lifestyle. It was clean, yes, but it lacked the little things, the touches that made a place feel like home.

Standing at the bathroom sink, the scent of antibacterial soap filled his nostrils as he scrubbed away the blood, watching the pink suds swirl down the drain. He treated the blood stains on his sweatshirt then slipped into a fresh one, the fabric soft against his tender skin, and snatched his car keys from the hook by the door.

With the stars as his silent witnesses, he set off, the cold air nipping at his cheeks. The night's earlier events replayed in his mind, each step a beat in the rhythm of an evening that had veered into the unexpected in every way.

Not knowing what else to expect, he hoped to make the trip quickly so he could finally settle in for the night and fill the gaping chasm of his empty stomach.

Mia

MIA'S APARTMENT WAS LESS her home and more a holdover place during a time of transition.

Several built-in shelves sat mostly empty. She hadn't collected anything worth displaying since she'd moved to Oak Harbor, aside from a few pieces of sea glass and a handful of broken shells she'd picked up down by the beach when she first moved to town. They were few, but they were undeniably hers, small anchors in a new life that was slowly taking shape.

It was the walls that were most telling. The large blank walls only accentuated the lack of personal photos and artwork. It wasn't that she didn't have the memories or people to fill those frames; it was simply the fallout after a relationship's end that kept those frames relegated to boxes in the storage room of her parents' basement.

She hadn't gotten around to making any new memories since she'd moved to town, so the walls held space for adventures yet unknown.

Even still, with its hand-me-down couch, and a coffee table and chair that spoke more of functionality than style, her little apartment was all she needed until she could find a more permanent place to put down some roots. Those things gave her somewhere to sit and read, somewhere to lie down to watch her shows, and somewhere to put her coffee and yarn while she worked on her crochet projects.

Outside her fourth-floor window, Oak Harbor, a five block by five block square on a small peninsula sticking into the ocean, unfolded like a movie set. Its waterfront district was a collection of every small business a person could want. The dual-purpose buildings, with businesses below and living spaces above, were a microcosm of the town itself—a place where the pulse of daily life beat strongest just beyond the tourist's gaze.

To the right, Center Street stretched into the town's heart, while to the left, the main thoroughfare called out with the promise of coffee, pastries, books, and gifts. Ahead, the town reached out toward the ocean, its restaurants and shops a man-made border along the vast Atlantic.

It was nearing nine o'clock, the savory scent of baked chicken filled Mia's apartment, a comforting contrast to the chill of the night. There was an extra unexplained energy in the swing of her hips and the sway of her body that moved in time with the angsty tunes of The Cure, her voice rising and falling with the haunting lyrics of "Fascination Street." As she sang along, Robert Smith's evocative voice wrapped around her like an embrace. Her own voice grew louder with his encouragement.

A sharp rap at the door jolted her, a sudden silence falling as she hurried to pause the music. She wasn't expecting company, especially at that time of night. Outside of her family, nobody even knew her new address.

A swift relief poured through her as she realized it was probably one of her neighbors coming to tell her to settle down with the singing and dancing. She approached the front door, wiping her hands on a towel as she walked.

Mia placed one hand on the deadbolt, ready to unlock it so she could apologize to her neighbor—most likely Mrs. Aldrich, the older lady down the hall—and pressed her eye to the peephole.

The bruised and butterfly-bandaged face of Jesse looked back at her. Stumbling back a step, she gripped the deadbolt tighter in one hand, and squeezed the hand towel in the other.

Had he gotten off the bus behind her and she missed it? Had he followed her home? How long had he been standing outside her door? And how the hell did he get inside her building?

Another knock. "Mia?" A pause. "Hey, it's me, Jesse... from the bus." More silence. "Sorry to bother you this late, but I found this on the bus, and I thought you might want it back."

She flung herself at the peephole and saw Jesse holding up her wallet. What the hell? When had she dropped that?

"Hold on," she said, tossing the towel onto the back of the living room chair. She'd dropped her backpack there when she came home earlier. With furious movement, she yanked it open and ripped out her book, her extra sweater, her hair elastics, a few pens, and her first aid kit.

No wallet.

Back at the peephole, she started to open the door. "Wait," she said, stilling her hand on the deadbolt again. "How did you even get in my building? And how did you get my wallet in the first place? I don't carry much cash in it, but you probably noticed that." Her eye stayed pressed to the peephole.

His eyes widened, at least as much as they could with all the swelling around them, and he said, "The pizza guy was on the way out, so I came in when he left. You must've dropped the wallet when you were digging through your bag because I found it on the floor under your seat when I was getting off at my stop."

He paused to suck in what looked like an angry breath. "And whatever was in it when you dropped it is still inside it. Because I'm not a fucking thief. But, hey, if it'll make you feel better, I'll just leave it out here," he said. After tossing the wallet unceremoniously to the floor in front of her door, he turned to leave.

Mia's heart sank as she watched Jesse's retreating figure. Why had she been such a jerk to him? His face was an obvious testament to the rough night he'd had, and here he was, returning her wallet when he probably would have preferred to be home in bed.

"Wait," she called out, her voice softer than before. She cracked the door open, jamming one foot behind it, just in case. "Sorry for being a dick," she admitted when he turned back. "It was seriously decent of you to bring this back."

She crouched down and grabbed the wallet with slightly shaky hands, hoping her nerves weren't as visible as they felt. "It would have been a complete pain in the ass to replace all this stuff."

Jesse stood with his hands shoved in his hoodie pocket, his gaze fixed on her as if he was trying to figure her out and not having much luck.

"What?" she finally asked, breaking the silence that stretched between them.

He smiled, a silent acknowledgment of her apology. "Have a good night," he said, and for the second time, he turned to leave.

Her heart hammered behind her ribs as he walked away. Was she so desperate for conversation her body was freaking out at the thought of him leaving? A sudden urge to keep the conversation going seized her. "What happened to you?" she blurted out. "Your face, I mean. How did you get all those bruises?"

"It's what I do. I'm a fighter," he said without turning around. His voice carried a hint of pride. "I'm not big-name famous or anything, but when the opportunity comes up, I take it."

"How about the other guy?" she pressed. "How bad does he look?" She was still talking to his back.

He finally faced her again, a wry grin on his lips. "Well, once they washed off all the blood and stitched him up, I'd say he looks sort of like this. Maybe a little worse." He shifted his weight from one foot to the other. "But if you're asking who won, I did. Submission by rear naked choke at two-seventeen of the fourth."

Whatever the hell that meant.

"Congratulations. I think."

"Thanks."

Mia's heart raced as Jesse made to leave again. The loneliness of her life in her new town pushed the words right out of her mouth. "Are you hungry? Did you have dinner yet?"

"Umm…" He hesitated, uncertainty flickering in his eyes.

"Sorry," she said. "That was weird. Never mind," Mia said, backpedaling and feeling the flush of embarrassment in her cheeks. She looked from her wallet to his face. "Thanks again for bringing this back."

"Don't worry about it," he said, stepping closer. "It's no big deal. But, to answer your questions, yes, I am hungry, and no, I haven't eaten yet."

The softness returned to his gaze, his unspoken question hanging in the air.

Inviting him inside her apartment would be a bold move, especially for her.

As life would have it, though, she found herself in need of a friend. Who was she to be picky about the way the universe provided? Mia took a deep breath, her decision made. "It's nothing fancy," she said. "Just baked chicken with a side salad."

For a moment, he paused, perhaps gauging the seriousness of her offer. "I like chicken and salad," he finally said.

After the briefest hesitation, with a nod, she opened the door wide, inviting Jesse into her world.

Mia

I N THE QUIET OF Mia's kitchen, the contrast between her and Jesse was almost poetic—she had made a career out of healing people, and he had made his out of taking them apart. The irony wasn't lost on her that the first guest to step into her personal haven was someone who fought for a living.

It was a weirdly ironic dynamic.

"It smells incredible in here," Jesse remarked, breaking the silence as he washed his hands. "Need a hand with anything?"

"You can slice cucumbers," she said, setting him up with a cutting board, a small knife and three mini cucumbers. He got to work slicing while she went to check on the chicken in the oven, a sense of camaraderie building between them.

Yet, as Jesse paused to survey her apartment, Mia felt a twinge of vulnerability. Through his eyes, the minimalistic decor of her space seemed stark, almost spartan. She quickly second guessed her decision to invite him inside.

"This is a great place," he said, following his gaze toward the windows. "The view is something else." The yellow streetlights lit the street in either direction, casting a warm hue over the quiet street below.

Mia smiled, a bit of pride seeping through her uncertainty. "Sometimes I pull the chair over and drink my coffee sitting there," she said. "I put my feet up on the windowsill. It's a great place to watch the sun rise and to do some people watching."

Jesse nodded appreciatively as he looked out the window. "The sunrise must be incredible," he mused, turning back to her with a curious tilt of his head. "Ever watch it from the beach?"

She'd thought about it but never had the nerve to walk the three blocks by herself in the predawn hours. His question sparked a pang of longing for such a simple adventure. "I haven't. Not yet, anyway. Maybe someday I will," she replied, the possibility hanging between them like a promise.

His eyes swept through her apartment, and she felt strangely exposed. Her furniture seemed so drab in the open floor plan. With two walls of exposed brick, the apartment should have looked a whole lot better than it did.

"I've only been here a couple months," she said, a hint of defensiveness in her voice, "and I haven't really done any decorating yet. I don't really have many visitors."

His eyes found hers as they walked back to the kitchen to finish cooking, a flicker of surprise in them. "Really?"

"You're the first one, actually," she admitted with an uncomfortable laugh.

"I feel honored then. But I've got to admit," he said as he tossed the cucumbers into the bowl, "I'm a little disappointed you didn't put that playlist back on."

She laser-focused on the pepper she had started slicing, trying to keep the smile from completely taking over her face. Laying her knife on the counter, with a smile, she turned to him.

"Are you making fun of my music? Because I'll have you know The Cure more than holds their own against some of the crap that passes for music today."

Jesse's laughter was soft, not mocking. "Easy, killer, I'm not making fun of anything. I could hear it through the door when I got here." He took a handful of cherry tomatoes and began to slice them into halves.

"You heard that?" Inwardly, she groaned, because she already knew the answer.

"What? You have a nice voice. It suits their music." A small smile pulled at the corner of his mouth. "Don't hear them all that often, but I always liked them."

Mia sighed. "I guess it could have been worse, right? At least you didn't see me dancing."

He quickly shot a glance at her ass before returning to his task, a playful spark in his eyes. "That definitely would *not* have been worse."

The not-so-subtle compliment pleased her and warmed her entire body like a shot of whiskey on a cold night.

Jesse tossed the rest of the tomatoes into the bowl, and she gave the salad a quick toss before placing it onto the small Ikea table in the center of the kitchen. The plates she handed to Jesse were plain, matching the blank slate feeling of her new beginning in Oak Harbor. She placed the plate of grilled chicken next to the salad bowl.

"Have a seat. I'll grab the salad dressing," Mia said.

They settled across from one another, brought together by happenstance, and about to share a meal together. She motioned to the salad. "Help yourself."

"Not happening," he said, his refusal gentle but firm. "I'll wait for you."

It was a small gesture, but it was a nice one. "I'd almost forgotten what good manners look like," she said with a laugh as she spooned some salad onto her plate. "Thank you for that."

His eyes narrowed a fraction. "Umm... you're welcome for not being a classless oaf?"

As they ate, Mia found her attention drawn to the vivid bruises marring Jesse's face, a stark contrast to the softness in his eyes. "Does it hurt too much?" she couldn't help but ask. "Having bruises like that?"

Jesse set his fork down, leaning back with a wince that betrayed the pain he downplayed. "Having them? Yeah, a bit. But it's getting them that's the real bitch." He smiled at her. "If you can help it, don't go around getting punched in the face. It's really not as fun as you'd think it might be."

Their laughter mingled as they enjoyed a shared moment of levity despite the night each of them had had. "I don't think that looks fun at all! I don't understand how anyone can possibly enjoy doing that for a living. In fact," she said, rising from her chair, "can I get you some ice or some ibuprofen? A shot of whiskey maybe?"

"Don't drink," he said. "But I wouldn't say no to a couple Advil."

She fetched him water and pain relief, and as they resumed their meal, the conversation flowed effortlessly.

"You said you've been in town for a few months," Jesse said, spearing a cherry tomato. "And I can't believe you were on the same bus as me, tonight of all nights."

"My car's in the shop," she began, her voice trailing off as she avoided his gaze. "I had a date tonight, and the bus was my quickest way home."

Jesse's expression shifted, a flicker of concern—or was it disapproval?—crossing his features. "You mean your date didn't even offer you a ride home?" he asked, his laughter not quite masking the edge in his voice. "No wonder you thought I had such good manners. The bar wasn't set very high, was it?"

She sighed as she set down her silverware, the clink of metal punctuating her resolve to come clean. "OK, fine. I lied. I didn't have a date. Well, I did, sort of, but it wasn't a romantic date." She took a quick sip of water. "I met up with my sister to have a drink or two and it didn't go so well. We don't really talk anymore, and we stupidly thought maybe we could."

With a halfhearted shrug, she added, "Needless to say, we couldn't." Crossing her utensils on top of her plate she stood to clear her dishes.

He didn't need to know about her parents' big Fourth of July party last summer—the day everything changed. Mia had opened her heart, only to have it crushed in front of the assembled friends and family. And Lauren... she hadn't exchanged a word with her sister since. The thought of facing everyone this year again was a complete nonstarter.

"I'm sorry to hear that," he said, his voice carrying a sincerity that reached across the table and wrapped around her like a much-needed hug. "Family can be tough. I promise we'll never talk about it again. Unless you want to."

"Thanks."

Jesse finished clearing the table while Mia packed up the leftovers into a small reusable container. "I'll help you wash," he offered when she started rinsing the dishes.

"No need," she said. "I'm just tossing them in the dishwasher and letting it do its thing while I get some sleep. But I appreciate the offer."

Time had slipped away as they talked and ate, the clock now ticking toward eleven. Jesse's concern broke through again. "Shit, it's really late. I'm sorry, I didn't mean to keep you up," he said, checking his phone.

"There's nothing to apologize for. Tomorrow's Sunday, I don't have to work," she said. "It's me who's sorry for keeping you up this late after the night you've had. I wish I could at least offer you a ride home. If my stupid car wasn't in the shop, I would totally give you a ride. Do you live far from here?"

He stood with his hands in the front pocket of his sweatshirt, that soft look had returned to his eyes. "Don't worry about it. My car's parked right out front. And I don't live far from here."

"Why were you on the bus then?" Mia asked.

"I don't drive to a fight," he said, shifting his weight between his feet. "In case I'm not in good enough shape to drive myself home."

The gravity of that hit her. This man did a dangerous job. With the potential for bad things to happen.

Mia walked him to the door, her heart fluttering with an inexplicable nervousness. "Thanks again for bringing back my wallet. I really do appreciate it."

"Trust me, it was no problem at all." He stepped through the door and pivoted to face her. "Sorry if it was uncomfortable having me show up like that."

"No, actually, it wasn't. Well, maybe at first, but then it was cool," she said, her own surprise lingering. "I'm glad you were able to stay. It was kind of nice having someone to eat dinner with." A wave of loneliness washed over her as Jesse lingered on the threshold. "Thanks for staying."

His eyes fell away from hers for a split second and she figured he was about to turn and disappear from her life. Instead, he offered a hopeful grin. "I know I look like I got hit by a truck, but I swear I'll look a whole lot better than this in a few days."

He gestured to the bandages she'd applied. "Think there's any chance I could thank you for your help? Maybe take you out for dinner or a movie or something? I know you don't know much of the town but there's some cool places I could show you. The big farmer's market is happening soon if you like that kind of thing."

"I'd like that," she said, her pulse quickening. "But... there's just... I guess I need you to know..." The words were awkward, but necessary. "I'm not looking for a boyfriend right now."

A look of surprise flashed on his face before he recovered with a warm smile. "Friends are good, though, right?" he asked.

"Friends are perfect. We can eat dinner or see a movie or whatever. As friends. No strings attached, no expectations."

"Expectations?" he echoed, a playful note in his voice. "Expectations of what?"

Twisting her fingers together into the hem of her shirt, she suddenly felt like a teenager instead of the grown woman she was. "You know," she said. "Sex or whatever."

Jesse laughter echoed softly through the hallway. "Mia," he said gently. "Don't take this the wrong way but I've known you for like three hours. You might be a great person but I'm not expecting anything from you. OK?"

Excitement zipped through Mia's limbs; her fingers and toes tingled. "OK." Even with the bruises, his smile lit her up. "And for the record," she said, "the bruises don't bother me."

That was natural, right? It sounded like something one friend would say to another. Didn't it?

After they traded numbers, she closed the door behind him, then stuck her face against the peephole to watch him walk away. Her heart stuttered when he turned around and smiled before disappearing into the elevator. Did he know she was watching? Or was he just smiling because he enjoyed being with her?

It appeared Mia Reed had finally made her first friend in her new town, outside of work. Her hand stilled over her phone, ready to fire off an excited text to her sister to tell her all about it. But, because Lauren had chosen Brandon over her, the message remained unsent.

Jesse

J ESSE EVENTUALLY ROLLED OUT of bed sometime in the early afternoon, his body a map of aches—arms, legs, back, face, not to mention the tender skin beneath his stitches. He'd gone to bed looking forward to a full day of lying on the couch, stuffing his face, and recuperating.

Instead, he got a couple hours of relaxing, snacking, and minimal healing. By dinnertime he needed to be in his parents' kitchen, getting ready for the weekly Sunday dinner with the family. Neither his parents nor his brothers had been at the fight on Saturday, and they were all waiting for him to show up to tell them how it went down.

Since she hadn't been there in person, his mother would more than likely show up at his front door to check on him anyway. Might as well go and get the benefit of a good home cooked meal out of it.

He pulled on some clean clothes after a slow shower where he'd tried his best to avoid his stitches. It hadn't been the twenty-four hours the doc had recommended but it was close enough.

The ten-minute drive took him to the far edge of Oak Harbor, to the home where he and his three older brothers and their younger sister all grew up. Pulling into the huge circular driveway in front of the house still brought a feeling of *home*.

The sprawling, two-story purple house with the gingerbread details was literally his mother's dream home. Their father had built it in stages over the course of their lives until their mother was completely happy with it.

When Gaelen needed a new bunny hutch, Pat built it. When she wanted to keep chickens because she read about it in a book, Pat had the coop constructed by the end of the weekend. And when Chester and Clark, Gaelen's beloved Huskies, needed some new digs, Pat had two giant dog houses built and set up out back by the shed within the week.

The best part was that everything his father had built had been constructed and finished to look like miniature versions of their house—same color, same details.

"Oh, Jesse," Gaelen said when Jesse walked in and sat at the high counter in his mother's kitchen. She put the lasagna pan onto a wood board on the counter, pulled her oven mitts off and hurried to his side.

"Look at this beautiful face," she said, taking hold of his cheeks, mindful of his stitches. "When are you going to stop this and do something less... less..."

"Dangerous?" Jesse finished for her. "Painful?"

"Yes." His mother had always been supportive of his choices and his career—until the first time she saw his face all battered and bloody. From then on, she'd been after him to give up fighting and come work at Murphy Construction.

"Sister Mary Ellen told me last night I should start using my head for more than target practice," Jesse said with a laugh.

Gaelen made the sign of the cross and turned back to finish getting dinner ready. "Smart woman," she said. "You should listen to her. She knows what she's talking about."

"I'll think about it, Mom," Jesse said, putting a handful of crackers and a stack of cheese slices onto his small plate. "How's that sound?"

Gaelen peered at him over her shoulder. "It's a start."

Jesse grinned. He and his parents hadn't always seen eye-to-eye when he was growing up, but they were good parents. Good people. "So, who's coming for dinner tonight?"

Jesse's brothers all lived in the area and worked for the family company. His sister was the baby of the family and had moved away after high school to "spread her wings." He couldn't keep track of where she lived because she seemed to move every few months.

"Shane and Seth are coming, but Gretchen's parents are having early Easter today, so she and Owen and the girls won't be here." She yanked open the refrigerator and pulled out a big silver bowl and put the salad tongs in it. "Here, honey," she said, handing it to Jesse with a wink. "Be a dear and put this on the table."

"Is Seth bringing Rylee?" he asked as he carried the bowl to the big farmhouse table in the dining room. He always kidded that his niece was part rabbit because of the crazy amount of vegetables she ate. If she was going to be there, he'd put the salad closest to her chair.

"Of course," his mother called from the kitchen. "I made her favorite apple crisp for dessert." Convenient for Jesse, since that was his favorite too and now that he wasn't trying to cut weight, he'd have a big helping for dessert. Maybe two.

All the granddaughters had their own smaller chairs in Gaelen's dining room. His nephew, Brant, used to have one as well, but since he'd hit puberty and was now bigger than Jesse, he'd graduated to a regular size chair.

"How about Brant? Am I setting a place for him too, or is he with Eleanor this weekend?"

Gaelen was quiet for a second. "I don't know," she said slowly. "Maybe just set a place for him and if he doesn't show, we'll put it away."

"Yes ma'am."

As Jesse gathered plates from the wooden hutch along the long wall and carried them to the table, the front door opened, and Rylee's voice pierced the quiet house. "Hi, Grandma! I'm here and I brought you something."

His mother's delight was audible. "Oh, Rylee, sweetheart, those are beautiful," Gaelen said. Then to Jesse's brother Seth, she said, "Hi, honey. Glad you could make it."

Gaelen and Seth talked for a few minutes in the kitchen while Jesse continued to set up the table as the sound of footsteps grew louder.

"Hi, Uncle J!" Rylee flung herself at him and he barely had time to toss the silverware onto the table so he didn't accidentally poke her with a fork. "I missed you," she said, as her little arms wrapped around his middle and squeezed.

Jesse held his breath against the pain rather than let the five-year old know he was injured. "Hey, Rylee Faye," he said, returning her hug. "I missed you too. How did your week go?"

"It was good," she said disengaging from the hug. Peering up at his bruised face, a crease formed in her brow. "Better than yours, I think."

"Rylee," Seth warned as he stepped into the room.

"Nah, it's good," Jesse said. "She's not wrong. Unless she got in a fight, too, and ended up with twelve stitches in her face."

Rylee giggled. "I didn't." Then she whisper-shouted at Jesse, "But I would've won if I did."

"Damn right you would've," Jesse said, holding out his hand. She bumped his fist with hers.

"All right, you," Seth said to his daughter. "Why don't you go help Grandma for a few minutes."

"But I want to help Uncle J," she said.

Seth gently spun her around by her shoulders. "That may be," he said. "But I asked you to go help Grandma. Now go."

Looking over her shoulder, her gaze met Jesse's, her eyes wide and imploring.

"Don't look at me, buddy. Dad's the boss here," Jesse said with a shrug. Her face pulled into a frowny pout and Jesse felt like shit for letting her down. "How about if I put your chair next to mine and we can eat dinner together tonight?" he asked.

"OK!" She sprinted toward the kitchen.

"Thanks, man," Seth said with a laugh as they listened to Rylee tear through the house yelling for her grandmother. "So, how'd last night go?"

To his surprise, Jesse realized he didn't want to talk about the fight. His brain tried to pull him into telling Seth about his impromptu dinner with Mia instead. What was that all about?

Steering his mind back to the fight, he shrugged. "At least I won."

"That's awesome, kid. Congratulations."

It didn't matter that Jesse was in his thirties, all his brothers had called him "kid" for as long as he could remember. Now that he was thinking about the future, about what it meant to grow up and look at what comes next, the name didn't fit quite the way it used to.

Not that any of them would give up the nickname, because... *brothers*.

"Thanks." He was quiet for a minute before he leaned over, resting his forearms on the back of the chair and searched his brother's face. "Is thirty-two too old to be doing this?"

The most thoughtful of his brothers, Seth considered the question, his response measured. "I don't know how to answer that. I know there are a lot of guys hitting their stride at thirty-two. So, I guess the real question is, at thirty-two, is this what you want to be doing with your life?"

Dinner was fantastic, always, and once it was over, Gaelen was more than happy to relinquish clean up duties to the others while she and Rylee went outside to check on the bunnies and the dogs.

Jesse's oldest brother Shane had showed up for dinner, but Brant hadn't come with him, leaving Jesse, his brothers and their father to clear the table, put away what leftovers there were, and load up the dishwasher.

"Hey, Dad," Jesse said, seizing his moment, after Shane and Seth left the kitchen to check the score of the baseball game on the TV in the living room. "I've been doing a little thinking lately and I was giving some thought to maybe, finally, taking you up on the offer to work for the company."

Pat Murphy, a giant of a man who was built like a tank, stopped mid-motion, hovering a dirty dish above the dishwasher rack. "For real?" he said as he slowly lowered the dish. "You're really going to give up fighting? To come work with us?" Pat's voice was thick with emotion that momentarily stunned Jesse into silence.

Jesse found his voice again and said, "Well, I mean, nothing's written in stone, but I've been thinking that I can't keep doing this forever." He pointed to his less swollen but still very black eye. "I've never thought past this point before, and I don't really know what I'm supposed to do now."

Seth and Shane popped back into the kitchen, as if they'd been summoned by Jesse's words. "Ho-ly shit," Shane said to Seth and slapped him on the chest. "You weren't kidding. Our baby boy's finally growing up." Seth laughed and Shane pretended to wipe tears from his eyes.

"Fuck off, you guys," Jesse said.

"Hey! No language like that in this house," Pat said, his eyes darting around the room, scanning for any sign of Gaelen. Despite being someone who swore like the proverbial sailor, he maintained a strict code of conduct when it came to avoiding that language in front of his wife.

"You do know Mom and Rylee are outside with the dogs, right?" Shane said. "They can't hear you."

Pat shrugged. "Fine. But none of that when they come back in. You get me?"

The brothers all nodded, each stifling a laugh.

"What kind of job do you think you can do with us?" Shane finally asked. "We don't have much need for combat on job sites. Although," he teased, "maybe we could have you drive from site to site and scare a little more productivity out of some of the crews."

"Honest to God, you guys," Jesse said. "I have no fuckin' idea what I can do. Maybe there's nothing."

"Well, your mother is looking to retire," Pat said. "She's looking for a new office manager as we speak."

Pat's suggestion hit Jesse like a cold wave. Aside from the fact that he was completely unqualified to do that job, the thought of sitting at a desk all day scared the shit out of him. He'd always been active. He needed the rush of activity to feel alive. There was no way he could sit in an office all day long.

But there was no other job with his father's company for which he was even remotely qualified either.

"I'm thinking that might not be the best match for him," Seth said, obviously seeing the look of sheer terror on Jesse's face. "But maybe he could shadow one of us for a few days and see if there's something he wants to learn."

"Yeah," Jesse said, quickly jumping on his brother's suggestion, "let's start with that."

Even though the job situation wasn't looking any brighter, at least Jesse had stopped thinking about Mia for a couple of hours.

Mostly.

"**A**RE YOU SURE YOU don't want to come with us?" Lexi's voice floated across the small office, as she sat, reclining in the chair opposite Mia's cluttered desk.

Several people from work had organized a casual evening of pool and drinks at a beachside restaurant. Lexi Greeves, the school's office administrator, was Mia's sole "sort of" friend among the staff—a social butterfly who flitted effortlessly through friend groups.

"I don't know." Mia thought about the upcoming weekend. "I have so much to do tomorrow," she said. "I'm not sure a hangover is such a good idea."

Lexi waved off her concern. "Well, that's easy. Just skip the drinks."

It had been a relentless week. A handful of nosebleeds, six fifth graders with lice after attending the same sleepover, a couple of kindergartener tummy aches, and a busted lip on a fourth grader who had taken a playground ball to the face—Mia had seen and dealt with it all. Add the usual stream of medications, headaches, sore throats, and general complaints, and her plate had more than overflowed.

Going out with people from work should have been a no-brainer. After all, she'd been working at Dyer Elementary for months and she'd been wishing and hoping for friends. It seemed like the perfect time to step out of her self-imposed hermit lifestyle.

Teetering on the brink of saying yes, Mia paused when her text notification went off.

Always eager for the scoop, Lexi leaned in, stealing a glance at Mia's screen. As she sat back, her expression shifted from shock to confusion to curiosity—a subtle transformation Mia almost missed.

Slipping her phone into her bag, Mia met Lexi's knowing gaze.

Lexi grinned. "Did I just see Jesse Murphy's name on your screen?"

Jesse, her enigmatic friend who had been radio silent. After their connection had sparked on the bus and flickered during dinner, Mia hadn't heard from him all week. She'd begun to think their friendship began on the bus and ended when he walked out the door after dinner.

After the disappointment of dismissing him as a potential friend, seeing his name light up her screen unexpectedly lifted her spirits.

"You know him?" Mia asked, cautiously hopeful about what Lexi would say.

"If it's the same Jesse Murphy that's lived in Oak Harbor all his life, I do," Lexi said.

Mia had no idea how long Jesse had lived in town, but she assumed they were talking about the same guy. "Is there something wrong with him?" Her belly wobbled from a shot of anxiety.

"No," Lexi said quickly as she leaned back in her chair. "There's nothing wrong with him. Nothing at all."

"What then?"

"Nothing. It's just... I had no idea... How do you know him?" Lexi said.

Oak Harbor was a small-ish town, so it didn't surprise her that Lexi knew Jesse. It did unnerve her, however, that Lexi was being as cryptic as she was. Obviously, she knew things about Jesse that Mia didn't, and she couldn't help but be uncomfortable with that knowledge.

"I fixed up his stitches last weekend," Mia said, keeping the story vague.

"What, like you were at his fight?" Lexi's heavily mascaraed eyes popped open, her eyebrows reaching toward her hairline. "I never would have picked you as a fight girl."

Mia gave Lexi the Cliffs Notes' version of the story, leaving out most of her side of things, instead, focusing on Jesse. "He was really nice," she said.

"Oh, he's *very* nice," Lexi agreed.

Mia's suspicions had been piqued by the way Lexi spoke about him. "How do you know him? Did you guys date or something?"

Lexi laughed. "No, no, no. Nothing like that," she said. "I used to babysit for his younger sister, Hannah, years ago. So, I've known Jesse since he was like ten years old. I grew up a couple blocks from their house. And I graduated high school with his oldest brother, Shane."

That wasn't such a bad secret, Mia thought. She'd been waiting for more of a bombshell than that.

"So..." Lexi said. "Are you thinking long-term when it comes to Jesse, or are you just having a little fun with him?"

Mia couldn't help but laugh. "I don't even know how to answer that," she said. "I only met him a week ago. We're just friends, so I guess my answer would be that I'm not thinking anything about him. Other than the fact that he's kind of cute." Her face screwed up in thought. "At least I imagine he'll be cute when all the bruises fade."

Lexi laughed again. "Trust me. He'll be very cute when the bruises fade." She leaned forward, resting her hands on Mia's desk. "Just be careful if you ever start thinking long-term with him. I don't think that's really his thing."

Nerves worked in Mia's belly again. "I really don't have *any* plans as far as he goes. Other than the occasional hangout. Maybe a movie."

Jesse's past and his dating habits were none of her business, but curiosity got the better of her. If there was a reason to stay away from him, she'd rather know it now and save herself the trouble down the road.

"What do you mean he doesn't do long-term? Is there something I need to know about him? Like should I not even try to be friends with him?"

"Oh, no, girl. Nothing like that. At least not as far as I know. He's dated a few women I know, and they all liked him a lot. But things with Jesse Murphy just don't seem to last." Lexi was quiet for a few seconds. "He's *really* into the whole fighting thing. It doesn't leave a lot of room for much else."

Mia's belly settled right back down. That sounded perfect. He'd be busy with his stuff. She'd be busy with her stuff. They'd hang out occasionally. No strings. No expectations. "Well, that's no big deal," she said. "It sounds like we'll get along great." She gave Lexi her most confident smile. "No matter how cute he turns out to be."

Lexi's lips quirked up on one side. "All those Murphy boys grew up to be pretty easy on the eyes, Jesse included." She tipped her head, as if lost in thought, then she sighed. "But... he's too young for me."

"Aren't you married?" Mia teased, sure that her friend had mentioned a husband at one point.

"Quite happily, actually," she said. "But that doesn't mean I can't notice things like how cute those brothers turned out." With a dramatic flourish, Lexi hopped out of her chair. "Oh well. Time to get back to work."

She stopped one more time on her way out the door. Her perfectly manicured fingernails and flawless makeup made her look more like a model than an elementary school admin as she turned to look back at Mia. "Hopefully we'll see you tonight. And feel free to bring Jesse with you."

She flashed a mischievous grin before disappearing out the door.

Once the bell rang at the end of the day, Mia could practically hear the weekend calling to her. Equal parts downtime and research time awaited her over the next forty-eight hours. Sitting in the car while she waited the few extra minutes for it to warm up, she pulled out her phone and looked at Jesse's text.

> Plans tomorrow?

> Sorry for the delay. Was working. Might be busy looking at open houses tomorrow.

She waited to see the three bouncing dots while he typed a reply, but he surprised her by calling instead.

"Hey!" she said as the call connected.

"Sorry to call." His voice filled the interior of her car. "I figured it would just be faster than trying to type out all the questions I wanted to ask." He chuckled and Mia decided she liked the sound of his laugh just as much as she remembered it from last weekend.

"Questions?" she said. "What questions could you possibly have for me?"

"Let's see. Open houses? Does that mean you're moving? If so, where are you looking to go? Have you given up on Oak Harbor already? When are you moving? Do you want some company while you look?" He was silent for a second then said, "I think that's everything."

Mia laughed at the onslaught of questions that she had no hope of remembering but tried her best to answer. "I like Oak Harbor just fine and I'm hoping to stay here. I don't even know if there *are* any open houses this weekend that fit what I'm looking for. And I have no idea when I'll be moving because it depends on what's for sale." She tried to remember everything he asked but wasn't sure if she'd heard him correctly on the biggest question. "Did I miss anything?"

"Only the most important one."

A gentle warmth crept up her neck. "Oh, which one was that?"

"I asked if you wanted some company while you look." She hadn't imagined that part. He really did ask about going to look at houses with her. "Friends do that sort of thing, right?" he said.

Under normal circumstances it would have been Lauren going to look at houses with her but since that was so far out of the question, she thought it might be nice to have the company.

With her newfound information about Jesse's serial dating habit, she was confident they could look at houses together and remain firmly in their safe space without pushing them into 'more than friends' territory.

And, quite frankly, having someone to pal around and chat with sounded a hell of a lot more fun than going by herself. "I guess they do," she said. "Do you really want to come look at houses with me?"

"I wouldn't have mentioned it if I didn't. Besides, I was wondering if you were up for doing something together—*as friends*—sometime over the weekend."

Mia considered the prospect of having a friend in town and decided she quite liked it. "The open houses are usually from ten to two, so any time after that I'm free to do whatever. Have anything in particular in mind?"

As soon as the words left her mouth she panicked and waited for Jesse to jump on her offer and turn it into something other than what she intended. Something that definitely did not fall in the category of friendship.

"Hmm," he said. "Since I'm not a hundred years old, dinner at two in the afternoon might be a tad early. But if you wanted to hang out for a while after your open houses, we could grab some dinner at night."

Had he not heard her make the offer to do 'whatever' with him, or was he honestly on board with the 'just friends' thing? Her heart kicked up at the thought of hanging out with someone else for a change. But she needed to be sure. "Dinner sounds good, but hang out where until then?"

"No clue. Hadn't really given it any thought," he said. "If you like being outside we could go for a hike. There's a couple of good trails nearby. If you're more of an indoor girl we could hang out at my place, or yours if it makes you more comfortable. I'm pretty easy going. For the most part, anyway." He chuckled, leaving Mia to wonder what he meant by that last bit.

Her car had warmed up enough and she was ready to head home. Yet something about having Jesse on the other end of the phone call kept her sitting in her car, while all the other cars had long since pulled away.

Aware of overstepping her self-imposed boundaries, she threw out a suggestion. "What do you have going on tonight? We could always hang out tonight if you wanted to."

"Ahh... I can't tonight, sorry about that. Friday nights I have a standing training time with some of the guys at the gym."

Another type of heat washed over her as she realized she probably came across as desperate and lonely and she wished she could take back her invitation. "Oh," she said. "No worries. I might be going out with some friends from work tonight, anyway."

He was quiet for an extra second, and she wished she had something to say that would make her feel less ridiculous. Nothing came to mind, so she stayed quiet and waited for him to say something else. For some reason she didn't ask him about Lexi.

"Cool," he said, finally. "But I'll definitely see you tomorrow?"

It wasn't what she expected him to say. Not that she knew what she was expecting—it just wasn't that. Was he holding back from her? Did he want to say something else but decided to brush it off instead?

"Yeah. Meet me at my place around quarter of ten?" she said. "Or is that too early for you? I don't know when you wake up in the morning." Of course she didn't know what time he got up in the morning. Why would she know that? Now, why did she suddenly want to know?

"Quarter of ten is fine," he said. "I'll see you tomorrow."

Jesse

F RIDAY NIGHT WAS OPEN gym night. Instead of formal classes, a group of athletes would come in on their night off to further hone and perfect their craft. The evening always started with a relaxed vibe, but once sparring began, the intensity ramped up. After the final round ended, the atmosphere would gradually come back down to its more laid-back state.

The first few workouts of his week had been after hours, while he gave his body time to recover. Nobody else in the gym meant no temptation to push himself harder than he was ready to go. But by Friday, the itch for full-contact sparring gnawed at him, held back only by the line of stitches still holding his face together.

After he warmed up with some jumping jacks, some stretches, and a few laps around the gym, Jesse wrapped his hands, the fabric snug against his knuckles, and approached a bag in the back corner of the room.

Blood pumping and muscles singing, he worked a few rounds of striking for speed and accuracy. His punches and elbows landed exactly where he wanted them to, time and time again, and his muscle memory took over as he started to place his kicks and land his knee strikes in the middle of the bag.

By the time he finished his speed rounds, his body had loosened up enough to start throwing for power. Combinations that had been seared into his memory over years of training landed on the bag with resounding thumps: *Jab, cross, low kick. Jab, cross, hook, elbow. Throw a kick, check a kick*. Over and over his limbs flew without conscious thought.

As the sweat poured from his body, his mind drifted out of the gym and back to the bus ride home from his fight, specifically his introduction to Mia. From the bus, his mind wandered to her kitchen, loving how she blushed when he looked at her ass. Then it wandered further to the high level of cuteness he'd heard when he'd talked to her on the phone earlier that afternoon.

Sweat dripped into his eyes, burning the ever-loving shit out of them. Having lost his focus, whether from his burning eyeballs or from thoughts of Mia, he yanked off his gloves and wiped his face with a towel he pulled from his bag.

"Jesse!" His Uncle Mark approached from the far side of the room with a wave. "Hey, I'm glad you're here tonight. I was going to be reaching out to you at some point over the weekend. This came across my desk a couple days ago." Mark handed a flyer to Jesse, *Savage Combat Productions* printed across the top of the page.

Jesse scanned the paper for the date of the upcoming fights. Looking back to his uncle, he said, "You guys want me to take this one? It's still what, nine, ten weeks away or something like that?" A river of sweat poured down the side of his face, over his uninjured cheek and he shrugged his shoulder to wipe it away.

Ten weeks was more than enough time to get ready for the fight; that wasn't his problem. His problem was deciding whether he wanted to take the fight to begin with. Did he want to go through the grueling weeks of training camp, the food restrictions as he cut weight, the endless days of training, eating, sleeping, and nothing (and nobody) else?

"They asked for you specifically," Mark said. "Willing to double what you made on the last one."

Money—the universal motivator. Jesse wanted to think he was above giving the idea any merit simply because of the payout. But, the way it did for everyone else, money made his world go around. He'd be an idiot to pass up double the payday simply because he was getting burned out on the sport.

With another week of modified training, he'd be fully healed, his stitches would be out, and he could be ready to train hard again. And, honestly, money was money. And still without any sense of what to do next, the paycheck he took home from that fight could give him a little more time to figure some stuff out.

He still had to take up Seth's offer to shadow him on a job site for a few days. The complete lack of enthusiasm he had for that idea was probably his biggest indicator that working for his dad's company was not going to be his way forward.

"Yeah, I'm in," he said, handing the flyer back to his uncle.

"I'll tell them." Without another word, Mark turned and left Jesse to get back to his workout.

Except he couldn't get his mind back into gear. The harder he tried to focus on his form, the further he needed to reach into his memory for a solid combination. Finally, he was able to snag an old familiar: *jab, cross, hook, slip, uppercut.* Jesse threw the combination a few times before his inner coach was completely drowned out by the sweet voice of Mia Reed: *We could always hang out tonight if you wanted to*.

He threw a lackluster version of the combo a few more times before he gave up for the night. His last uppercut had nothing on it and his hands stilled before falling to his sides.

"You good, Jesse?" his cousin Danny asked. "Kinda looks like you're still struggling a little bit." Equally drenched and exhausted, Danny dropped to the ground behind him, back against the wall. "How you feeling?"

Outside of his brothers, Danny was Jesse's best friend. They'd grown up together, their bond forged in blood and bruises. From childhood wrestling matches to teenage sparring sessions, they'd honed their skills side by side. He was a good fighter and an even better man.

"I'm all right," Jesse said. "Actually, feeling pretty good. Just can't get my head into gear."

The fact that Mia had gotten into his head deep enough to screw with his training was concerning. He had work to do and now a fight to prepare for. There was no way he should be letting her take over his thoughts like that. Especially since the only thing the future held for them was friendship.

"Yeah," Danny said, a shit-eating grin on his face, "girls will do that to you."

Jesse threw his cousin a look. "Who said anything about a girl?"

With his head leaned back against the wall, his arms draped over his knees, Danny laughed. "With that shit you were throwing, what the hell else could it be?"

Mia had invaded his mind, disrupted his focus. And he'd barely even spent any time with her. What would happen after he spent time with her? Or worse, if he let himself fall for her?

Danny pushed himself to his feet. "What do you say, cousin? Have you checked out for the night, or you wanna throw hands for a round or two?"

Determination renewed, Jesse strapped his sweaty gloves back on. "Hell yeah, I'm up for it. I've got to go light because of my face. Other than that, I'm ready."

The two men squared off before slipping into the familiar, controlled dance of sparring.

"**W**ow," Mia said, opening her apartment door to see a smiling Jesse on Saturday morning. "You are seriously punctual."

Since Mia had seen him last, Jesse's face had almost entirely healed. The swelling was gone, his bruises were not much more than shadows, and the stitches looked like they weren't doing much anymore and could probably come out.

"I've been outside for a few minutes," he said, grinning. "But we said nine forty-five, so I waited before I buzzed."

When he smiled, Mia suddenly had to remind herself to breathe. She had imagined he was a nice-looking guy underneath all the injuries, but her imagination had nothing on reality. Obviously, Lexi hadn't been kidding when she said he was cute under all those bruises.

Dark, scruffy hair covered a solid chin. His eyes, a bluer blue than she remembered, seemed to be holding something deeper behind them. Calm like the surface of a lake but teeming with life just below.

He stepped inside the apartment and took a deep breath as his baby blues zeroed in on her coffee maker. "You wouldn't happen to have any more of that, would you?"

"Help yourself."

He moved freely through her kitchen, looking in cabinets for a coffee mug, grabbing the milk from the fridge, setting up her coffee maker as if he'd done it a million times. As if he fit perfectly in her space. How was she going to keep herself from being attracted to this man when he could make that so difficult simply by existing?

She didn't want to think too much about it, but the hint of swagger in the way he carried himself was almost all self-confidence, and very little, if any, arrogance. And it was sexy as hell.

The more she tried to look away from him the more he effortlessly drew her attention. And his coffee hadn't even finished brewing yet.

None of that matters, she chided herself. It didn't matter because she wasn't interested in him like that.

Although, looking at it from a different perspective, it would make it a lot more fun to look at him while they hung around together.

"This place is so cute," Mia said as they pulled up in front of the quaint Cape Cod style house. It was set back from the street, nestled among a stand of tall trees. From its gray shingles to the decent sized front yard and nice landscaping, it exuded charm. Even the mailbox that looked like a giant fish added a touch of whimsy.

"That mailbox adds a nice touch," Jesse teased as they got out of the car.

From the looks of it, she and Jesse were the only ones there aside from the real estate agent.

Mia's laughter bubbled up, and she nudged his arm. "Maybe your first job as my friend could be to replace that. Rumor has it you have connections in the construction industry," she said, smiling, as they walked the length of sidewalk toward the driveway.

"I might have a connection or two," he said, opening the mailbox, then closing it up again. He shook his head. "Because that abomination absolutely has to go."

"But what if I like it?" Mia said, jokingly challenging him.

Jessed pivoted like he was going back to the car. "Then we can't be friends anymore," he teased.

She grabbed his arm and pulled him with her toward the house. The one thing she absolutely was not paying attention to was how solid his arm felt beneath her fingers. She was also not paying any attention to how easy it was to touch him. Or how much she liked it.

"It's kind of a small place," Jesse said as they walked up the driveway. "Is that what you're looking for?"

"I'm not a hundred percent sure yet," she said. "This is only the second house I've looked at. But how much room do I really need? It's literally just me. You've seen my apartment. I've got next to no furniture, so a bigger place doesn't feel like it makes a lot of sense."

Whatever dog she ended up adopting, assuming it wasn't some giant breed, would fit perfectly with her in a house that size.

He knocked on the door then turned the knob and waited for Mia to enter in front of him. "I guess," he said. "It just seems awfully small."

Inside, the layout matched the exterior's charm. A stairway to the second floor lay directly ahead, and to their left was a cozy living room. Straight ahead, past the stairs, a small dining area beckoned.

"Hello, how are you?" A tall woman in dress pants and a purple sweater approached from the room to the left of the dining area—probably the kitchen. "Welcome to fifty-six Harmony Ave. My name is Cindy." She stuck out her hand and Mia stepped forward to shake it.

"Mia Reed," she said, then gestured toward Jesse. "This is my friend, Jesse Murphy."

Cindy's eyes widened as she shook Jesse's hand. "Murphy?" she exclaimed. "Are you related to Owen Murphy by any chance?"

"Guilty," he said. "Owen's my older brother."

Cindy's face lit up. "Oh man," she said. "I graduated with him. How's he doing?"

As Cindy and Jesse exchanged stories about Owen, Mia couldn't help but notice the easy camaraderie between them. It turned out Cindy had a crush on Jesse's brother at one point during their high school careers. If Owen was even half as good-looking as Jesse, it wasn't a mystery why.

"So," Cindy said, pulling the conversation back to the house. "This home was built in the early sixties but has been recently updated. All new heating, electrical, and plumbing. The roof was replaced about five years ago." She brought them into the kitchen. "The kitchen was remodeled last year and obviously they chose all stainless-steel appliances."

"It's beautiful," Mia said. It really was. It lacked the breathtaking view her apartment had, but she could easily picture herself cooking in the little kitchen, then curling up on her couch in the living room to eat dinner.

Jesse stepped out of the kitchen and came back a few seconds later. "Is there a bathroom on this floor?"

Whether she meant to or not, Cindy winced slightly. "There is one full bathroom down here and one full bathroom upstairs."

"Where is it?" Jesse pressed.

Cindy guided them into the master bedroom which took up the entire right half of the first floor. At the top of the room were two doors, one to the bathroom and one to a small walk-in closet. "This is a nice sized room," Mia said, taking in the bedroom. It would more than fit her bed and bureau. "There's even plenty of room to set up a reading nook," she said. "I could get a recliner and a small bookshelf and put them near the window. It's a pretty space."

Jesse's eyes met hers, and for a moment, the label of "just friends" felt flimsy. "Do you mind if we look around a little bit?" Jesse said to Cindy.

"Absolutely. I'll be in the kitchen if you have any questions."

Cindy walked out of the room, leaving Jesse and Mia alone in the bedroom.

"I really like this house," she said. "What do you think of it?" In the grand scheme of things, his opinion wouldn't sway her decision, but she couldn't help being curious.

It surprised her when he said, "It's all right. I still think it's really small."

"I know it's small. But I think that's what I want." She laughed. He still looked unimpressed.

"Let's take a look around," he said, gesturing toward the bedroom door. "You haven't even gone upstairs yet."

Stopping in the doorway, he waited for her to walk through. She didn't remember to hold her breath as she slipped by him. Instead, she got a whiff of the warm scent that came off him in waves—a blend of clean laundry and something uniquely Jesse—that wrapped itself around her.

Relieved to be out of reach of his scent, she led the way upstairs.

Directly at the top of the landing was a full bathroom. To either side was a bedroom, mirror images of each other.

"Let me guess?" she quipped. "Too small?"

"Way."

The angled ceilings created cozy alcoves by the dormered windows. Mia stepped into one, gazing out over the neighborhood. His scent followed her, an invisible thread that wound through the air, brushing her shoulders and trailing down her body. Her eyes fluttered closed as he stepped into the space with her, his body tantalizingly close, to look over her shoulder. "Not as nice a view as your apartment has," he said, his breath warm against her skin, "but it's OK."

She was as aware of Jesse behind her as she'd ever been about anything in her life. Sure, his body was big and took up space, but it was his presence that couldn't be ignored. More to the point, it was the way her body tingled from head to foot when he was near her that couldn't be ignored.

"Yeah," she murmured, her eyes still closed. "It's nice."

"Still think it's too small."

"You're seriously hung up on that," she said, turning to face him, ready for a playfully heated debate. Their eyes locked, and her breath hitched. And judging by the way his smile tipped to the side, he'd heard it—the unspoken hesitation. "Why is that such a big deal?" she managed to squeak out.

He shrugged one big shoulder. "Think about it," he said. "If people come to visit, the dining room looked like it might hold five or six people, max. And if any of those people needed to use the bathroom, they'd have to go into your bedroom to get there."

She hadn't thought about that. "So," she said. "What's wrong with that?"

"I don't know that there's anything *wrong* with it," he said. "So much as I don't think I'd want people in my personal space like that. A bedroom is like a , you know? The things that happen there are personal. The thoughts you think there are personal. Whether or not you put your clothes in the hamper or leave them in a pile on the floor is personal."

Neither of them had moved an inch yet somehow there was even less air to breathe as he held her gaze. "Know what I mean?" he said.

"How's everything going up here?" Cindy's bright voice popped their little bubble, and Jesse instinctively took a half step backward.

"We're good," Mia replied. To Jesse, she said, "I still want to look at the yard though."

Without a word, he stepped out of the alcove, clearing the way for her to come through. "After you."

The backyard was perfect. It was a small, fenced-in square of grass with a row of flowers along the back edge. "OK, I know you're going to tell me this is too small, but I think it's amazing," she said.

To her surprise, Jesse stood with his hands on his hips, looking appraisingly over the yard, then shook his head. "No, I'm not going to say that at all." His eyes fixed on the small cement pad over to the far side near the garage. "That little patio might be the biggest selling point of the whole house."

"It's perfect, right?" Mia's excitement bubbled over. "I could put some outdoor seating there. A grill. Maybe a fire pit. There's so much I could do with that space."

One dark eyebrow angled up. "You're out of your mind," he said. "That is the perfect place to build a small frame and hang a heavy bag. Maybe even hang a speed bag from one of the supports."

Mia couldn't help but laugh. "Don't you already go to the gym? Why would you want all that stuff in your house, too?"

He slapped a hand over his heart. "You're killing me, Mia. You know that don't you? Killing. Me."

Jesse

T HE PLANS HE AND Mia had made to hang out in the afternoon and then grab dinner ended up getting scratched when his uncle texted and asked him to cover the two Saturday afternoon classes at the gym.

Jesse noticed the subtle shift in Mia's demeanor as he prepared to leave her apartment. Her eyes, once bright with excitement over her house prospects, now held a hint of disappointment. She fidgeted with the edge of her sweater, her fingers tracing patterns on the fabric.

He tried to explain the need to cover the classes. "It's my uncle's gym," he said. "And there's nobody else to cover them."

She nodded, her smile a little forced. "It's no big deal," she said. "It's not like we had definite plans or anything. Don't worry about it."

As he stepped toward the door, he caught her gaze—a fleeting moment of vulnerability. She blinked, masking whatever emotions brewed beneath the surface. But Jesse had seen it—the way her lips tightened, the way her shoulders slumped ever so slightly.

Mia acted like it didn't matter, but he wondered if that was true. Maybe she just wanted to hang out as friends until dinner, or perhaps she actually enjoyed being with him. Maybe he wasn't misreading her expression; maybe she truly felt disappointed that their day had to end so suddenly.

It was less than ten minutes from Mia's place to the gym. Even though he looked forward to the familiar feel of the mats beneath his feet and the creak of heavy bags swinging from thick chains, he hated that he'd already disappointed her.

Normally, walking through the front doors of his uncle's gym was enough to strip away everything else happening in his life, giving him the ability to focus on his workout, or the class he was teaching. Somehow, Mia had changed that, even in the brief time they'd known each other.

It was nothing she'd done, nothing she'd said that had him out of sorts. It was just... her. He liked her and he liked being around her. He liked the way she looked at him and the way her breath caught when they were together looking out the window of the smallest house he'd ever been inside.

Jesse laughed to himself as he pulled the gym door open. What Mia saw in that miniscule house was beyond him. She said he was the first person to visit her apartment, so maybe she didn't need that much space, but still... And that mailbox. If she did end up buying the house, he'd make sure that was the first thing to go.

A dozen elementary aged kids sat lined up against the padded wall at the back of the room, "Thanks for coming in, man," Danny said. "I hate having to cancel."

Danny normally taught the Saturday classes with one of the other instructors, while Jesse's domain was more the young adult classes that met during the week. "Don't worry about it," Jesse said. "Your dad said Robby's got food poisoning or something."

Frowning, Danny nodded. "Poor guy couldn't even text me himself. His girl had to text me from their spare bedroom. Dude's in a world of fucking hurt." They approached the kids together and Danny added, "I hope I didn't drag you away from anything important."

"Nah," Jesse lied. "Nothing major."

Danny had a natural rapport with the kids, and Jesse found himself falling into sync with him. To work on their reflexes and speed, Danny had them play a simple game of tag before focusing on balance—having them stand on one leg like flamingos. Jesse followed Danny's lead through the rest of the class.

Rather than have the kids hitting the heavy bag, or one another, they had them split into two lines, one before Danny and one before Jesse. The two adults wielded lengths of foam pool noodles they used to "attack" the kids, giving them practice in defense before holding them up as targets for honing their striking skills.

As they almost always did for Jesse, the class flew by in a blink. Before he knew it, the gym was almost empty. All the kids had been picked up but one. His mother was hustling into the building as Jesse was giving the floor a onceover with the sanitizer after playing host to all those bare feet.

"Bye Mr. Jesse," the kid yelled as his mother gathered up his belongings.

Jesse waved at him, and his mother caught Jesse's eye. Under normal circumstances, her flirtatious smile would have certainly caught Jesse's interest and he would've flirted back. But having met and spent time with Mia, his circumstances felt nothing like normal. So, rather than encourage her, Jesse looked back to the little boy. "Great work today, buddy."

The kid beamed as he followed his mother out the door, leaving Danny and Jesse alone until the next group of kids arrived.

With a questioning look, Danny raised his eyes to Jesse's. "What was that about?"

"What was what about?" Honestly confused, Jesse kept cleaning the mats.

"Kyle's mom practically tripped over her own tongue when she saw you, and you, who would normally have jumped all over that, ignored her entirely," Danny said, suspicion dripping from every word. "What aren't you telling me, cousin?"

Unable to suppress a smile, Jesse shrugged. "Nothing to tell, cousin."

"Like hell," Danny said, stepping out from behind the desk. "You never did tell me her name last night." He stood leaning against the desk with his arms folded across his chest.

Not willing to keep lying to his cousin, Jesse stilled his cleaning. "Her name is Mia."

Danny's face split into a grin.

"Before you go getting all goofy on me," Jesse said, "she's just a friend of mine. Nothing more than that."

His cousin looked entirely unconvinced. "A friend?" he echoed. "Dude, I've got friends too. And none of them have me losing focus when I train or ignoring beautiful women who are throwing signs at me, so don't be handing me that line of crap."

"It's not crap, man. We met the night of my fight. We've barely even spent any time together. I swear to God, she's just a friend of mine," Jesse insisted, not believing his own words any more than his cousin seemed to be.

Later that night, after a shower during which Jesse thought of nothing but Mia, he sat on the couch and waited for his dinner to be delivered. It wouldn't be too long and he'd be training for a fight again, and takeout wouldn't be an option.

Lounging in his sweatpants and his favorite hoodie, he picked up his phone.

> Sorry again about bailing on you tonite

Her reply was quick.

> Don't worry about it

> How was your class

His mind, which had been so agitated, started to settle down again as he and Mia fell into a rhythm of text messages.

> It was good

> Kids are funny

> lol yes they are

He put the phone down when the delivery driver knocked on the door. As he sat on the couch and started to unwrap his sub, disappointment flooded him again. He and Mia were supposed to be eating dinner together.

Sitting by himself eating a sandwich kind of sucked.

> **Hey – got any plans tomorrow**

> nope

> **wanna hang out**

This time her reply was not as quick, and he wondered if he'd been too forward. She'd said she wanted to be friends and he may have just scared her off.

> sorry – timer went off

> had to get dinner out of the oven

> would love to hang out

> what do you want to do

Relief flooded into every one of his cells. Until he realized he didn't really have a plan for what to do. He just wanted to see her, to be near her.

Thankfully, an idea popped into his head.

> **want to walk to the farmer's market**

> yes! that sounds like fun

The desire to keep up their conversation pulled at him. But the threat of saying too much or saying the wrong thing overtook him. He liked this woman. A lot. The last thing he wanted to do was drive her away.

great. see you tomorrow

pick you up around 10?

sounds perfect

If she only knew how perfect she sounded. What was happening to him? Was this all part of his what-the-hell-comes-next panic? He'd never thought about a woman as much as he thought about Mia, let alone been afraid of driving one away. Before Mia came along, that had never even been a thought.

Mia

FOR THE SECOND MORNING in a row, Jesse was in her house, drinking her coffee. This time he brought it to the couch and made himself even more at home.

She wondered if it was too much, too soon. Despite her total body freakouts every time he was within a foot of her, he hadn't expressed any interest in her. Well, aside from the way he looked like he might have kissed her in front of the window at the open house yesterday.

There was no way that's what he'd been thinking, though. They'd decided *together* to be friends and nothing more.

After swallowing down a large mouthful of coffee, he said, "Well, I know it's not as exciting as looking at the smallest houses on the east coast, but the farmer's market up at St. Michael's Park is still pretty fun."

Twenty minutes later, they were out in the cool morning that held the promise of a warm afternoon. Not that she didn't warm up quite nicely on her own every time Jesse looked at her.

She really needed to get a handle on this. He was not her boyfriend. She didn't want a boyfriend. And if Lexi was right, he didn't really do the girlfriend thing all that well. If she couldn't act like a normal person around him, she'd have to stop hanging around with him altogether.

The crisp air woke her up as they walked inland a few blocks to a huge grassy field across the road from a giant white church. The park was enclosed by a black wrought iron fence while the interior was set up with rows of tables and tents and food trucks. A decent crowd had already begun to gather.

As they walked, they talked. "I've never known anyone who does what you do for a living," she said. "How did you even get into fighting in the first place?"

An impish smile stole across his face. "That's a story I haven't told in a long time."

"Which means now you have to tell it."

Loads of people seemed to recognize Jesse as they walked through the crowd. A few people waved at him, while others looked from him to her then went back to whatever they'd been doing. Jesse waved back at the ones who initiated but didn't seem to notice the rest of the eyes that followed them as they walked.

"Did you see the older lady on the bus the other night?" he asked.

"Yeah," Mia said. "She's a nun, right?"

"Sister Mary Ellen, that's her."

"A nun got you into fighting?" Mia said, throwing a little sass his way.

"In a roundabout kind of way," he said, his tone playful. "I was a bit of a troublemaker when I was a kid. Hard to believe, I know. But it's true. One day my cousin and I thought it would be a good idea to sneak into the church and steal the wine they use for communion." He flicked a glance toward the white clapboard building with the steepled bell tower on top.

She gasped and hid her open mouth behind her hand. "No, you didn't."

He cast his eyes down as he nodded his head. "Oh, we did. Except, you know, it's locked inside this big box thing, and when we tried to break it open, Sister Mary Ellen happened to be there and heard us."

With a big grin on his face, he said, "I thought nuns were supposed to be these calm, peaceful old ladies, but Sister Mary Ellen was *on fire* when she caught us there. I thought we were gonna catch a beating from the sister right then and there."

Jesse's laughter was contagious as he recounted his tale. "Somehow Danny talked her down and even got her to not call the police on us. I think he used to be an altar boy or something. Either way, he saved our asses—big time—that night."

"So, what? You took up fighting to protect yourself from angry nuns?" The image that painted in her head cracked her up.

"Not a bad guess," he teased. "But it turned out that part of the deal for not getting turned in to the cops was Danny and I having to do a shit ton of work on the rec center on the other side of the church. Turns out a couple of fifteen-year-old kids could do a decent amount of work when they had somewhere to focus their attention.

"And when our parents found out what happened, Danny's dad—my Uncle Mark, who was a professional boxer—thought the two of us might need a little bit of structure once our time on the rec center was done. So, he got us into boxing.

"Fast forward eighteen years, and here we are," he said, spreading his arms wide.

Mia couldn't help but admire what she saw—again. She knew she shouldn't be looking at him that way, but it was impossible not to. He was tall and lean, and his body was tight with a perfect amount of muscle. His arms stretched the fabric of his shirt sleeves and his slim cut jeans didn't leave a lot to the imagination.

They were not the observations one friend made of another and she knew she had to keep that line firmly between them because it was getting blurry—fast.

"But it's got to be a tough gig," she said.

"It's not always easy." He looked at one of the food trucks selling cannoli. "For one thing, stuff like that is off the table for me most days." He laughed so easily, Mia envied his easygoing nature. "For real, it's pretty hard. There's the training. I'm at the gym pretty much every day. When I'm leading up to a fight, I'm in the gym every day twice a day for like a month or more. I've got to watch what I eat, partly to make sure I hit my fight weight, but also to make sure I've got fuel in the tank."

Thankfully, he seemed oblivious to the way she looked at him.

A couple of men came up to them and interrupted their conversation. "What's up, Jesse?" one of the guys said.

Jesse shook his hand. "Hey, good to see you, man. How's things going?"

"Good. You know how it is."

The men looked from Jesse to Mia.

"Mia," Jesse said, "these are a couple of friends of mine from way back. Gus, Irv, this is my friend Mia. She's new to town and I'm showing her how awesome Oak Harbor is."

"Nice to meet you, Mia," Gus said, extending his hand for a shake.

"Welcome to town," Irv said. "It's kind of small, but it's a decent place to live."

After a few more words between them, Gus and Irv walked on, heading toward a couple of women and small children that Mia assumed must be their families.

"You know a lot of people in this town," Mia remarked as they resumed their walk through the rows of vendors. And if Lexi was right, he'd probably dated quite a few of the women there.

"It's not a very big town." He stopped at one table and bought a small basil plant.

"Besides," he said, leading her down another row where people were selling hand crafted items, "like a quarter of the people in this town are related by blood or by marriage so it's almost impossible to go anywhere and not know someone."

They stopped at one table where Mia picked up a bar of hand-made soap designed with a yellow daisy in the center. Not only was it adorable but it had a nice, bright scent. She bought it, thinking how cute it might look in her bathroom.

"What about you?" he asked as they kept walking. "Being a nurse can't be the easiest job there is either?"

"It's not easy, no," she said. "But working in a school isn't nearly as hard as being an ER nurse. The worst thing I deal with now is the occasional kid with a stomach bug who can't quite make it to the bathroom."

"Nasty," Jesse said. "I think I'll take my chances in the ring."

"No, it was really sad," Mia said, recalling the little girl who'd thrown up all over the floor of her office. "The poor little thing terrified herself because she'd never thrown up before." She laughed, thinking back, then admitted, "But, yeah, it was nasty."

They walked past another vendor selling individual Boston Cream pies and she saw the longing in Jesse's eyes as he looked at them. In all her life, Mia had never been jealous of a pastry until that very minute.

Pulling herself back, she continued their conversation. "I don't think I could do anything else, though," she said. "I really love what I do, despite the occasional grossness of it."

"It's a hard thing to think about, isn't it? What to do next?" he said. "I'm kind of in that boat right now."

Without any conscious thought or planning, they had ended up in line for a ring toss game. Mia fished a couple singles out of her wallet and bought them each a round of play. "You're giving up fighting?" she asked as she tossed a hoop, hoping to keep her surprise unseen. "That's huge."

Jesse

MIA'S RING BOUNCED AROUND the bottles and landed on a non-winning one.

Jesse leaned over and tossed one of his rings, also landing on a non-winning bottle. "I've been thinking about it for a while, I just have no idea what I'd even do next. I have no idea what's even out there for me to do."

"I get that," she said. "Sort of." She tossed another ring that bounced over the bottles and landed on the ground.

He paused before he tossed the next ring. "You do?"

"Actually, yeah. I left my old town and came here kind of on a whim because the job at the school was available. But it's only available because the regular nurse is on maternity leave. So, when the school year ends, so does my employment."

"Do you want to stay with nursing?" he asked as he eventually tossed the ring and watched it land on a red painted bottle.

"Winner!" the young man with the apron called out. "Take your pick," he said, pointing to a row of small stuffed animals on a table behind the ring toss game. "Anything in the first row."

Jesse looked at Mia. "Which one you want?"

"The bear with the daisy on her belly," she said.

Of course she picked that one. "Got a thing for daisies?" he asked.
"They're my favorite flower."

"We'll take the bear with the daisy, please," Jesse said to the young man.

Mia threw her remaining ring, but it clattered over the bottles and flipped over the side of the table onto the ground.

"You never answered my question," he said as they headed toward the break in the fence that led out of the park, his basil plant in one hand, her bar of soap in the other while Mia cuddled the stuffed animal.

"Oh," she said. "About staying in nursing?"

He nodded.

"Yeah, I'll definitely stay in nursing, but I really don't want to go back to a hospital. The hours are tough, and the work can be really intense. I don't know where I'll end up, but I really need to get to work finding something if I want to buy a house here."

They had a couple sandwiches and a bag of chips delivered to her apartment. Jesse sat beside Mia on the couch, and they ate while they watched an episode of *Cake Wars*. "This is what you like to watch?" he said, glancing up at the screen.

"I love this stuff," she said. "It's easy to watch one episode and not get sucked in all day. It's fun, it's entertaining, and... you know what?" Her back straightened and she held his gaze. "Yes, I like watching cooking shows. And I don't need to explain myself or the things I like to do."

Initially, he had seen her as kind of fragile, but now he recognized a different side to her—a spark that intrigued him. As they sat together on the couch, sharing sandwiches and chips, her eyes held determination as she defended her interests.

Jesse appreciated her confidence. He liked it. "Good for you," he said, and he took another bite of his sandwich. Once he swallowed it down, he said, "Never apologize for the shit you like. I was just teasing you. My mom and my sister-in-law love this stuff. And even though they'd die before admitting it out loud, I'm pretty sure a couple of my brothers like it too."

"I've been meaning to ask you about that," she said as she lifted her glass to her lips. "Exactly how many brothers do you have?"

"Three. All older than me," he said. "And a younger sister."

Mia sipped from her water glass, then put it down on the table. "Five children," she whispered. "I can't even imagine what that was like." She turned to him. "Was it awesome growing up with that many siblings? I'll bet it was awesome."

He hadn't thought about it much. It was just the way life was. It was the only family he'd ever had and, as much of a pain in the ass as they could be, they were his and he loved them all.

"It was fun," he finally said. "Having four boys in the house always kept things interesting anyhow." He leaned back against the couch. "How many brothers and sisters do you have?"

"Just the one sister."

"The one you don't talk to anymore?"

Her smile faded and she nodded. Grabbing the garbage from the table, she crumbled it all up in her hands then carried it to the trash can in the kitchen. He understood her cue to let the topic drop.

She came back to the couch with a couple bottles of seltzer and handed him one. Sitting beside him, she leaned back, mimicking his posture. "If you want," she started, then stopped. "I don't know if it's anything you even want help with," she said, "but... I could give you a hand trying to find something else to do once you're done boxing." Her face scrunched up in thought. "That's what you do, right? Box?"

"I do box," he said. "But I'm an MMA fighter which means I also fight other forms."

"Other forms of what?" she said, confusion in her eyes.

"Martial arts," he said with a laugh. "Obviously I box, but I also train Muay Thai and Jiu Jitsu, with straight up wrestling all thrown in at the same time. Though I favor Muay Thai and boxing because I'm more of a stand-up fighter." He held her gaze as she sipped from her seltzer, realizing she probably had no idea what the difference was between all those things. Why would she? "But if you're serious about helping me, I'd have to be an idiot not to accept."

"Oh, good," she said putting the seltzer down on the coffee table, appearing to be back in her comfort zone.

It wouldn't take much for a guy to get lost in a smile like hers. He'd wanted to kiss her in that stupid little house she was looking at yesterday and he wanted to kiss her sitting next to her on the couch right then.

It also wouldn't take much to make her kick him to the curb after telling him she only wanted to be friends.

He needed to get out of her apartment before he made things awkward by saying, or doing, something he shouldn't. He looked at his phone. "Thanks for coming out for some exercise with me. That was really fun." Standing, he picked up the remaining garbage from the table and carried it to the trash.

As he approached the door to leave, he said, "This weekend was nice." He pulled the door open and stopped in the doorway. "It's pretty cool having a new friend in town."

The look in her eyes told him she might be thinking of him as more than a friend and it shook him. While her words still said 'just friends,' the way she looked at him at the open house, then at the farmer's market, and then again in her doorway, said 'more.'

"New friends are good," she said, then took a long drink from her seltzer bottle. "This is good." He wanted her to say more, to tell him she wanted him to kiss her, to say anything at all that would get him to stay. "I'll text you during the week and we can set up a time to start doing some what-comes-next research."

Out loud, he said, "Cool. Sounds good." On the inside he was thinking that she couldn't text him soon enough and he couldn't wait to see her again. With his basil plant clutched in his hands, he left her apartment and headed home to change before going to Sunday dinner with the family.

Jesse

"**W**HEN DO WE GET to meet your new friend?"

"Nice to see you too, Mom," Jesse teased as he stepped into the kitchen to offer his mother some help.

"Gaelen," his father said, a touch of gentle warning in his voice, "would you leave the kid alone? He's been in the house for three seconds." Pat rolled his eyes, looked at Jesse, then lifted his chin toward the living room. "The girls are all waiting for you."

The Murphy house was full that Sunday evening. Between all four brothers, one sister-in-law, three nieces, and one nephew, there was no doubt his mother was in her glory.

With a laugh, Jesse left his parents to get dinner ready while he went to search out his nieces. With all of them there that week, he wouldn't get a moment's rest until they sat down to eat. Maybe not even then.

His siblings were chatting amongst themselves, his teenage nephew sat scrolling through his phone, and the three girls were lying on the floor amidst a pile of papers and a basket of magic markers.

Jesse watched the scene for an extra heartbeat, taking it all in. When his brother Owen noticed him, Jesse lifted a finger to keep him from saying anything, then pointed at the girls.

For whatever reason, his nieces loved when he pretended to be a monster and chase them around the house. Working up his best growl and pulling his face into a sneer, he stood just outside the living room door.

Within a second, the girls started screaming. He jumped into the doorway and threw his hands in the air with a roar. Markers and papers went flying, little girls scrambled to their feet, laughing and screaming hysterically as they tripped over themselves to get away from the monster.

"It's a beautiful day today!" Jesse's sister-in-law Gretchen yelled over the cacophony. "Maybe take it outside."

All three girls sprinted out of the living room toward the kitchen, then out the back door while Jesse did his heavy-footed monster march behind them.

As soon as he reached the backyard, he scanned to find where the girls were hiding. Though, he didn't need to use his eyes so much as his ears because no matter how many times he told them he could hear them, they still insisted on shushing each other—loudly—the closer he got.

He sniffed dramatically and growled, "I know there are little girls out here somewhere," in his deepest, most monster-like voice. "I wonder if they're over by the chicken coop." They were nowhere near the chicken coop and he knew it, but what fun would it be to catch them right away? The further he walked away from them, the louder their giggles became.

Trying to keep himself from laughing, he growled in frustration at not finding them by the chicken coop. One of the girls whisper-shouted to the others, "He can't find us," and they all started giggling again.

He made a great show of stomping around the yard, looking under the patio furniture, around the side of the bunny hutch, and behind the chicken coop. On the far side of the house, still inside the fenced-in backyard, his parents had a small shed to hold the supplies they needed to maintain the menagerie of animals his mother had collected over the years. It was the one place the girls always hid. No matter how many times he'd found them there, it was the place he always would.

Movement from the interior of the house caught his eye. His mother waved at him in from the other side of the sliding glass doors. She was letting him know dinner was ready. He nodded and motioned to give him one minute to round up the girls.

"I am so hungry!" With exaggerated stomps and deep growls, Jesse stomped his way toward the shed.

One of the girls whispered, "Here he comes. Ready?"

He stifled another laugh, wondering what they were getting ready for. With a roar, Jesse jumped to the far side of the shed and at the same time, three little girls jumped out and roared back at him, waving their hands and baring their teeth.

It was chaos as Jesse dropped to the ground, pretending to be terrified at the horde of little girls. His nieces flew through the air, jumping on him, clinging to him, and trying to wrestle him to the ground.

Unable to stop himself, Jesse laughed long and deep as they defended their ground from him with such unbridled zeal. Eventually, he managed to get to one knee. Ava, his oldest niece, clung to his back like a monkey, while he grabbed Rylee in one arm then pushed up to standing. Chloe, the littlest one, roared at him and charged full steam. In one quick motion he scooped her up and tucked her under his free arm and began the trek back into the house.

Gretchen opened the sliding door and stepped onto the patio, laughing as she took in the sight of them. "Grandma says it's time to eat." Chloe immediately stopped her roaring and flailing arms, Rylee's eyes popped open, and Ava released her choke hold on his neck and almost fell to the ground. He precariously lowered himself and let the horde escape. "Go inside and wash your hands please, girls," Gretchen called out as they rushed by her.

As Jesse attempted to step through the door after the girls, his sister-in-law gave him a pointed look, her eyes narrowed a fraction and a smile tugging at the corners of her mouth.

When he was younger, Sunday dinners were a hassle. Only emergencies excused a person from eating dinner with the family on a Sunday night. *"It's the only time we get to be all together,"* his mother used to say. *"It's what your mother wants, so get your ass in the chair,"* his father had always said.

Now that he was older, he'd grown to appreciate the time with everyone. Once kids started entering the picture, and significant others that came and went, it was a different gathering of people almost every week. He'd even been known to bring a girlfriend a time or two. More than anything else, though, the ritual of family dinner every week added a layer of security to Jesse's life.

Conversation was lively, as it always was. Owen and Gretchen fussed over their girls and Seth did the same for Rylee. Shane and his son sat side by side but didn't say much of anything to one another.

"So, Jesse," his mother said as she scooped a serving of mashed potatoes onto her plate, "can you tell me about this new friend of yours yet?"

He'd forgotten she'd asked about Mia when he first walked in the door. His father had saved him then, but the old man was caught up in a conversation with Shane over one of the jobs they were currently working, so he'd be no help.

"What friend is that, Mom?"

Gaelen arched her brows in the way that moms do, telling him she wasn't an idiot and to start talking.

"How do you even know about her?" Jesse asked, thoroughly confused as to how she could possibly know about Mia.

"Danny said something to Uncle Mike. Uncle Mike told Aunt Nadine and Aunt Nadine told me. We have a very big family in a very small town." She passed the potatoes to Seth then picked up the bowl of green beans. "So, who is she and why isn't she here tonight?"

"Well," Jesse said with a laugh, taking a few slices of ham from the platter in front of him, "her name is Mia. I met her on the bus a few weeks ago after my fight. We're *just friends*. And she's not here because I don't invite my *just friends* to family dinners. If I did that, this place would be overrun with people."

Conversations around the table petered out as everyone turned their attention to his conversation with his mother.

"You've got a girlfriend?" Gretchen said, wearing a bemused expression. "Well, that's exciting. You're going to be an amazing dad someday, J, you know that right?"

Jesse went still as a statue as he digested the words his sister-in-law tossed out so easily. Him? With kids? And why did Mia's face pop unbidden into his mind when he thought about that? "Kids?" he said. "We're not having any kids. Because she's not my girlfriend."

"Why not?" Shane asked in that irritating way he had that implied Jesse was a dumbass for not making Mia his girlfriend. As if it was up to Jesse...

"Is she pretty?" Rylee asked. "I'll bet she's pretty. Right Uncle J?"

"When can I meet her?" Ava asked.

"Me too?" Chloe added.

All eyes were on him. Even Brant and Seth were watching to see how he would answer all these questions. And for the first time since he was a kid, he wished he'd chosen to skip family dinner night.

He shoved a piece of ham into his mouth and chewed, giving himself time to think. "Look," he said after he washed the bite down with a drink of lemonade, "I told you already. She's just a person I met on the bus. I popped a stitch and she's a nurse, so she helped me out. That's it. She's a nice woman and there's nothing more to tell."

Gretchen, who was normally on Jesse's side with all things family related, made a slightly guilty face. "Actually, I already knew about you two. I heard you were kind of cozy down at the farmer's market today." She had the decency to look ashamed of spreading gossip, but it didn't change the fact that his entire family was talking about his new *friendship*.

"Yeah, I heard that too," Brant said. The kid never said much of anything to anyone. He had to choose that moment to start?

"How the hell did you hear about anything?" Jesse asked his normally quiet nephew. He threw his gaze around the table. "How did any of you hear anything about this?"

He'd told Mia he lived in a small town where most of the people were related by blood or marriage, and it seemed it was truer than he even knew.

"Calm down, honey," his mother said. "You know how it is in a town like this. People love to talk. And when it comes to the potential for young love, they love it even more."

Everyone at the table laughed, except Jesse.

"Young love, Mom? I'm thirty-two years old, not seventeen."

"Yeah, he's old," Chloe chimed in.

From across the table, he shot his four-year-old niece an amused grin. "Thanks."

From right beside him, Rylee tapped his arm, tugged him close, and whispered, "Is she pretty, Uncle J?"

Unable to lie to the kid, he sighed, nodded, and whispered back, "Very."

Jesse

J ESSE STEPPED OUT OF the shower area and into the gym's main locker room on Wednesday morning. He checked his phone for the millionth time to see if Mia had texted him. She'd said she would during the week. The week was half over, and he still hadn't heard from her.

He wondered if he'd made it obvious that he was into her the last time they were together and maybe that had something to do with her silence.

Could he help it if he liked being around her? He'd never made a move on her, never even tried to hold her hand, so why she was keeping him at a distance was kind of a mystery. She'd told him she only wanted to be friends and he'd respected that.

Unless she *was* interested in him but was too afraid to say anything about it. He'd seen the disappointment when he had to leave early last weekend. And, if he wasn't mistaken, she'd been checking him out while they walked around the farmers' market, even though she pretended like she wasn't.

Or maybe she found out how small and gossipy Oak Harbor really was all on her own. The way people talked in this town, who knows who said what to her. For all he knew, half the town had them engaged by this point.

His heart raced as he stared at his phone, contemplating whether to send a message instead of waiting for her. What if she didn't respond? What if he was misreading everything? The cursor blinked, waiting for him to type, but his fingers felt like lead.

Jesse's mind played out scenarios—each one more nerve-wracking than the last. His safe place was in the gym or in the ring. In those places he was cool, calm, and collected. Even with other women he'd never felt this uncertain, this unsteady. The feelings he was developing for Mia were uncharted territory.

> Been thinking about my next move. Dinner and talk tomorrow?

She didn't need to know he meant that in more than one way. In truth, he meant it in only one way; he wanted his move to be taking a step closer to her. He hadn't given one second's thought to whatever his next career move might be. She could read the text any which way, it was all good to him.

> Working now, dinner tomorrow is good. Where and when?

Shit. He'd forgotten that she had a regular job with regular hours.

> Your place 6pm?

She responded with a thumb's up emoji.

He stuffed his phone into his bag as a couple of the younger guys exited the shower area and started packing up their gear. Jesse had just taught their early morning class and he knew a few of them had college classes later in the day and the rest all had to go to their day jobs.

"Nice work today, Eddie," Jesse said to one of the guys. Eddie had his gear bag slung over his shoulder and was heading off to school. "That spin elbow is badass, man. Keep working on it."

"Thanks, Coach. You coming with us tomorrow night?" A bunch of the guys were going together to check out some local fights, maybe stop for a bite to eat.

"Can't. Got plans. I'll see you back here on Monday, though."

"You got a date, Coach?" Eddie asked, a shit-eating grin plastered on his face. "Is she hot?"

A question only a kid could ask him without getting his ass kicked. "See you Monday, Eddie." Jesse grabbed his gear and headed out the door.

"**T**HANKS FOR COMING OUT with me," Mia said as she and Lexi loaded up their bags into the trunk of Mia's car. "It's fun having someone to go shopping with."

Dressed like she was going out on a hot date instead of a night shopping with Mia, Lexi smiled. "We're not done yet, though, right?" she said. "My Mastercard is just getting warmed up. Besides," she said as they hopped into Mia's gray Mazda, "shopping makes me hungry, and we still haven't eaten yet."

Aside from the few times she'd hung out with Jesse, this was the first time she'd hung out with anyone since she moved to Oak Harbor. Keeping Jesse out of her mind was proving harder to do and she'd been looking for someone else to hang out with.

She'd texted Lexi during her lunch hour and within five minutes, the trip was a "go."

They had driven down the coast a bit to hit the nearest mall where they both bought clothes and shoes, and a few new decorations for their homes.

The highlight had been what Lexi described as the area's hidden gem of a consignment store. Set a few miles inland, somewhere along a road that meandered through several towns, Ace of Space sounded more like a NASA program than an adorable place to buy cute accent pieces for her apartment. She didn't even need to dip into her house savings account to be able to afford them.

Mia's backseat was a testament to the great little finds she and Lexi couldn't resist. Mia had grabbed a small end table and a couple framed prints in various hues of blue and green that reminded her of the ocean. She'd also found a cute set of wooden lighthouse bookends and she couldn't wait to get her books off the floor and up onto those built-in shelves.

As the women drove back into Oak Harbor, Lexi pointed to a small Italian restaurant near the edge of the waterfront district. "Pull in there," she said, indicating the entrance to Morello's parking lot. Mia happily obliged.

"I haven't been here yet," Mia said. "Is this another hidden gem I should have known about?"

Lexi unfolded herself from the passenger seat. "Oh, no. This is probably one of the food highlights of this town. Everyone knows this place." She looked around the parking lot that was probably about seventy percent full. "The only reason we'll get in here without a reservation tonight is because it's a Wednesday." She flipped her thick black mane of hair over her shoulder and said with a grin, "And because my husband is best friends with the owner."

As the host escorted them to a small table, a tall man dressed in dark pants with a crisp white shirt and black tie approached them with his arms held open for a hug. "Mrs. Greeves," he said to Lexi, "it's great to see you."

Lexi laughed as she returned his hug. "I know it's been more than two years, but the whole 'Mrs.' thing still sounds weird to my ear."

"It suits you perfectly," he said then turned his eye toward Mia. "Hello," he said, extending his hand. "Michael Morello."

"Mia Reed." She shook his hand. "Your restaurant is beautiful," she said, looking around the spacious, yet somehow cozy, dining room.

"All the more so now that you lovely ladies have arrived." It was no wonder Morello's was a popular place among the locals. The owner was charming, and handsome, and probably had a PhD in flirting. Mia liked him.

A young woman dressed similarly to Michael, except with the addition of a black apron around her waist, came by with a bottle of water for their table. With a gracious smile, Michael said, "I will leave you in Kelsey's capable hands. And make sure you leave room for dessert."

After ordering a bottle of Chianti and a plate of bruschetta to share, Mia and Lexi took a few extra minutes to look over the menu. Mia leaned forward to whisper across the table. "Wow," she said, "so, the owner sure is a charmer, huh?"

Lexi leaned in to whisper back, "He is such a great guy. And not too hard on the eyes, that's for sure."

The women giggled and Mia said, "Is it hard having him as your husband's best friend?"

"No," Lexi said. "Well, except on my wedding day. Michael was our best man and if you think he looks good in plain old suit pants, you should see him in a tux. If my husband wasn't a total hottie, I might've had a hard time not walking down the aisle into the arms of the best man."

Lexi giggled again and Mia wasn't entirely sure if she was joking. Lexi must have sensed Mia's confusion because she laughed harder. "Relax, Mia. I'm kidding with you."

Mia smiled into her wine glass, loving the relaxing feeling of laughing with a friend.

"So," Lexi said as she put her own glass down "speaking of hotties..."

The server returned and placed a wood cutting board with a loaf of fresh bread onto the table. She took their order and walked away, leaving Mia to have to respond to Lexi's comment.

"What about them?" she said, feigning innocence.

"Not 'them,'" Lexi said, "so much as one particular hottie I was thinking about."

What could she say? That she and Jesse were only friends, but they'd spent both days of last weekend together and would probably do the same this weekend? Because that was a totally normal thing for friends to do.

"Which one would that be?" Mia asked, putting off the inevitable one last time.

A sly grin stole over Lexi's face. "How are things going with you and Jesse?"

"Fine," Mia squeaked, then cleared her throat to dislodge the frog that had settled there. "Fine," she said again. "There's not much to say though, because we're just friends, so..." She tipped her glass and let the savory tartness of the wine coat her tongue as it warmed a trail straight down her middle.

With eyebrows reaching toward her hairline, Lexi leaned back in her chair. "You have *seen* Jesse Murphy, haven't you?"

Mia chuckled. "Of course I've seen him."

"If you're telling me you can hang around with him and some-how—miraculously—remain friends, I don't think you've looked close enough. That man is yummy with a capital Y, Mia."

She wasn't wrong. And having her friend say it out loud only seemed to enhance it.

"He is very good looking," Mia admitted, trying her damnedest to sound diplomatic and slightly detached from Jesse on a more... *intimate* level.

"Good looking?" Lexi said. "Girl, the fact that you haven't been in each other's pants yet is downright criminal." Holding Mia's gaze with wide open, unbelieving eyes, she placed her palms on the table and leaned in. "Lock-you-both-up-and-throw-away-the-keys kind of criminal."

Lexi's words hung in the air, a playful challenge that stirred Mia's thoughts. She swirled the wine in her glass, contemplating how to respond. Jesse was more than just good-looking; he was magnetic, with a charisma that drew people in.

Mia's heart fluttered. She'd felt that pull, the unspoken tension between her and Jesse. But fear held her back—the fear of becoming another name on Jesse's list. Falling for someone and then being left behind was not something she wanted to repeat. Ever.

She took a deep breath. "I can't just be another notch on the bedpost, Lexi." Not with Jesse, she couldn't.

Lexi's expression softened. "Maybe it'll be different this time. Maybe you'll be the one to break that chain." She shrugged one shoulder. "And just maybe, he's waiting for someone like you to show him that there's more to life than fighting."

Mia considered Lexi's words while they ate their dinner, switching the conversation back to talk of work. For the rest of the evening, Mia couldn't stop thinking about Jesse for more than three seconds at a time.

That might be a problem...

S ATURDAY NIGHT, WHEN MIA opened the door, Jesse stopped
for an extra second to take her in. She had dressed in dark jeans, a
cream-colored tank top, and an open, blue-patterned cardigan, to try
to keep her look casual. She was trying extra hard not to give him the
wrong idea about their budding friendship.

"You look nice," he said when she moved back to let him in. "I like
your hair in a ponytail." It had been an attempt at another way to keep
things casual, to make it seem as if she hadn't put much effort into her
appearance while she waited for him to show up.

"Thanks," she said, fighting off the wave of nerves that had suddenly overtaken her. Her hand trembled slightly as she pushed the door
closed. Lexi's comment about getting into his pants now lived rent free
in her head and the harder she tried not to think about it, the more she
had to avert her eyes from traveling below his belt.

"Hey, that's new," he said, pointing to the side table next to the
couch. It was the one she'd picked up earlier in the week with Lexi.
She needed somewhere to put a lamp when she worked on her crochet
projects and Ace of Space had exactly what she needed. "So is that." He
pointed to the folded-up blanket draped over the back of the couch.

Running his fingers over the soft woven yarn, he asked, "Did you make this?"

"It's nothing," she said. "Just something I do when I'm bored."

She sat on the couch and pulled her feet up beneath her. If things were going to stay on the friend level, she should probably steer them that way. "I know you said you've been doing some thinking about what comes next for you, but I was able to find some things too, if you want to take a look."

Since she had dinner with Lexi on Wednesday, she'd been worried about how things would go when she saw Jesse again. She'd spent a few hours doing research for him, which was justifiable time spent thinking about him. Then she actively tried to avoid thinking about him by crocheting.

It had been the quickest blanket she'd ever made.

Grabbing her laptop, she flipped it open and waited for it to boot up.

"That's great, I'd love that," he said taking the seat next to her on the couch.

She closed her eyes and breathed in his scent, immediately setting off alarm bells in her heart. Shaking off the fog, her back stiffened and she pushed the laptop between them so no parts of their bodies touched, even accidentally.

"Is everything all right?" he asked.

She glanced at him briefly. "Of course. Everything's fine. Why do you ask?"

"I don't know. You just seem a little... off," he said leaning away from her to look her over from head to toe. It didn't make any of her discomfort dissipate. "Did I do something or say something to make you nervous?"

She shrugged and smiled. Aside from being kind and taking an interest in her and being really good looking and smelling like the air after a summer rainstorm, he hadn't done a thing.

And there it was, the inconvenient truth she couldn't ignore—he was sweet, and fun to be around, and he was as hot as the sand at the beach in the middle of August—and it was all but impossible not to notice.

"No, you didn't do anything. Promise." Forcing a smile, she spun her laptop toward him and said, "So, I don't really know what kinds of things you're interested in, but I found a couple sites that had some pretty good suggestions."

Mia had typed a list of potential careers into a spreadsheet. Next to every one of them was the average salary, the amount of schooling necessary to attain each job, and examples of people who currently held those jobs. It had taken her a few hours to compile.

He moved closer to her in order to see the screen. Mia's body temperature jumped as he leaned behind her and braced one hand on the arm of the couch on her far side. Everything in her body clenched as his arm rested against her back. "When did you do all this?" he asked.

She shrugged again. "It's no big deal, really. I just looked around a couple different websites for athletes that wanted to make careers from their passions." The look of appreciation on his face had her heart and her belly doing funny things. "I know it probably won't be all things you're interested in, but I figured we had to start somewhere, right?"

Mia scrolled down the list and asked him questions about the ones he said held interest for him, such as Coaching, Strength and Conditioning Coach, and Physical Therapist. She typed notes so they could keep track of his thoughts. Several of them were easy enough to scratch off the list—Wellness Consultant and Sales—so they spent some more time researching and taking notes on the other options. A few quick clicks gave them all the information they needed.

"Personal trainer," he said. "I've given that one some thought already. I kind of have a foot in that world and I think getting certified would be a huge benefit. A friend of mine asked if I'd be interested in teaching a self-defense class at his gym. A bunch of the women who go there were asking for one. It's cool that he thought of me."

"Have you done that before?"

"I mean, it's kind of what I do."

She adjusted her seat on the couch, her body finally starting to relax around him as the conversation stayed business focused. "Sure, it's what you do. But have you ever taught it to someone else? From the perspective of self-defense? Doing and teaching are different skill sets."

"I teach classes down at the gym all the time. As far as self-defense goes, I'd have to come up with some kind of program, but it wouldn't be all that different than what I do now." He stood and held out his hand to her. "Come here. I'll teach you some right now."

She hesitated because she had no idea what to expect from this encounter. Could she trust that he wasn't trying to hit on her or gain any ground toward a relationship?

Mia reminded herself Jesse was simply a guy who wanted to share what he knew. In truth, she knew *Jesse* was the one who should be on guard against *her* if they wanted to maintain the boundaries of friendship.

"All right." Slipping her hand into his she stood then shrugged out of her sweater.

"Turn around," he said. "Like you're walking down the street and I'll come up behind you."

It was all pretend, but her traitorous heart kicked up its beat just the same. Just knowing he would be putting his hands on her had her body heating up in all the usual places.

She stood with her back to him, waiting. He approached and wrapped his arms around her midsection, his hard chest pressed against her back. "I'm not wearing any protective gear, so don't actually kick my ass," he said with a laugh.

"OK. What do I do?" she asked, focusing on his words, and trying her best to ignore the hardness of his body and the strength in his arms as he held her. She feared she might actually melt into a puddle and slip right through his grip.

"First, you're going to grab onto my arms and push your hips back like you're pushing me away with your ass."

Heat built in her everywhere all at once, but she managed to steady her breathing and do as he asked.

"Now, you're going to push your hips to one side and then *pretend* to swing your arm into my crotch." He held her extra tightly for a second and said, "Don't actually hit my junk, Mia. This is just *learning*."

A bubble of delight swelled in her chest as she felt the power shift from him to her. "OK." In one swift movement, she slid her hips over and broke free of his grip then swung her arm through the air, stopping before she made contact. "Like that?" she said.

"Just like that." He leaned forward as if he'd been struck. "So, you've hurt me, right? Now spin around, lock your hands behind my neck and pretend to throw your knee into my face."

From his bent over position, he moved his hands from his knees to his forehead.

Hoping she was doing it correctly, she spun, clasped her hands together, pushed his upper body down, and aimed her knee at his head, making the tiniest contact with his hands.

He straightened up. "That was awesome." His smile alone started to melt away her hesitation. "All right, now, imagine that in real time with some force behind it. I don't care how big and tough the guy is; if you smash him in the nuts with your fist and then in the face with your knee, he's hitting the ground like a big bag of rocks."

Adrenaline surged through her and blanketed her with a sense of power. "That was fun," she said. "Not getting attacked, I mean, but experiencing what it feels like to go through those motions. It's... what's the word I'm looking for?"

"Badass?"

"Yes! I feel like a badass. That was unbelievably empowering." She squared her shoulders. "Can we try it again, but this time don't tell me what to do. Let me see if I can do it on the fly."

Jesse

I T WAS AWESOME SEEING her come out of her shell the way she did. And it didn't hurt that he got to hold her in his arms, even if it was only so she could practice crushing his manhood. "Absolutely. Just make sure you don't actually kill me, yeah?"

Her body shivered with excitement, and it was the cutest fucking thing he'd ever seen. They went through the scenario a few more times until she felt comfortable enough with it that he didn't have to call out each step to her.

"What else can you teach me?" she asked.

So many things, he thought. She meant it from a self-defense point of view, but he could have answered it from another so easily.

Afraid of scaring her away, he kept his less pure thoughts to himself and focused on the task at hand. "Most likely, if you're going to be attacked, it's going to be by someone bigger than you, right?"

She nodded, eyes wide and hands curled into tight fists.

"So, you don't want to depend on your *punching* strength. At some point I'll teach you to throw a mean kick, but right now I want you to get comfortable throwing an elbow."

Somehow her eyes grew even wider. "Seriously?"

"Yeah, seriously," he said. "I'm going to pretend to choke you and when I put my hands around your neck, I want you to throw one arm straight up in the air and then twist as hard as you can to the other side to break my contact. Got it?"

She nodded, stood directly in front of him and let him put his hands gently around her throat. Her skin was so fucking soft, and the steady beat of her heart tapped against his fingers. Every ounce of his awareness was focused in his fingertips. What the hell was this woman doing to him?

"One arm up, right?" she asked.

"Yep," he said, forcing himself to be in the moment and not lost in some fantasy.

She threw her right arm in the air then twisted to her left to drag his hands off her neck. His hands fell against her breasts, and he ignored every instinct in his body that screamed at him to notice how soft she was.

"Now, bend your arm and swing your body back, *slowly*, aiming your elbow at the side of my head."

She swung her elbow gently and stopped as it touched the hand he'd put up to shield his temple. "Did I do that right?" She vibrated with excitement.

"One hundred percent."

Fuck, this girl was going to be the death of him. He'd gone from teacher mode to wanting to see her naked in a blink.

He thought he could do it. Just being friends with her sounded innocent enough, easy enough, as natural as breathing for someone like him, who didn't *do* relationships.

Yet, there he was, in Mia's apartment, touching her, teaching her self-defense, and suddenly wondering how to convince her how right they could be together.

Relationships weren't something he'd spent a lot of time nurturing over the years. Something told him that doing that work with Mia would be worth the effort.

Mia's belly gurgled. It actually sounded like she growled at him, and he couldn't help but laugh. Her eyes went huge, and she crisscrossed her arms over her stomach. "Oh my God! That was so embarrassing," she said. "I didn't realize I was that hungry."

That made two of them.

"What do you say? Want to make some dinner?" he asked. "I know how to cook a mean chicken breast with brown rice and broccoli."

She pulled her face into a silly frown. "No offense, but that sounds quite terrible, actually."

"What? That's the building blocks of just about every athlete out there."

She nodded, her face still scrunched in a frown. "Maybe so, but it still sounds terrible." She held her hand out toward him. "Come on," she said. "My turn to teach you something."

Taking hold of her hand, and before he could stop the words from tumbling out, he said, "I like the sound of that."

She stopped walking and turned to face him but didn't let go of his hand. "Down, boy," she said. "I meant I would teach you how to cook something other than that blandness you threatened me with. That's all." With her free hand she gestured back and forth between them. "Just friends, remember?"

The fact that she hadn't dropped his hand spoke volumes.

"For now," he said.

A heavy pause hung between them, but Jesse decided he wouldn't be the first to budge. He liked Mia and he was certain she liked him too. He was willing to wait for her, even if that kept them in the territory of friends for a while longer. But not forever.

"Maybe we should go to the market and grab some stuff for dinner," she said. "I think maybe the fresh air might be good to cool you down a bit."

Her cheeks had flushed a deep red that reached all the way down her neck and into her chest. She wasn't fooling anyone; she needed that cool air just as much as he did. Maybe more.

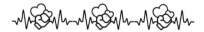

The elevator door opened, and they stepped inside. Being alone with her in such a small space made it impossible to ignore the delicate scent of her perfume. Mia was right, he definitely needed to be in the fresh air to clear his head.

"How long have you lived here?" he asked as the elevator made its descent. "Close to a year, right?"

"About eight months," she said. "Why?"

They walked out of the elevator and crossed the hallway toward the front of the building. "And how many times have you been to the ocean since you've been here?"

"In the past eight months?" Her brow pulled into a sharp crease. "Maybe half a dozen or so. Why are you asking me about the ocean?"

"Humor me," he said. They stepped down onto the sidewalk then he tugged her hand, leading her across the street, instead of inland toward the store.

Swiveling her head in one direction and then the other, she said, "Where are we going?"

"To the store."

"The store is that way," she said, looking backward over her shoulder.

"We're taking the long way." Still holding her hand, he led her forward. "How many of those trips to the ocean were during the first month or so that you lived here?"

Mia made a face as she thought. "Probably most of them." She was quiet for a few seconds. "Maybe all of them."

"That's what I'm talking about. How far do you live from the water? Two blocks?"

"Three," she said, sounding slightly defensive.

"You live three blocks from the Atlantic Ocean." He stopped walking and turned to face her, holding her upper arms. "You should be here every day. Fine, maybe every other," he conceded when she frowned at him. "But my point stands."

"Jesse," she said as they started walking toward the water again. "I don't think you ever actually made a point. Aside from telling me I'm living my life wrong by not coming down to the water more often."

From his place by her side, he smiled. "No, that's pretty much my point."

With a laugh, Mia shook her head, and they walked the rest of the way in silence. The wind picked up as they neared the water, the dampness and smell of salt heavy in the air.

It was an early May evening which meant that close to the water it was still pretty cold. And when the wind whipped up, it was even colder. Mia pulled her sweater tighter and wrapped her arms around her middle. The tide was on its way out and Jesse wanted to walk in the wet sand with her.

"Take your shoes off," he said. He let go of her hand to lean against the sea wall and pull off his own shoes. She surprised him by taking off her shoes and not arguing against it. Once the four shoes were lined up, with socks tucked inside, he took her hand again and led her down the stone steps and onto the cool sand.

"It's kind of chilly," she said as he brought them down to the water's edge. "I don't know how long I can stay out here."

"You're fine," he said. "It's just a little salty air. It won't do anything to you, except make you sleep better tonight."

About thirty yards down the beach was an outcropping of boulders where every kid in town had played at one point in their lives. He tugged her hand in that direction. "See those rocks over there?"

She nodded as the wind whipped her ponytail. Long tendrils of hair that weren't held in place anymore swirled around her face as they walked toward the rocks.

"My brothers and I used to play pirates on them when we were kids. My oldest brother was always the captain and the rest of us were his crew." He smiled as the memories played in his mind. "Though my sister would never be a pirate. She would only ever be a *beautiful mermaid*. Drove my brother Seth crazy."

"Why? Did he want to be the beautiful mermaid?"

Jesse laughed long and hard at that. When he finally regained his composure, he said, "No, he just didn't like that Hannah got to do whatever she wanted to do while Shane made *us* do all his pirate work."

Jesse climbed up onto the large boulder that never really disappeared, even during high tide. He held out his hand and helped Mia climb up behind him. Sitting down with his back against the rock, he waited for Mia to sit next to him. She surprised him for the second time by choosing to sit between his legs and lean against his chest.

Friends, my ass, he thought. He had a lot of friends. And the number of friends that sat between his legs and leaned against his chest could be counted on zero hands.

The smooth skin at the curve where her neck and shoulders met tempted him to lean in and place a kiss. Instead, he rested his chin on her shoulder and looked out over the ocean with her in silence.

"You can't live this close to the ocean, to the smell of the salt air, and let it become mundane," he said after a long while. "You have to see what you have right in front of you and embrace it. You've got to see if for the gift it is."

She was quiet for a few seconds. "Are you talking about the ocean or are you talking about yourself?" she said, tilting her head to see his face.

He wrapped his arms around her and gave a little squeeze. Choosing to avoid her question, he said, "Think about how many people have never even seen the ocean. And all you have to do is walk three blocks and look up. That's not something to take for granted."

Breaking contact with him briefly, she dug her phone out of her sweater pocket, leaned back against him again, then held her phone in the air. "Smile," she said, and snapped a quick selfie of them. Before he could ask to see it, she stuffed the phone back into her pocket and rested against him again.

Maybe half an hour after they climbed onto the rock, Jesse hopped down, then held out his hand to help Mia back onto the sand. His ass had gone numb sitting on the cold rock and his feet were turning to blocks of ice in the wind.

"What do you say? Head up to the market and get the stuff for dinner?"

She pulled her sweater tight again and smiled as her feet hit the ground. "I'm starving," she said.

Me too. In more ways than one.

Mia

T HE WALK TO THE market was exactly the thing she needed to clear her head and let things simmer down between them. What had she been thinking snuggling in his lap like that? How had she let the romance of the ocean push her to do something so bold?

Self-defense was one thing, but sitting on the beach, watching the waves crash, with his arms wrapped around her? Forget about the line between them getting blurry. That line was in danger of being obliterated.

The air warmed significantly as they moved away from the water. She couldn't even imagine what state her hair was in after the wind tore most of it free from her ponytail. Somehow, Jesse only looked better now that he was a little bit windblown with his cheeks reddened from the chilly air.

"What are we making tonight?" he asked as they neared the market's front door. "I'm guessing no chicken, broccoli, and brown rice?" His smile was warm and like everything about him, it promised affection. But she'd been burned by a pretty smile before and she'd be damned if she'd let it happen again.

"I was thinking maybe some steak tips and roasted root vegetables, maybe sweet potatoes and parsnips. And then a salad on the side. What do you think?"

He pulled a small basket from the stack as they walked through the sliding doors. "I've never had parsnips, but I think it sounds amazing. I also think it sounds like a guy wouldn't have much luck inviting you to dinner because your food sounds better than most of the restaurants around here."

Her shoulders tensed slightly as she grappled with what her heart and her gut each wanted. Her heart hoped he wouldn't ask her to dinner while her gut absolutely wished he would. "Then don't ask me out to dinner," she said with a stilted laugh, trying to appear unaffected by him. "That's an easy fix."

Without waiting for a response, she beelined to the produce section to find some sweet potatoes, onions, yellow potatoes, and parsnips. He followed behind her, and one after the other she placed the vegetables into the basket that hung from Jesse's arm. "We need a sprig of rosemary," she said and headed toward the fresh herbs.

Thankfully, he didn't push the idea of asking her out any further as they finished their shopping. He brought the conversation back to the self-defense moves they'd practiced. "You know, if you want, you can come down to the gym with me and I can teach you some more moves. I'll have you throwing punches and knees like a savage in no time."

"Just what my mother always wanted for me," she teased. "A daughter who can drop a man with a well-placed knee." She thought about what she had just said and her inner badass had a small revelation. "Now that I think about it, maybe that's exactly what she'd want for me. I'm thinking all women should learn how to drop a man with a well-placed knee."

"Damn straight, they should," Jesse said. "Have you met most guys?"

She had to admit she enjoyed the sense of empowerment she felt around Jesse. It was something she wasn't entirely used to, but it was starting to feel good.

When they made it back to her apartment, she started her favorite eighties playlist, full of all the old artists she loved; R.E.M., The Cult, Violent Femmes, heavily sprinkled with her absolute favorite of all time, The Cure.

Jesse chuckled as she began to sing but it wasn't enough to stop her. "Sorry, I have to turn this up. 'Lovesong' is probably my favorite song on earth," she said as she clicked up the volume. The way it always did, the ethereal music had her hips swaying in time with the song as she went from task to task getting dinner prepped.

He chopped vegetables while she preheated the oven, then gathered the olive oil and other spices they would need.

Pushing chopped sweet potatoes into the bowl, he turned toward her. "You're kind of killing me here, Mia." He laid the cutting board and knife on the counter. "I *knew* I was missing something that night I heard you singing through the door. The dance half of the performance is exactly what I imagined it would be."

With a bottle of olive oil in one hand, salt in the other, she stood, stock still, in the middle of the kitchen. She put those things down on the counter and snatched her phone, quickly scrolling through to play a less suggestive song. "Sorry," she said as she scrolled. "I'll stop." Landing on a 'Making Dinner' mood playlist, she clicked play and put the phone back down.

"That's not what I was saying, Mia. I don't want you to stop being you or doing what you do. I just... " He sighed. "I like you. You're a nice person and I like being around you. And watching you dance around your kitchen? Well, that's sort of the icing on the friendship cake, isn't it?"

Her heart ached. She wanted to be able to admit to liking Jesse the same way he liked her. She wanted to open herself up to whatever it was he was offering, but she couldn't do it. Nothing good ever came from making herself vulnerable to another person.

She steeled herself for whatever the fallout might be. "Jesse," she said. "You're a really great guy. I like spending time with you, too. But I've already told you, I can't do more than friendship right now. If that doesn't work for you, maybe we ought to just call a stop to this whole thing."

The last thing she wanted was to lose one of the only friends she had, but if it meant getting rid of the pressure to be more than she was ready for, what other option did she have?

With a gentle smile on his face, Jesse approached but didn't touch her. "I like having you as my friend too. I'm not letting that go."

She exhaled a deep breath, and he stepped closer. Her fingers trembled; certain he was going to try to kiss her.

He tipped her chin with one finger but rather than kiss her lips he turned her head slightly and pressed a soft kiss to her cheek. When he removed his finger from her chin, she felt the emptiness where their bodies had connected, even for such a short time.

"Can we make dinner now?" he asked, his body still impossibly close to hers. "Because, *my friend*, I am quite hungry." His eyes held hers and she felt the double meaning of his words in every cell of her body.

Jesse

W HATEVER HAD HAPPENED BETWEEN her and the last guy
she was with had certainly fucked up her heart.

She had the look of a trapped animal when Jesse kissed her cheek
in the kitchen. But, if he wasn't misreading it, she also looked like it
wouldn't have taken much to convince her to go for more.

That wasn't his intention, though. At least not his only intention.
He didn't just want her physically, though that was certainly part of
it. He also wanted to get to know her better, to get her to open up to
him, to let him get close enough to prove he wasn't a threat to her or
her heart.

Their dinner together had turned out fine, but she never quite
loosened up to the level of being able to dance to The Cure again and
he wanted to kick his own ass for opening his mouth and ruining what
they had going on. He wanted her to be comfortable around him, to
feel free to relax and to dance and to just be free.

He leaned into his surefire way to forget his problems; heading to
the gym, and—on the heavy bag or on the mat—working himself to
exhaustion.

His entire week unfolded the same way, with the heavy bag in the
corner taking the brunt of his frustration. The people working out all

around him knew better than to get in his way as he threw combinations of punches, kicks, knees, and elbows at the uncomplaining black leather bag.

By the time his workouts ended each day, sweat poured off his body and some of his bad mood had been left in the drops of sweat scattered all over the floor. More often, though, it stayed firmly lodged where it had started, right in the middle of his heart.

"You alright, Coach?" Eddie asked him on the fifth day of his self-imposed punishment. "You seem a little more *aggressive* than usual this week."

Jesse had already showered and was sitting on the bench in the locker room putting on his shoes when his student approached. Looking up from his laces, he said, "Yeah, man, I'm fine."

"Looks like it." Eddie sat on the bench but was smart enough to leave some space between them. "Something going on you need to talk about?"

That was one thing Jesse appreciated about the young men he coached; they didn't have any kind of weirdness about talking things through the way his own brothers did. It was refreshing, even if he didn't necessarily want to talk about what was going on in his mind.

"It's a girl, isn't it?" Eddie asked when Jesse hadn't answered him. "It's almost always about a girl when a dude works out like that." There was no judgment in Eddie's voice, only empathy, maybe even sympathy.

Thinking back to Danny saying something similar, he laughed. "How old are you?" Jesse asked.

"I'll be twenty next month."

Jesse nodded, confirming he wouldn't be contributing to the delinquency of a minor. "It's definitely about a girl," he conceded. "And I'm not sure what to do next."

"What do you mean?"

"I like her. A lot. I'm pretty sure she feels the same but something's holding her back. I think she's afraid, you know?"

"Afraid?" Eddie asked, his brow creased. "Like, afraid of you?"

"Fuck, I hope not," Jesse said. "I think maybe her last boyfriend fucked up her heart and she's a little hesitant to get back in the ring, so to speak."

"That's a tough one." Eddie was quiet for a second. "Have you told her how you feel?"

"I told her I like her, if that's what you mean."

"What'd she say?"

"That we can be friends but that's it."

"And you don't want to be friends." Eddie said, checking his phone when it chimed. He rolled his eyes at whomever was trying to reach him and tossed the phone into his bag. "Can you maybe push it a little? Like, try to make her jealous or something and see what she does. If you flirt with some other chick in front of her and she doesn't care, you'll have your answer."

Jesse looked up at his devious young friend. "But if she does care..."

"Well, then you'll have a different answer, Coach." He grabbed his bag from the floor and stood to leave. "My ride's here. I gotta run. See you tomorrow?"

Jesse nodded and waved Eddie out the door, then grabbed his own things.

A plan began forming in his mind as he crossed the crowded gym, feeling more optimistic than he'd felt in close to a week. Could he do it, though? Could he do something as devious as tricking her the way Eddie had suggested?

Did he have any other choice?

He'd never felt about a woman the way he felt about Mia, and it was going to kill him to set her up, to force her hand and wait for the fallout. Whatever way she chose he would live with, but his heart one hundred percent wanted her to choose him.

Before he walked out the door into the late May evening, he sent her a quick text.

> Haven't seen you in a while. Hang out with me Sat?

He shoved the phone into his pocket and headed for his car.

S HE COULD DO THIS. It wouldn't be difficult to hang out with Jesse and stay friends. After all, they'd been doing it so far. Granted, it got a little weird while they were cooking dinner last week. But they were both adults. There was no reason they couldn't put whatever they thought they'd been feeling into perspective. They were friends and that was all.

She'd been looking forward to seeing him since his text came in on Friday night and she couldn't wait to show him the expanded list of career choices she'd pulled together for him.

When she opened the door to see him standing there, her resolve to keep things friendly slipped to the floor and she had to mentally pick it back up and pin it in place.

Wearing fitted jeans that hung low on his hips, a t-shirt with some sort of fight organization logo on it, and an unzipped leather jacket, once again Jesse fired up all the parts of her she'd been trying desperately to keep cool since she had her heart publicly stomped to smithereens.

Except, it wasn't working so well anymore.

"Come on in," she croaked, then cleared her throat. "It's great to see you again."

"I can't wait to see what you've got for me," he said as he walked past her, leaving her to follow in the wake of his cologne like a bird following a trail of birdseed.

They settled onto the couch like they always did, her laptop open again to the list of potential jobs. "There's a few new ones I added since last time."

He leaned toward her, and she tried to stop breathing so his scent wouldn't keep caressing her the way she wished his hands would.

"Massage therapist?" He cocked one dark eyebrow in her direction. "You think I'd be good as a massage therapist?" A slow smile worked its way across his face.

The heat in her belly fanned out to include her legs, her arms. "I... I don't know. It's just another thing to think about." And then she couldn't stop thinking about his hands on her body, rubbing her down with oil, exactly the way she'd imagined it when she added it to the list the day before.

"It's definitely something to think about," he said. The look in his eye told her he was thinking very similar thoughts to her own.

She shifted in her seat, angling her legs away from him, trying to prevent any accidental touches.

"What else did you add to the list?" he said, leaning close again.

They spent half an hour looking through her list and talking again about what each job would require of him as far as education and knowledge, as well as the average salary for each position.

"So far, I think I'm leaning toward Personal Trainer or Strength and Conditioning Coach. Those probably offer the most upside from where I'm sitting. But I haven't ruled out Massage Therapist yet. I think there would definitely be a serious upside to a job like that."

She imagined him working as a massage therapist and very quickly developing a long list of female clients. All of a sudden it wasn't such an appealing option. "I guess," she said. "But the pay for Strength and Conditioning is like fifty percent higher, so you have to keep that in mind."

The side of his mouth tipped into a knowing grin, and she knew her jealousy wasn't as hidden as she'd hoped.

"Thanks for doing all this for me," he said, leaning back into the couch. "It's really decent of you." He turned to face her, rested his hand on her thigh, scorching the place where their skin connected. "Let me take you out for a drink?"

"You don't drink," she said. "And I'm not drinking alone. How pathetic would that make me?" If he was trying to get her to lower her resistance with alcohol, he could think again.

"All right. How about if we grab a quick bite to eat and maybe shoot a couple rounds of pool or something? Have you been to York's Landing yet?"

"No, not yet. Some of the people from work invited me a while back but I never went." She knew exactly where it was because she'd passed it countless times but never bothered to check it out.

"Great," he said. "Let's head down there. The guy, Sean, who owns the place is a good friend of mine. I've known him for years. They've got wicked good food and it's just a really cool place. I think there's supposed to be a cool local band playing tonight. At least that's what my brother Shane told me."

It sounded like something friends would do together. An easy dinner, shooting pool, and listening to live music would be a perfect way to forget all about her massage fantasies.

"I'd like that."

Mia curled into her sweater to ward off the chill of the evening. But a clear sky that promised a spectacular view of the stars, when the sun finally set, made the cool walk worth it.

York's Landing was cuter on the inside than she'd guessed it would be from the times she'd walked by it. It was a casual place with a long, beautifully polished bar. High tables filled the bar area while booths and tables took up the rest of the space. There was a stage set up along the far wall and the entire street side of the building was made up of giant windows overlooking the busy downtown street. Off to the side, behind the bar, was a separate space set up with scattered high tops surrounding a half dozen pool tables.

It wasn't a surprise that a handful of people waved to Jesse as they passed through on their way to play pool. He introduced her to a few of his friends, including his cousin Danny, while they waited for an open table. Jesse was incredibly attractive, and his cousin was almost as easy on the eyes. She could only wonder what the rest of his family looked like.

She needed to stop thinking about Jesse in any other way than as a friend. And the way their night was going gave her the confidence that he was finally in agreement with her. He introduced her as a friend of his and he never put his hands on her or stood close enough to give anyone the impression they were together.

"It was nice to meet you, Mia," Danny said as she and Jesse made their way to an open pool table. "Maybe I'll see you at Sunday dinner one of these weeks?"

Jesse tensed ever so slightly. "You haven't been to one of those in like six months," he said to Danny. "You gonna start coming back?"

"Who knows what the future holds, cousin." With a smile, Danny turned his attention back to the group he was with, then took out his wallet as they divided up the bill.

"What's Sunday dinner?" Mia asked. "Is that like a family thing?"

"Yeah," he said, pulling a couple cues from the rack on the wall. "I told you we have a big family. My parents have been hosting a Sunday dinner since before I was born. It was always my brothers and my sister and me but sometimes the aunts and uncles and the cousins would all show up. Sometimes they still do."

"Your parents must have a really big house for all those people."

Jesse laughed. "They do. And as soon as my mom wants it bigger, my dad gets to work."

"What?" Who just asked for a bigger house and got it? Like life was that easy.

It was only Mia and her sister Lauren growing up so there were no big family get-togethers. The busiest their house ever got was when her favorite aunt would show up and eat with them once a month or so. They would usually only see the grandparents on the holidays. "Your family sounds amazing," she said. "I'd love to meet them sometime."

"Sure," he said with a smile. "But now, we play pool. I'll rack, you break," he said, rolling the pool balls inside the wooden triangle to get the game started.

Her breaking shot was pretty good but not the best. She didn't sink any of the balls, so Jesse took over.

He leaned his long body over the pool table, cue in hand, lining up his shot. His attention was completely focused on his task. Sitting on the chair at the high-top table, she crossed her legs and squeezed them tighter as he lined up and took his shot.

Everything about him, the way his hands held the cue, the way he smiled at her once the purple number four ball sank into the side pocket, threatened to consume her if she wasn't vigilant against it.

When the server came by, Mia ordered herself a lemonade and Jesse ordered a Coke. The young woman wasn't shy about watching Jesse and Mia didn't know what to think or do about it. He wasn't her boyfriend. She might as well have had it tattooed across her forehead. But it still bothered her that some other woman was so blatant about her *admiration* of him. Jesse and Mia could have been a couple for all she knew.

Wordlessly, the server handed Mia her lemonade. Then she swayed her hips and her ass as she made her way over to Jesse and put his soda on the table behind him. "I'll leave this here for you," she said, "so it's there when you're ready for it."

Mia almost gagged on her drink watching this woman flirt so openly, trusting that Jesse would never flirt back when he had been so open about his feelings for Mia.

"Thanks," he said, then stood and turned to talk with the woman. Leaning his ass against the pool table, he crossed his arms over his chest, highlighting the definition in his forearms and stretching the cotton shirt with his broad back. His manner was entirely too cool, like he did this every day. It was like it was no big deal to flirt with one woman while he was obviously out with another.

We're only friends, she reminded herself as she turned away from the scene, her face burning in familiar humiliation. And this is what he does, she reminded herself. Lexi warned her about that from the very beginning. Now she was able to see it with her own eyes. It hurt like hell.

"I've seen you in here before, right?" the woman said, standing entirely too close to him. "You definitely look familiar."

Mia sucked down her lemonade as she eavesdropped on the conversation, figuring out the best way to make an exit without acting like a jealous girlfriend. A red exit sign hung over the door, and she readied herself to make a hasty exit the first chance she got.

"Oh yeah," Jesse said. "My brothers and I are in here a lot to shoot pool."

The woman's voice changed, became quieter and much more suggestive and she said, "I knew I'd seen you before. You're pretty good."

It was a good thing her lemonade glass was strong because Mia's death grip would have shattered it otherwise.

"Thanks," Jesse said. "You play at all?"

There was no need to be jealous. Jesse was not her boyfriend. She had no claim on him, and he was a red-blooded male talking with a very pretty woman.

If only someone could help get the message from her brain to her heart.

From across the room a nice-looking guy made eye contact with Mia. He flicked a glance at Jesse, gave her a questioning look then waved her over to his table. It wasn't something she normally would have done but considering the circumstances...

She banged her glass on the table beside her, yanked her sweater from the back of her chair, and stormed away to go make *another* new friend.

"Hey," the guy said as she approached his table. Two other guys sat around the table and gave her a cursory wave. "Is your boyfriend seriously flirting with another woman right now?"

"Hey," she said in return, trying to keep her voice light and cheerful. "And he's not my boyfriend so he can flirt with anyone he wants to." Her voice quavered, betraying her true feelings, and everyone at the table sensed it.

"I'm Alex," the new guy said as he stood and pulled over a chair for her. "Care to join us?"

"I'm Mia," she said then looked at his two friends.

"That's Jim and Ricky."

Everybody said their hellos and Mia sat down to talk. Despite her previous hesitation, Alex and his friends turned out to be nice guys to talk with for the few minutes they had together. According to Alex, they'd been friends since middle school and made it a point to catch up over drinks and dinner a few times a year. It was their way of making sure they never lost touch with each other.

It was a terribly sweet story that only made her lonely heart ache more.

She shared vague details about her life, and they were nice enough not to pry. Then Ricky flicked his hand into Alex's arm, causing all of them to look up and Mia to turn in her seat. A seriously pissed off Jesse was quickly approaching.

"I think your 'not boyfriend' might be looking for you," Alex said, and his friendly face suddenly looked angry as he watched Jesse coming toward them.

Mia huffed and stood from her chair, just as pissed and ready to square off with Jesse but hoping it wouldn't happen in the middle of a crowded restaurant.

"Who's your friends? People from work?" Jesse asked, his smile so fake it looked painful on his face.

"Not that it's any of your business, but these are my *new* friends, Alex and..." In her fury, she'd forgotten their names.

"Jim," Jim said.

"Ricky," Ricky piped in.

"Alex and Jim and Ricky," she repeated. "They're very nice people and we were having a very nice conversation." She folded her arms across her chest in defiance of the possessive look in Jesse's eyes. "Is there something I can help you with?"

Mia

T HE MUSCLES IN JESSE'S jaw twitched and for the first time she had the slightest hint of worry for her new friends.

"I was thinking maybe you'd had enough pool and you wanted to get out of here," he said through gritted teeth.

"Pool?" The shock of his statement reverberated through her body. "First, I didn't even shoot any pool. You got distracted by a lovely woman with a ponytail and a nice ass and didn't even notice that I left." She waved her hand haphazardly behind her. "And luckily for me, Alex was kind enough to invite me over to hang out while you were busy getting her number."

Jesse's eyes darted from her to Alex and then back to her. "He sounds like a great guy, Mia." His eyes flared and for a brief moment she worried he might jump past her and go after one of the guys. "I would certainly hate to have to rip his fucking arms off for nothing he did wrong." He took a step closer to her, but she didn't back down. "Is that what you want for poor Alex here? A life with no appendages?"

He stepped closer again. "I think maybe it's time to go."

The sound of chairs scraping across wood behind her alerted her that Alex and his friends stood up to come to her aid. The eyes of every person in the restaurant fell on them and the ambient noise died to a hush.

This whole situation had gone far enough. Nobody was going to be fighting anyone. They weren't kids getting ready to throw hands in the schoolyard and she had had enough. "Are you serious right now?"

Jesse didn't flinch.

Turning around to Alex and his friends, she said, "I'm really sorry, you guys. Please excuse my friend's behavior. It was nice to meet all of you. Thank you for inviting me over when you saw I needed a friend."

Slowly, Alex turned his attention from Jesse to her, worry marring his otherwise kind features. "You sure you're going to be all right with this guy?"

She felt Jesse's posture change, like a caged animal ready to spring. She reached over, placed a hand gently on his forearm. "He's just a little overprotective, but otherwise harmless—at least to me, that is."

Alex took her hint and he and his friends sat back down, and she slid her hand from Jesse's forearm down to take hold of his hand.

They snaked through the crowd until they made it out the back door into an alleyway that ran alongside the restaurant. As soon as the door closed behind them, she turned on him, fury rolling off her in waves.

"Don't you dare do that to me again!" She jabbed her finger into his chest, as she walked him backward across the alley. "Do you understand me? I don't even know what to make of what just happened in there! I've never been so embarrassed in my entire life!" She pushed at his chest, and he barely took a step backward.

He shoved his hands into his coat pockets and his nostrils flared. "You were flirting with that guy, Mia, and I couldn't take it."

"We are *not* a couple, Jesse. I can flirt with anyone I damn well please! Exactly the same way *you* were flirting with that waitress!"

Blood pounded through her veins and heat flooded her face, but she would not cry. She'd spilled enough tears over men, and she refused to let even one more fall.

"*You* said we weren't a couple, Mia, *not me!* I have never wanted anyone or anything in my entire life more than I want you."

She'd heard that before and knew better than to believe it. "And the waitress?" she yelled. "What was she? Your backup plan?"

He leaned back against the brick building, folded his arms over his chest, no hint of a smile on his face. His voice came back down to a normal volume. "No, she wasn't my backup plan. She was my only plan."

Mia's threw her hands in the air and turned to leave Jesse where he stood. It was time to wash her hands of this whole friendship.

"She's a friend of my sister's," he called out to her as she walked away. "And she was my way of figuring you out," he said, still talking to her back. Her feet refused to take another step no matter how hard her brain yelled at her to keep walking.

She turned back, crossing her arms over her chest, mimicking Jesse's stance. "I don't understand."

"You said you wanted to be friends."

"Yes."

"I don't believe you. I think you're lying to yourself and you're lying to me." Pushing himself away from the building he stepped toward her.

Lowering her arms, she stepped backward. He continued walking her backward across the alleyway until she bumped into the building behind her.

"I'm not lying," she whispered, wondering where her fury and indignation had run off to. "I *don't* want to be more than friends with you."

He lifted his hand to her hair, let the strands fall through his fingers.
"You're lying to me again."

"I'm not." She was. "I just can't."

"Why?"

"Because."

"That's not good enough, Mia."

"Yes, it is, Jesse!" Tears threatened again but she held them at bay.
"What I say and what I want *are* good enough. Even if *you* don't
understand why." She shoved at his chest, pushing him back a couple
steps. "You don't get to have me just because you decided you want
me."

"That's not how it is," he said, his words threaded with emotion.

"Oh? Then what the hell just happened in there?"

His lips pressed tightly into a thin line across his face.

"What?" she said. "You thought it would be cute to flirt with some
other woman to try and make me jealous so I would suddenly wake up
and realize how much I want you?" Her voice had begun to tremble.
"You humiliated me, Jesse. That was a horrible thing to do to me."

He scrubbed his hands through his hair. "You're right," he said
behind his hands as he dragged them down his face. "You're absolutely
fucking right. It was a shitty thing to do, and I have no idea what I was
thinking." He blew out a huge sigh. "I am so sorry, Mia." He closed
his eyes. "Fuck!"

When he opened his eyes to look at her again, he said, "I'm really
sorry about that. About everything."

"Can you just please tell me what you were thinking? Why would
you do something like that to me?"

His chest expanded as he sucked in a huge breath. Then his whole
posture slumped as he blew it out again. "It wasn't supposed to go that
far," he said, his voice quiet. "Annabeth was supposed to flirt with me

and make you jealous. That was it. It was supposed to stop there. But when she told me you'd gotten up and were sitting with a bunch of other guys..."

He shook his head, unable to look her in the eye. Staring at the ground, he said, "I've never been jealous like that before." He raised his eyes to hers. "I know you probably don't believe me, but it's true.

"Seeing you with those guys just did something to me, Mia. It snapped into something that I've never felt before."

It was a nice story but hardly believable.

"Are you trying to tell me you've never been jealous over a woman before?" she said.

He shrugged. "Not really. If any woman I was with had gotten up to sit with someone else, that would be the end for us."

"Just that easy?"

He nodded. "Just that easy."

"Then why did you threaten him?"

"Fuck, I don't know," he said, running his hands through his hair again. He moved toward her. "Actually, I do know. It was seeing what I did to you. Seeing the hurt and the anger in your eyes when I walked over there? It just about killed me. I was fucking pissed, Mia. But not at any of you. Not even at fucking Alex." He sighed again. "I'm really sorry."

Her chest ached, but for the first time in a long time, it was not from loneliness. Seeing his honesty, his vulnerability shocked her.

"I don't know what to say, Jesse." She was being honest with him because she was at a complete loss for words. "Even if I accept your apology, that absolutely does not excuse what you did to me."

"I understand that," he said, taking a step closer to her. "There was no excuse for what I did, other than I'm a dumbass."

"Please don't ever do that to me again," she said.

His eyes darted from her lips to her eyes and back again. "I won't."

"I can talk with anyone I want to," she said as she reached out and laid her hand on his chest. "Because you are not the boss of me." Her words sounded less confident out loud than they did inside her head.

"Understood," he said as he stepped closer again, his eyes ablaze with unspoken thoughts.

Her back was only inches from the wall behind her so there was no way for her to retreat any further. There was nowhere to go to get any distance between them and she could feel the energy pulsing around them. Or maybe that was her own blind lust threatening to overwhelm her.

In a flash of movement, his arms were around her waist, hers were around his neck and his mouth crushed hers in a bruising kiss. His tongue demanded entry to her mouth, and she willingly, eagerly, parted her lips to let him in. They clashed in a tangle of hands and lips and tongues.

His hands roamed from her waist to hold the back of her head, then flew back down to grab her ass, yanking her off the ground. Her legs wrapped around his waist, gripping the hard planes of his body with her thighs. He continued to taste her and suck on her bottom lip.

"Tell me again you don't want me," he growled into her ear when he eventually stopped kissing her. "I'll put you down and let you go right now."

She felt good in his arms, safe and protected, and so fucking hot she swore she left scorch marks on the bricks behind her. His arms made the slightest move, as if he was about to put her down and she tightened her grip on him. "Don't you dare," she said.

The warm breath of his exhale tickled her ear and the side of her overheated neck. He hiked her up and held her body flush against his own. "I never would." He kissed the side of her neck and then up to her cheek, his fingers gripping her ass and getting ever closer to igniting a spark that would take a lifetime to put out.

Voices broke into their intimate space as a group of people turned down the alley and Jesse lowered her gently to the ground. "But I don't think this is the right place for this to happen."

F OR TWO BLOCKS, SHE pulled him along by the hand, stopping every few feet to push him against a wall or a closed-up storefront to steal a kiss.

She was going to be the one in charge and he needed to know it.

Jesse was practically glued to her body while she stood on the stoop in front of her building and fumbled with the key to unlock the door. His hands reached beneath her skirt and grabbed her ass while he buried his face in the hair at the base of her neck. "Hurry up, Mia," he whispered into her hair. "Or your neighbors are going to be in for one hell of a show tonight."

Her belly tightened and she shoved the door open, ripping the key from the lock as he pushed her through the open doorway, toward the elevator.

Only because Mrs. Aldrich was waiting by the elevator did Jesse actually behave himself. Sort of.

Once they were all in the elevator, he pulled Mia's body backward against his own. He gripped the fabric at the back of her skirt and slowly inched it just high enough that he could easily stroke his fingertips along the delicate skin where her thighs met her cheeks.

Mia swallowed down the moans that threatened to escape her lips when one of Jesse's fingers slipped beneath the fabric of her panties.

As the elevator rumbled to a stop at the fourth floor, Mia swatted away Jesse's hands and smoothed down her skirt. She tried to take a step away from him but his hand across her midsection held her firmly in place. The elevator doors opened, and Jesse finally released her.

"Have a nice night, Mrs. Aldrich," Mia said as they went their separate ways.

"You too, dear. And thank you for taking my garbage down to the dumpster for me yesterday."

"It was no problem at all." Mia smiled at her neighbor then unlocked the door to the apartment.

When she closed the door behind them, Jesse heaved a sigh. "Jesus Christ, I thought you two would never stop talking."

Before Mia could explain the conversation only lasted three seconds, Jesse had his hands all over her, in her hair, down her arms, over her breasts, down her belly to the skirt he'd been so anxious to get off her. Kneeling in front of her, he unlaced her boots and pulled them off before he pulled her socks off and tossed them to the side.

"What if my feet get cold?" she teased.

He didn't respond. Instead, he picked up one foot and gently turned it to the side, staring at the inside of her ankle. His eyes traveled up her body until he met her gaze. "I didn't know you had a tattoo."

"Two of them, actually."

His eyebrows lifted and he grinned. "You know I have to find the other one now, right?" From his position in front of her he slid his hands up her thighs and yanked her underwear down to pool around her feet. "But not quite yet." Dragging his fingers up her inner thighs, he pushed her legs apart, then stroked her center, dipped one finger inside. "Fuck, Mia, you're already so wet for me," he said, his voice thick with need.

She didn't mean to whimper at his touch, to turn to a bowl of jelly when his fingers slipped into her over and over again in a slow and steady rhythm, but she couldn't stop herself.

Getting to his feet, he pulled her away from the wall that was her only means of support, since her legs had lost the ability to hold her upright, and with a gentle nudge, he pushed her toward the couch.

All her intentions of being the one in charge seemed to have gone the way of her underwear, tossed in a heap on the other side of the room, and she happily let Jesse take over.

"Kneel on the couch and lean over. Put your hands on the back," he said. One second after she did as he asked, her skirt was lifted over her hips and she was completely exposed to his gaze, his hands, his mouth.

"Holy fuck," he said, letting his hands roam her naked bottom, fingers sliding into her again. "I just love how wet you are." He took his fingers from her and spread her cheeks, sending waves of intense longing through her core.

She couldn't see him behind her, but she could see the warm, yellow streetlights outside her building as she felt him kneel behind her. Without any warning, he grabbed onto her hips, holding her still as his tongue lapped at her, licked her until she was a writhing, whimpering mess. Her fingers held a death grip on the couch to keep from floating off into space.

The world outside her windows kept moving. Cars drove by, people walked up and down the sidewalks. The bus shuddered to a stop at each enclosed shelter along its route. In the distance, the wild Atlantic Ocean crashed against the rocky shore as Jesse Murphy spun her world on its axis.

Then, without warning, he brought it to a screeching halt.

"No," she moaned, pushing her body back to find him again. "Please, please, please don't stop."

She couldn't see it, but she could hear the smile on his face when he said, "Don't worry, Beauty, I'm not done with you yet."

Her aching center felt entirely too empty without him there.

And then that one word registered in her brain, took root, and settled in: *Beauty*. He'd called her Beauty. Not *beautiful*, as in what she looked like on the outside, but rather, Beauty, how he saw her as a whole person.

A little hitch in her heart caught her unaware and before she had time to think about it, his hands were on her again, running up and down her thighs, outside and in before gliding up over her ass and back down between her legs, right where they belonged.

"Stand up so I can take these clothes off you," he said, removing his hands from her center and giving a tug on her hips.

He could have asked her to stand on her head and do one arm pushups and she would have done it, so strong was her fascination with him, her desire to see what the rest of the night held in store. Her skirt fell back down over her lower half as she stood and faced him, unable to focus on anything aside from his commanding presence.

His chest rose and fell with each deep breath. His jaw twitched as he reached his hands out to slide the sweater off her shoulders, letting it fall to the floor. Stepping closer, he bunched up the skirt and pulled her whole dress up and off her body, leaving her standing in front of him wearing only an emerald-green lace bra.

The reality of being intimate with a new man hit her when Jesse pulled her close, buried his face into her cleavage and kissed the tops of her breasts. He grabbed onto her ass with one hand and wrapped the other around her waist. Her whimpered gasp encouraged him to keep exploring her body.

Both of his hands slid up her back and unhooked her bra while he nuzzled into her hair. "I found it," he whispered against her ear.

"Found what?" she asked through the haze of need that settled into her brain like fog rolling over the water.

His left arm drifted down, and his fingertips lightly stroked her right thigh. "Your other tattoo."

When he smiled, his scruffy beard pulled gently on her hair and she melted against him, needing to not be the only naked one in the room anymore.

Her peaked nipples needed to be pressed against his skin. "Can I take this off you now?" she asked, pulling at the hem of his shirt.

His fingers wrapped around her wrists, stopping her from getting what she wanted. "Nope," he said. "I told you; I'm not done with you yet." He pulled at her unhooked bra and tossed it onto the couch behind her.

The way he touched her, rough but not harsh, the way he looked at her, and especially the way he made her feel when he put his mouth on her, made any lingering feelings of uncertainty evaporate like mist on a summer morning.

Without a word, he wrapped his arms around her again and hoisted her off the floor. She wrapped her legs around his waist, and he tugged his shirt up just enough to allow the skin-to-skin contact she craved, her heated center against the velvety smooth skin of his abdomen.

Grabbing both sides of his face, she leaned in and took his mouth, devouring him with kisses as he carried her toward her bedroom. She whimpered against his lips when one of his hands slid between her opened legs, fingering her as they walked.

He didn't bother shutting the door, just walked in and set her feet on the carpet by the head of the bed. "I want you on your knees like you were on the couch. Hands on the headboard."

It wasn't a request, but a command. Her heart thumped in her chest as she quickly did as he said.

"Spread your legs for me, Beauty."

If words could cause orgasms, those were the ones that could do it.

She pushed the pillows out of the way and widened her kneeling stance, gripping the top of the headboard, ready and willing for whatever came next.

The bed moved as Jesse climbed onto it, then slid himself between her legs, his face directly beneath her, his eyes as intense as she'd ever seen them. "Give me that sweet pussy, Mia. I need you in my mouth again. I need the taste of you on my tongue."

Those words might have worked too.

As she lowered down to sit on his face, he grasped her hips and pulled her down, his mouth moving on her, kissing, licking, sucking. He angled her body so he could lick her clit, suck on it, until her legs quivered, on the verge of not being able to hold her up her anymore.

Her toes and fingers tingled and the muscles in her feet tensed as her orgasm started to build. Any pretense of being quiet went out the window as she whined and gasped and grunted, her breaths growing shallow and rapid as he continued to please her.

His own growls and moans vibrated through her core as the coiling sensation quickly tensed her entire body. With a scream, her eyes screwed tight as flashes of lightning erupted behind them and she exploded into a million stars in the sky. Her body trembled and her fingers scratched and clawed against the headboard.

Instinctively, she pulled herself up and away from his face, her sensitivity level close to overload. Gasping, she rolled off and flopped down beside him, staring at the ceiling in awe of what he'd just done to her. Scrubbing her hands over her face, she breathed deeply to get her heart to slow down.

Beside her, Jesse yanked his shirt over his head, pulled a foil packet from his jeans pocket then discarded the rest of his clothes. She had never seen a body like his up close and she was thankful she hadn't seen it before. He looked like he had been carved from stone, and she felt quite soft by comparison all of a sudden.

Grabbing for the extra blanket on the floor next to the bed, she draped it over herself.

"You cold?" he asked, wrapping an arm over her.

"No," she admitted, glancing from his body down at her own. "Just feeling a little outclassed here."

He ripped the blanket off and tossed it to the floor. Throwing one leg over her middle, he straddled her, grabbed her hands, and held them tightly above her head. Shaking his head slowly, he said, "Don't ever say that. You are the most beautiful woman I've ever known. The fact that *you* are so openly sharing yourself with *me*? Trust me when I say I'm the one who's outclassed here."

Her heart couldn't take much more before she finally gave in completely to him. She struggled to keep even a hint of emotional distance between them. "Are you kidding?" she said. "Look at you. I have literally never seen a body like yours in real life before. You're a little intimidating." She huffed out a small laugh, but his stern expression didn't change.

"It's just a body, Mia. It's only as good as the person it belongs to."

The urge to reach out and run her fingers along the cutouts of his muscles had to stay unfulfilled because he was not letting go of her wrists. "Are you?" she asked.

"Am I what?"

"Are you a good person?"

Jesse

H OW THE HELL DID he answer a question like that? He'd always thought of himself as a good person but it's tough to justify oneself to someone while sitting naked on top of them, holding them immobile beneath you.

"I don't know. I guess you'll have to spend more time with me and come to your own conclusion on that."

She smiled up at him, and the overwhelming urge to suck her pink nipples and hear the noises he brought out of her, hit him as hard as any punch ever had. Without letting go of her hands, he moved down her hips and lowered his mouth to her, sucking and licking her nipples until they peaked in his mouth. Her moans of pleasure made his dick twitch to be inside her.

He knew what she tasted like, now he needed to know what it felt like to bury himself inside her and hear his name fall from her lips while he took her. Lifting his head, he looked up to see her watching him, her eyes practically begging him to keep going.

"You want me keep sucking on you, Beauty, or do you want something else from me?" He reached down and stroked himself against the softness of her belly and felt her shuddering breath as she tried to open her legs wider for him. "Are you spreading your legs for me, Beauty?"

She nodded but didn't speak.

"Does that mean you're ready for me to take you? To make you mine?"

Her eyes flashed. She was scared.

"Because that's what this means," he said. "If you give yourself to me, I'm taking it all. I want you, Mia. I want to feel you beneath me. I want to feel your pussy wrapped around me." He kissed her belly.

"But most of all," he continued, "I want you to trust me. I want you to trust me to be good to you, to take care of you, to never hurt you." He leaned down and kissed her nipples, sucked them gently, first one and then the other. "Can you do that, Beauty? Can you trust me enough to let me fuck you and make you scream my name and ruin you for every other man on the face of the fucking earth?"

The fight happened behind her eyes. Unbridled lust and pure sexual need warred with her clearly bruised and broken heart, each gaining the upper hand for a flash, before the other took over again.

He worried that he might have pushed her too far, pushed her to make a choice he wouldn't like. It would hurt like hell to leave her untouched, but if that's what she wanted, that's what he'd do.

Readying himself for the reality that his only relief would come from jerking off in the shower by himself later, he waited for her to answer.

Then she nodded her head and tried again to push her legs open. "OK," she whispered. "I trust you."

Like a man possessed, he dropped his head to her chest again, secure in the knowledge that he would do everything he could to please this woman, in every way, as long as she would let him. Sitting back up, he nudged her legs a little wider, took hold of his cock and stroked it against her. "Are you on anything or do I need a condom?" he asked.

"Both," she said on a whisper. "I'm on the pill but I don't know anything about your past or who you've been with." She wriggled her hips and stared down at him. "Please don't take that the wrong way."

He knew he was clean, but he had to prove it to her, so the decision was made; at the first opportunity he had, he'd be taking a trip to the clinic and getting *all the tests*. He'd obviously wear the condom now, but the mere thought of fucking her bare almost had him running out the door to find an all-night clinic.

After a few more strokes he reached over and ripped open the packet, unrolled the condom down his shaft. Her eyes stayed fixed on his hands, following every move he made, making the normally mundane act erotic in and of itself.

He leaned over, hovering his chest above her breasts, and nudged his tip into her. This was what he'd been waiting for, he didn't want to rush and be done too soon. He wanted to savor every inch as he filled her. Slowly, he pushed inside, his hands flat on the bed on either side of her head. Her back arched to rub her nipples against his chest.

When he was buried deep, her hips open and accepting, he lowered his head to kiss the side of her neck as she twined her fingers into his hair, her gentle moans filling the otherwise silent room.

As he sank into her again and again, his mind filled with the scent of her hair, the stab of her fingernails as they raked up and down his back, the connection of her legs as they wrapped around his, the ridiculously silky skin between her neck and shoulder as he kissed it. His eyes rolled into his head as he slid into her with a quickening tempo.

The hottest fucking thing he'd ever heard was the sound of her moans morphing into gasps and cries which grew more urgent with every thrust of his hips.

"God, yes," she cried out, her hips bucking into his, her fingernails digging deeper into his shoulders. "Oh, my God, Jesse, please." Her plea was desperate. She was so close again, taking him as hard as he gave it to her.

"It's OK, Beauty," he whispered. "I've got you. You can trust me." The pressure was building in his balls, he just needed to push her over again before he could finally let go and come inside her, making her his own. "I need you to come for me, Mia. I need to hear you."

Her cries became grunts as she met him thrust for thrust until she clenched around him, buried her face in his neck. "Yes, Jesse, yes," she cried against his skin, her arms and legs clinging to him. Without giving her a second to rest he closed his eyes and pounded into her.

Her gasps were whispers in his ear as he slammed into her with one final thrust, his borderline animalistic sounds overwhelming hers as he found his release.

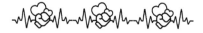

Sweat covered their bodies as they lay together. Mia snuggled against his side with one leg draped over him. The possessive nature of the position turned him on almost as much as bending her over the couch did. Almost.

"Look at you," she said as she lazily traced the outline of his abdominal muscles with one slender finger. "I could use your body as a marble run."

She giggled when he flipped her onto her back and pinned her to the bed. "I could use your body for a lot of things," he said. "So, if there's ever anything you want to do or try, you just let me know because I'm down for all of it."

Laughing, she pushed him off her, rolled him onto his back and then threw one leg over his hips, straddling him.

"You like cowgirl, do you?" he said, resting his hands on the roundest part of her hips. Her skin was achingly soft.

"I like a lot of things," she said, being intentionally vague and he already couldn't wait to see what kinds of things she liked. Spreading out her fingers on his chest, she ran them gently over the tattoo on his left pec. The black ink marked his skin in a geometric pattern. "It's beautiful. It's a mandala?"

He nodded.

"Does it have meaning?"

"No, nothing in particular. A friend of mine drew it and I really liked the design, so I went with it."

She trailed her fingers further down toward his waist to the other tattoo he had above his right hipbone. The words, *He will win who knows when to fight and when not to fight – Sun Tzu*, had been inked alongside a skeleton wearing hand wraps, and posed in the motion of throwing a knee strike. "This one must mean something."

He sucked in a quick breath as her fingertips danced over his skin. "The skeleton is a Muay Thai fighter, and the quote is one that I live by. Sun Tzu was a general, but his focus was on ways to avoid war if at all possible. That's how I am as a fighter and, I hope, as a man. It's how I want to be, anyway."

A sly grin worked its way across her lips. "It sure seemed like my friend Alex was in danger of losing his arms tonight. Are you saying that was a fight that was unavoidable?"

"For you, Beauty? Without a fucking doubt," he said, completely serious. "Alex would never have known what hit him." Reaching his hands up, he stroked her breasts, loving the way her eyes drifted closed as he teased her nipples. "Your turn," he said, thinking back to her ankle tattoo—a snake encircling a wooden staff. "What's your ankle tattoo all about? It's a medical thing, right?"

Taking hold of his hands, she stopped his movements and smiled down at him. "I can't think straight when you do that." As if his ego needed more stroking.

"So, what is it?" he said, dropping his hands to her hips.

Looking sideways down to her ankle then back at him, she said, "It's called a rod of Asclepius."

"The rod of who?" He traced small circles on her skin just to feel the goosebumps he raised.

"Asclepius," she said. "He was the Greek god of healing. And he was particularly good at his craft, to the point of bringing people back from the dead. And that pissed off Hades, who wanted those souls for himself in the Underworld. And it also pissed off Zeus, who thought Asclepius was messing around with the natural order of things. So, Zeus struck him down with a thunderbolt."

His heart tripped in his chest as he listened to her, naked, sitting astride him, telling stories of Greek myths.

"My Aunt Claire has been an ER nurse for her entire career. She's actually the one who got me into nursing to begin with. She's the one who told me that story." Her body curled inward over him as she started giggling. "When she would get a patient in the emergency room that should have died and they were able to save them, she would always look up and say, 'Not today, Zeus. Not today.'"

Jesse laughed with her. "I think I need to meet this aunt of yours. She sounds like my kind of people."

"Oh, she would love you," Mia said. "In fact, she might actually hit on you and literally try to love you."

His eyes popped open, and he slid his hands off Mia's hips and covered his suddenly uncomfortable penis, while she fell into another fit of giggles.

There was so much about this woman he wanted to know. He raised his hands to her hips again then trailed his fingers down her leg and stopped on the small bandage "X" tattoo over a noticeable scar on her thigh. "What's this one all about?"

"That," she said with a smile, "is a souvenir of my short-lived rebellious phase when I was in high school. My friend and I decided to go to a party that was happening in the woods not far from her house. And about an hour in, the cops showed up and we all took off like bats out of hell. Of course, there was a chain-link fence that bordered the yards that butted up against the woods."

"Oh, no," Jesse said, a grin blossoming on his face.

Hanging her head in shame, she laughed. "Oh, yes. My friend, Jenna, grabbed that fence and hopped it like a freaking rabbit. I, on the other hand, grabbed the fence, threw one leg over and somehow caught my other leg on a jagged piece of metal and gave myself a nice gash." She couldn't hold back the laughter as she continued. "Because I'd been drinking, it wouldn't stop bleeding. So, my parents had to take me to the ER to get stitches. I got the whole, 'we raised you better than this' speech on the way to the hospital, while I was getting the stitches, and on the way home. It was terrible."

"That was it for your career as a troublemaker?" he asked with a laugh.

"That was it. The beginning and the end of my bad girl stage in one fell swoop."

One of his eyebrows quirked up. "I don't know, after what went down here tonight, I'd say that bad girl might still be in there somewhere," he said, raising one hand and pressing a finger to her belly.

"Maybe she just needs a little more encouragement to come out?" His finger slowly worked its way down until he slid it between her legs, feeling how wet she was. "Maybe not as much encouragement as I thought."

"Only if you have another condom," she said.

She was getting closer to letting him in fully on an emotional level. But he understood that she still had to maintain her boundaries.

T HROUGH THE BRIGHT MORNING sunshine, Mia carried the
paper tray with two coffees and the bag with two bagels toward
her apartment. Still riding the euphoric high from the night before,
she barely felt the pavement beneath her feet, or heard the singing birds
in the trees along the road, or any other noise in the world around her.

Jesse had stayed the night, and they made the best use of the condoms he'd brought with him, joking that he might never walk again
if he'd brought four with him, instead of just the three. The air felt
warmer, the sun shone brighter, and Mia's body ached in the best way
possible from head to foot.

When she got back to the apartment, she heard Jesse moving
around in her bedroom.

Panic erupted in her brain and immediately burned through her
entire body when she walked in and saw him sitting on the edge of her
bed, pulling his shirt over his head, his jeans already on and buttoned.

He'd been asleep when she left and now, he was trying to sneak out
before she came back home. Her vision narrowed and she propped
herself against the doorframe, all power in her limbs flagging, as she
struggled to keep herself upright.

"Hey," she said, hoping to keep her voice calm and casual as her heart splintered in her chest. "I brought coffee and bagels if you've got time to stay and eat."

He looked up to see her, a big, happy grin on his face. "That's where you went," he said. "I was figuring you couldn't have been running out on me, since this is your place and all." Crossing the room in only a few steps, he took the coffee and bagels from her, set them on her bureau. He pulled her into a warm, snuggly bear hug, letting his hands roam up and down her back. "Good morning, Beauty," he said. "How'd you sleep? I didn't keep you awake or anything?"

Taking a steadying breath, she reminded herself that Jesse was not Brandon. But then Brandon wasn't Brandon when they'd started dating either. He had been quite charming and fun and sexy and—oh, right—in love with her sister.

"You didn't keep me awake," she said softly. "I liked having you in the bed with me. It felt nice. You felt nice."

He squeezed her hand then reached over for a cup of coffee, handed her the first cup, then grabbed his own. "I've got to get down to the gym this morning. Want to come with?"

It was a shock to be invited into his life so quickly and she didn't know how to respond. "Why would you want me to go to the gym with you? Like to sit and watch you work out?"

His laugh was loud in the quiet space of her room. "No, Beauty, I don't need you to come and watch me work out. I thought you might like to practice some more of those self-defense moves. Maybe learn a few more." He took a sip of his coffee while he waited for her to respond.

"I don't have the right clothes."

He narrowed his eyes a fraction then he walked to her bureau and opened the top drawer.

"What are you doing?" she said, hurrying to stop him from finding things she didn't want him to find. Maybe someday she'd be willing to show him the toys she had in her bottom drawer, but it wouldn't be the day after they had sex for the very first time!

He closed the top drawer and opened the middle one. After rooting around for a second, he pulled out a t-shirt and tossed it into her hands. She fumbled to catch the shirt without spilling her coffee everywhere.

Jesse closed the middle drawer and squatted down to pull open the bottom drawer. Before she could stop herself, she leaped forward and kicked the drawer shut, narrowly avoiding slamming it on his fingers.

His head snapped up. "What the?" Then he flashed a panty-melting grin. "Oh... I can't wait for you to show me what you keep in *that* drawer."

Heat flooded her cheeks and she asked, "What are you even looking for?"

"Sweatpants? Yoga pants? Whatever you wear to work out."

She pulled open a drawer under her bed and took out a pair of black yoga pants, held them up for him to see.

"Perfect. Put them on and let's get out of here." He sat on the edge of the bed and waited for her to change her clothes.

"Aren't you going to wait in the living room?"

A look of confusion washed over his face. "Oh," he said as the confusion gave way to playfulness. "It didn't even occur to me. You're right. I'll go wait on the couch. You remember the couch, right? The place where I bent you over, lifted your dress and had myself a little late night snack?"

"Jesse!" She buried her face in the balled-up T-shirt in her hands, feeling it get warm from the heat radiating off of her. "You can't just say things like that," she mumbled into the fabric.

Her eyes were closed but her body was keenly aware of Jesse suddenly standing right in front of her. He pulled her T-shirt-gripping hands away from her face. "So, it's OK to *do* those things, just not say the words? That doesn't make a lot of sense to me." Touching his finger to her cheek, he said, "There was nothing wrong with what we did last night. You know that, yeah?"

She certainly knew it last night. It was the hottest thing she'd ever experienced, and she couldn't wait to do it again. Shoving the T-shirt into his hands, she pulled off her sweater then unzipped her jeans and pushed them to the floor before she lost the courage to do it.

As she reached over to get her workout shirt back from him, he grabbed hold of her wrist, pushed her hand behind her back and held it there, causing her to arch her body into him. He held her close, nudged her ear. "You take my breath away," he whispered, then kissed the tip of her nose as he squeezed her panty-clad bottom with his free hand. "Don't ever forget that."

K EEPING UP WITH HIM when he was on a mission to get into the gym was a workout all by itself. His long strides ate up the distance from the car to the building and, despite her own long legs, Mia struggled to keep pace.

The gym was a ten-minute drive further inland to an industrial section of Oak Harbor. Surrounded by a window manufacturer, several medical businesses of some sort, and a landscaping company, Willis Combat Training was nothing more than a big gray box of a building. If you didn't already know it was there, it could very easily go overlooked.

"I think just getting in here was enough of a workout for me," she teased as he held the door open to let her walk through.

Once they entered the building, Mia was shocked at how different the inside was from the outside. It was bright and open and there was something happening every place she looked. Conversations and commands from trainers filled her ears as they approached the front desk.

The next thing she picked up was the faint smell of body odor in the air. It wasn't overwhelming, but was fairly unpleasant, nonetheless.

Jesse's face didn't show a hint of concern at the smell, and she realized it was probably a normal part of his experience every day.

Jesse's cousin Danny stood behind the front desk.

"Hey, you two," he said, looking curiously from Jesse to Mia and back to Jesse. "Coming in for a little workout between friends?" His mouth quirked up at one side and Mia dipped her head to hide her embarrassment. Danny slid a paper to Mia and had her fill out the waver form before she could head into the gym itself.

"Am I really in danger here?" she said to Danny as she signed her name on the line. She said to Jesse, "Because I can totally grab a chair and wait until you're done."

She walked to stay in shape and did yoga for strength; both of which she could do by herself without the added pressure of a room full of people. With a grin, Jesse slid the paper back to Danny, then pushed against Mia's back to head her toward impending doom.

Despite the early hour on a Sunday morning, the gym was busier than she'd expected. "There's a lot of people here," she said, stopping to watch a couple guys wrestling on the blue foam mats. Everywhere she turned there was motion and talking and heavy breathing and grunting. "Is it always this busy?"

"Sundays are open gym day, so yeah, it's usually pretty busy around now."

He had her leave her shoes next to his on a tall shoe rack before they stepped onto the mats. It was certainly not like any gym she'd ever been to with rows of gleaming machines and TVs hung from the ceiling. This place was different in every way.

In one corner a half dozen boxing heavy bags swung, suspended from the ceiling by thick silver chains. Opposite those was an actual boxing ring. There was nobody inside it and Mia had the urge to jump in the ring just to see how it would feel to be in there.

The most surprising thing though, was the crowd. There were men and women of all ages there, but there wasn't a lot of preening or showing off that she could see. Everybody seemed to be there to focus on their craft more than they were there to find dates.

In the far corner of the room, she saw a small group of people practicing wrestling of some sort. There was an older man who stood among the fighters, watching like a hawk, turning from one pair to the next to the next, saying things like, "Be mindful of Jose's shoulder, Mike," and "That's it, Lena, pull her hand away from her body." Suddenly, he yelled, "Yes! Now you're getting it, Henry. Push his knee! Keep pushing it! Push his hip now!"

Jesse came back from the locker room, where he'd changed from his jeans into his workout gear, and sat down on the floor beside her. "That's Jiu Jitsu," he said, sitting in a wide V, his legs outstretched to either side. He pulled his legs together and reached toward his toes. "Those guys have been doing this only about six months or so. Some of them are getting pretty good."

She kicked her foot up behind herself, grabbed it with one hand and stretched her leg before repeating it on the other side.

"It kind of looks like they could really hurt each other with some of that stuff," she said.

"They could if they weren't careful, but that's what Nick's trying to teach them. They need to know when they're training and when they're competing. There's a difference."

"Is that what you do? Fight like that? And teach other people to fight too?"

"Pretty much." He was back on his feet, and he grabbed her hand. "Come on, I'll show you some stuff too." He led her to an empty space on the floor, stood with his feet apart, one leg forward and the other back, his hands in fists by his face. "See what I'm doing here? Copy the way I'm standing."

She curled her hands into fists and tried to stand the way he was.

"Good," he said. "Now, keeping your fist loose, I want you to take a step with your left foot and at the same time throw your left hand for a jab, like this." He showed her what to do and again she copied him. "When you get to the end of your punch, tighten your fist." It took her a few tries to get the hang of it and then he said, "Awesome. From there, you're not going to step with your right foot. Instead, pivot on the ball of your foot as you throw a right cross, keeping your weight in your back leg."

She threw a couple slow-motion crosses, as awkward as they were. Eventually, he had her attempt to throw what he called a "simple one-two" combination of a jab and a cross.

It was a lot of instructions for what should have been a simple movement. Even after he showed her a bunch of times what it was supposed to look like, it took her a while to really grasp his instructions and throw the one-two at the air. Resting her weight on her back leg was awkward and harder to do than she thought it should be.

Eventually he was satisfied with how she moved, and he changed his position to stand facing her. He held his hands up, palms facing out on either side of his head. Holding his left hand a bit forward he said, "Throw a jab right here."

She threw the punch, and he caught it.

"Nice. Now throw the one-two," he said. "The one at my left hand, the two at my right. Got it?"

"I think so." She stepped and threw a punch with her left hand, then pivoted and threw one with her right, as a feeling of total badassery washed over her entire being. "I did it," she said, hopping on her toes. "Did you see that? I did it!"

Jesse grinned at her, encouraged her to keep going, and taught her how to keep her guard up while she threw her punches. "Imagine your hand is glued to your cheekbone," he said. Once she'd gotten the hang of that, he surprised her by jumping behind her, grabbing her, and pulling her body back against his own. "Do you remember how to get out of this?" he asked.

She took a few seconds to think about it, then talked it through out loud with him as she slid her hips to the side to break his grip on her, raised her fist and pretended to strike his crotch.

"You got it," he said, encouraging her. "Remember what to do next?"

Again, she talked her way through it as she spun around, locked her hands behind his head, and threw a slow-motion knee into his hands as he used them to protect his forehead.

"That was perfect," he said. "Let's do it a few more times. A little faster, but still no force, got it?"

"Got it."

For close to an hour, they practiced punching and kneeing and getting away from attackers. Sweat poured off her body, soaking through her shirt. It was exhilarating and empowering and exhausting all at the same time. And she understood firsthand why the air smelled like sweat.

"That's it for me," she said, gasping for breath when they finally finished their workout. "How come I'm the only one dripping sweat here?"

He wiped his face on a towel and smiled at her. "Do you mind giving me about a half hour or so? I've just got a little bit more to do before I'm done."

Every muscle ached, her back and shoulders couldn't move if she tried, and yet she was in no rush to get out of the gym. The vibe of the place fit Jesse perfectly and despite not knowing anyone, the vibe felt right, comfortable for her. "No, I don't mind," she said. "It'll give me time to rebuild my strength for the walk to the car."

"You're definitely going to need that strength later," he said with a wink.

Her response was cut off when a couple of younger guys approached them.

"Coach!"

Jesse spun and smiled at the newcomers. "Hey, what's up fellas?"

One young man looked from Jesse to Mia and back to Jesse. "Not much, Coach. What's going on with you?"

The guy's face broke into a huge smile that Jesse seemed to understand immediately. Jesse put his hand on the guy's shoulder and turned him toward the mat. "That's enough out of you, Eddie," he said as he pushed the guy away with a laugh. "And remind me to kick your ass later."

The next half hour flashed by as Mia watched the activity happening everywhere she looked. As fun as it was to see so many athletes of every shape, size, and color honing their skills, her eyes always found their way back to Jesse. His body moved with a smooth, effortless grace; every motion led into the next and the next, but with a startling amount of speed and power when he connected with the black leather punching bag.

"Hey, Coach, now that you're tired as fuck, you wanna go a couple rounds?" one of the young guys asked Jesse when he stopped to wipe his face and neck with a towel.

The look in Jesse's eyes had Mia feeling sorry for the guy already, and Jesse hadn't even said yes yet.

"Give me five to catch my breath and I'll meet you in there," Jesse said, nodding his head toward the boxing ring. He came back over to Mia. "Do me a favor? Can you go into the locker room for me while I grab a bottle of water? My gloves are in my locker. Number one-thirty-five, main wall, kind of on the bottom right."

"Combination?"

"Six. Seventeen. Twenty-two."

After pointing her in the right direction, he went to the cooler by the front desk while she entered the surprisingly clean and well-lit locker room. Two walls of lockers filled the space, a hallway on the right side led to the men's showers, and the hallway on the left led to the women's showers.

"Six. Seventeen. Twenty-two," she repeated as she caught sight of herself in the giant wall mirror, her ponytail barely holding any hair, a ring of sweat darkening her collar and her underarms. She looked like an athlete. She felt like an athlete.

Finding locker one-thirty-five, she twirled the lock until it opened, revealing a pair of boxing gloves in the otherwise empty box.

"Hey, Coach's girl," someone said as they walked into the room. She looked around to see who the young man was talking to. Being the only other person in the room, he was, apparently, talking to her. "What's up?"

"Uh... nothing," she said. "I'm Mia. It's nice to meet you."

"Robby," he said. "Nice to meet you too." He grabbed his stuff out of a locker and disappeared down the hallway on the right. She had no idea if that was a good meeting with Robby or a bad one. It sort of felt like a good one and it made her smile.

Jesse and the guy who had challenged him to a couple rounds sat side by side on the edge of the ring talking when Mia walked over with the gloves. Jesse elbowed the kid good-naturedly then stood to thank her.

"This won't be too long," he told her as he climbed through the ropes and into the ring.

Rather than go back to the chair where she had been sitting, she chose to sit on the blue mat outside the ring and watch from there. Like everything she'd experienced since she'd started spending time with Jesse, his sparring session was nothing like she expected.

Instead of two fighters trying to kill each other, it was two guys pushing each other to be better at a sport they love. With a controlled aggression from both men, punches connected, kicks landed, and the three-minute rounds flew by.

She waited for Jesse to finish talking with the guy before they fist bumped one another and stepped out of the ring. Holding up his gloves, he said to Mia, "Let me go put these away and we can get out of here."

A minute or so after Jesse and his friend disappeared into the locker room, an outburst of hooting and hollering and raucous laughter erupted from the other side of the wall. Among all the noise, she heard more than one voice congratulating their coach and she knew she was the reason for what she was hearing. An easy warmth spread through her body and ended with the smile on her face.

"Mind if we swing by my place?" Jesse asked as they exited the gym. "I wasn't thinking about getting dressed after a shower when I left your place this morning. And these clothes aren't going to cut it." His shirt looked like it could be wrung out, it was so wet, his hair was the same. It might have been the sexiest she'd seen him look yet.

"Of course," she said, wondering how long it would be until she could get home and jump in for a shower of her own. "I've never seen your place, I'm kind of looking forward to it."

"Great," he said as he tugged her hand, leading her out the front door into the cool morning. "We'll go to my place, take a shower, get dirty, and take another shower." He squeezed her hand. "Then you can come with me to Sunday family dinner night."

Mia was still coming to terms with the fact that Jesse had invited her to family dinner night when they made it back to his place.

Jesse

A S HE UNLOCKED THE door, he stopped and looked Mia in the eye. "Don't get your hopes too high. There's been a random assortment of people living here over the years. Most of us weren't big in the interior decorating department." He shrugged. "My place makes your place look like a department store display."

Rolling her eyes, she gave him a playful push to get them through the door. As soon as she stepped inside, her eyes roamed from one end of the apartment to the other. "You weren't kidding when you said you don't decorate," she said. "You don't even have curtains on the windows."

"Nobody ever bothered," he said with a shrug. "I figured somebody would end up with a girlfriend at some point and then we'd do something about it, but nobody's girl ever seemed to care about it." He held her gaze. "Does it bother you?"

"Not even a little bit." She followed him into his bedroom which was only slightly less bare than the rest of the place. At least he had a rug on the old wooden floor. "You made your bed," she said, not bothering to hide the surprise in her voice.

Turning to her with a look of fake hurt, he said, "I'm not an animal, Mia. I might not decorate but I know how to make a bed." He walked her backward until she bumped into his bureau. She sucked in a quick gasp of air when he stood toe-to-toe with her. The desire in her eyes burned so brightly he could almost see the flames.

But he needed a shower.

Putting one hand on either of her hips, he slid her two steps to the side, then opened the drawer she'd been blocking to grab out some clean clothes. He opened another drawer and pulled out a few more things and handed them to her. "They're going to be a little big on you, but it'll be a hell of a lot better than putting sweaty clothes back on."

Jesse took her hand and pulled her along behind him as he led the way to the bathroom, yanking a couple of bath towels from a laundry basket at the foot of his bed as he went. Obviously, he assumed she was taking a shower at his place. With him.

His apartment wasn't glamorous, but he'd always liked the bathroom. Not only was it a decent size for an old house, but it had a big soaking tub instead of the stand-up shower stall that most apartments had.

"Oh, I could soak in that for hours," she said on a sigh. "That looks heavenly."

The tub looked clean enough, but he had no idea when it had been deep cleaned last. "How about if I promise to scrub it out before you come over again and then I'll give you a bath in there myself."

He opened the tap and let the water run while he stripped out of his sweaty gym clothes, tossed them to the corner of the room. Taking two steps closer to her, he took hold of the hem of her shirt and pulled it up and over her head. He reached back and unhooked her bra, let it fall away and expose her delicious breasts. Once he had her yoga pants off and she stood before him entirely naked, he flipped the lever to turn the shower on and helped her step into the tub.

Her long legs, full hips, and an ass that fit perfectly in his hands...
It took all of his self-control not to press her up against the tub wall,
spread those luscious legs and drive into her. He was so fucking hard
for her; it was going to be a long three minutes of getting clean before
he could make her dirty again.

She stood beneath the stream of water, soaking her hair and wetting
her skin. He grabbed a bar of soap from the rack behind her head and
lathered up his hands. They switched places allowing him to get his
body wet before he ran his soapy hands over himself, washing away all
traces of his workout.

He quickly scrubbed in some shampoo, then rinsed it out as he
let the suds wash down his body. Putting his hands on her hips he
switched their places back so she could be under the water again.

"I liked watching you wash yourself," she said softly, then diverted
her eyes from his.

He leaned in, placed his lips lightly against hers. "I'm glad you liked
it." He reached up and grabbed the bar of soap again, lathered up his
hands and replaced it on the rack before he placed his hands on her
breasts, her hard nipples tickling his palms. "Now I'm going to wash
you."

The shower spray bounced off her back and shoulders and she let
her head fall back while he ran his soapy hands from her breasts down
over her belly and then around to her ass. He re-soaped his hands
before he knelt down in front of her. "Spread your legs for me," he
said, running his fingers up the inside of her thighs and washing her
everywhere that needed washing.

Her fingers curled into his hair as she moaned her enjoyment of his
attention. "Your hands feel so good," she whispered.

From his knees, he turned her to face into the water, letting the
spray rinse her clean before he turned her around again. Unable to

resist the sound of her sighs, Jesse leaned in, pressed his tongue against her center and licked.

"Oh, Jesse," she cried, reaching her hands to the sides but hitting nothing but a flimsy shower curtain. "Oh, I really like that."

Sliding one finger inside her, he pressed his tongue against her and licked again.

Her knees wobbled as she moaned.

He didn't want to stop but it had to be enough to tide him over for another couple minutes until he could get her into his bedroom where he had condoms. After forcing himself to stand again, he soaped up the rest of her body, feeling her silky skin beneath his hands. She tipped her head back and let him massage shampoo through her hair.

With the tips of her fingers, she reached out for him, touched the tip of his erection, sending a surge of need like a lightning strike straight from his dick to his brain and back again.

Wrapping his fingers around her wrist, he removed her hand. "Not yet, Beauty," he whispered into her ear, pressing his erection into her belly as he rinsed the shampoo from her hair.

She whimpered her protest but didn't say anything as he closed the tap, leaving them naked, wet, and pressed skin-to-skin in the shower.

After they stepped out onto the bathmat, he wrapped one towel around her shoulders then grabbed the other one to tie around his waist. She lifted her arms, letting him dry her from top to bottom, being careful to dry her everywhere, even between her toes, before he wrapped it around her body and led her back to his bedroom.

"Why are you so sweet to me?" she asked once they were back in his room with the door closed. There was a hairbrush on his bureau and Mia stood in front of the mirror and ran it through her hair. It was a small thing to have her use his hairbrush but there was something unimaginably intimate about the gesture.

"Why wouldn't I be?" he said, standing against her towel-clad back after letting his own towel hit the floor. Being nude was as natural as breathing to him. "I told you that you could trust me and I wouldn't hurt you, didn't I?"

She nodded, placed the brush back on the bureau, and whispered, "Yes."

"Well, part of not hurting you is treating you like the amazing woman you are, letting you know how sexy and beautiful and fun and touchable I find you," he said as he wrapped his arms around her waist and held her against his chest, letting his chin rest on her shoulder as he held her gaze in the mirror.

Tugging at her towel, the fabric between them dropped to the ground. His eyes raked her naked form and his dick responded immediately, pressing into her ass. She turned to face him, her warm, damp, silky-smooth body against his.

He dropped his head down to meet hers. Her mouth opened and her tongue darted in to dance with his. Her soft lips nipped at his lips, his jaw, his neck. The way her fingers lazily stroked his back, his sides, his ass, was a stark contrast to the eagerness and energetic frenzy of the night before.

The velvety smooth skin of her ass filled his hands as he lifted her from the ground and carried her over to his bed. He sat with her straddling his lap, her mouth hungry for his, her hips grinding, seeking to press her herself against his hard length.

"Beauty," he whispered through the haze of need that threatened to cloud their judgment. "I need to get a condom before you take me inside you like that."

She whimpered against his mouth but didn't stop kissing him.

"You do want me inside you, don't you, Beauty? Filling you up, fucking you, making you come for me?"

"Yes," she whispered. "But I don't want you to let me go."

He hoisted her in his arms and stood from the bed. Within five steps he was at his bureau, Mia still clinging to his body, and he grabbed a strip of condoms from the top drawer. Tossing the condoms onto the bed, he sat back down the way they had been, and she returned to grinding on him as they kissed.

She giggled. "That was kind of fun," she said against his mouth. "I've never had anyone carry me across a room like that before, you know, with both of us being naked."

"You asked me not to let you go, so I didn't." He leaned back to look into her eyes, hunger visibly burning there. "Besides I quite like you wrapped around me like that. I get to hold onto your ass that way." He squeezed her ass for emphasis before he moved them higher onto the bed.

"What's different about you?" she asked as she pushed him back to lay flat beneath her. "What is it about you that brings this out of me?" Her hips continued to rock back and forth, stroking him with her pussy. "I've never had sex with the lights on before, let alone in the middle of the day in a room with no curtains."

A distinct sense of conquest came over him, knowing he was the only one to ever see the way she looked in complete control of her body, her wants, her needs, embracing her sexual nature with abandon. If it was up to him, he'd be the only one to ever see it again because he had every intention of making this woman his own for all time.

"I don't know, Beauty, but if you keep grinding on me like that without actually riding me, I might have to throw you over and take you right now."

The sexiest smile graced her face, and she leaned forward, raising his hands over his head, holding her breasts directly over his mouth. "Think you're strong enough?" she asked. "I've been learning some pretty awesome self-defense moves from this really hot guy at the gym." She angled her hips and pressed herself onto the tip of his cock.

That same feeling of conquest threatened to drive him deep inside of her without a condom, just to feel her the way nature intended, soft and hot and wet. He had to force himself to stop things from going the way he truly wanted them to go.

Breaking free of her hands, he grabbed her hips, pulled her off and flipped her onto her back. Hovering above her, he pressed his cock to her belly. "Are you trying to tempt me into breaking your own rule, Beauty? Because we're coming awfully close."

Her eyes were wide as he held her gaze, his body barely holding on while he waited for her answer.

"No," she finally said. "We should definitely use a condom."

He pushed his body up to straddle her while he reached over to grab the foil packet and tear it open. Looking down on her, he wanted nothing more than to toss the condom into the trash can and sink into her body with one quick thrust.

"Can I do that?" she asked, stilling his hands before he could roll it on. "Lie down on your back."

Watching her, fascinated by her in every way, he rolled off and lay beside her. She stretched one long leg over him, straddling him the way he liked it and sat back on her heels. With one warm hand she stroked him, then rolled the condom all the way on while he watched, aching to be inside her.

Flattening her hands on either side of his head she leaned forward again, and this time he grabbed her breasts and began to indulge his appetite for her, ready to take his fill.

Her back bowed as he ran his fingers down the length of her spine, pushing her breasts into his face, stoking the fire that burned in his belly. His patience was running out as he waited for her. Finally, she wiggled her hips backward, taking him inside until he couldn't go any further. Their groans filled the mostly empty space of his room as she began rocking, grinding herself on him as she did.

The silky-smooth skin of her low back gave way to the silky-smooth skin of her ass, and he couldn't get enough of either as his hands roamed her body while she used his body for her own pleasure. She moaned and sighed as she rode him in a steady rhythm, her hands splayed on his chest for leverage, their bodies finding mutual enjoyment from one another.

Having Mia riding him with her eyes closed, lips pressed tight, as if she were moving to her own private soundtrack was so fucking hot that his desire to conquer her had to be held in check, again. It was about her, and he wouldn't do anything to fuck it up.

Her little mewling sounds transformed into quick, high breaths as her steady rhythm picked up in speed and intensity. His eyes switched focus from her breasts to her face as he waited for her to come undone while he had the undeniable privilege of watching it happen.

He'd only met her a few weeks ago and already he knew he wanted to see every flash of pleasure on her face, every orgasm—because he wanted to be the one to cause them all. He grabbed her ass and helped pull and push her hips as her body moved frantically, desperate for the orgasm he could see building in her and feel building in himself.

All at once she cried out as her hips ground against him, her fingers scratching at his chest. Her legs shook and gave way to her whole body trembling above him. With a whimper, she dropped her head to kiss his chest. Unable to hold back any longer, he flipped them over, so he was on top, then sat up, hooked her legs up and over his shoulders and drove into her, slamming against the backs of her thighs until his own orgasm ripped through him like a lightning bolt from his heart to his abdomen to his groin.

Gently, he lowered her legs, settled his body on top of hers and caught her whimpers with his mouth, kissing her deeply and thoroughly. In that instant, his heart bound itself to that of the beautiful women in his arms just as fiercely as his body had bound itself to hers only seconds before.

Jesse

I T HAD BEEN MORE than a few years since Jesse had brought anyone home for Sunday dinner. Anyone who wasn't a fellow fighter
that he met at the gym, anyway.

There had been plenty of buddies in need of a good meal that
found their way to the Murphy home, but the last time he'd brought a
girlfriend home was when two of his nieces were babies and the third
didn't exist yet.

Before they'd driven out to his parents' house, they'd each taken
a second shower, then stopped at Mia's house so she could grab her
own clothes to wear. He'd wanted the shower to be a together event,
but Mia had insisted they'd never make it on time. He was forced to
endure the loneliness of a solo shower, which was almost as torturous
as knowing what she looked like alone in there right before him.

"Oh, this is seriously purple," Mia said with a soft laugh, as they
pulled up in front of his parents' house. Her mouth hung slightly
open. "This is fantastic. I love this so much."

Jesse laughed as he parked his car behind Shane's truck in the big
driveway. "Just wait until you see the inside."

"No way," she said, a hint of excitement in her voice.

"When my mother loves something, she goes all in. And my dad is crazy about her and lets her paint and decorate however makes her happy. He always told us growing up that when she was happy, he was happy. And that's all he ever wanted in life."

They walked hand in hand up the porch steps. "Oh my God, that is the sweetest thing I've ever heard."

Jesse laughed again as they neared the front door. "It absolutely is. But it went the other way too. When she was unhappy, he was unhappy. Especially if it was one of us that caused the unhappiness." He shook his head. "And when *he* was unhappy, *nobody* in my house was happy."

Turning the knob, Jesse pushed the door open and waited for Mia to enter in front of him. She gasped quietly as she took in the pale violet walls of the main entryway, the various shades of purple in the rug, the flowers, the art on the walls.

Turning to him with an playful grin, she said, "You weren't kidding."

Unwilling to hold himself back from her, he leaned in and kissed her smiling lips. "I told you," he said as he let one hand drift down to squeeze her bottom. Then he placed his hand at the small of her back and guided her through the hallway and into the kitchen.

"Hey, Mom," Jesse called as they entered the giant eat-in kitchen where his mother and sister-in-law were currently drinking glasses of wine and sharing a cheese and cracker plate. "Hey, Gretchen," he added when the women looked up.

While Gretchen couldn't hide the shock at seeing Jesse enter the house with a woman, his mother's face was a study in pure joy when she looked from Jesse to Mia. She rested her wine glass on the counter and hurried across the room to pull him in for a big hug. "Hi, honey," she said, placing a kiss on his cheek. "I'm glad to see those stitches are gone." Turning to Mia, she said, "Hi, I'm Gaelen." She pointed to Gretchen and said, "That's my daughter-in-law, Gretchen."

Jesse was about to introduce Mia, worrying that she might feel overwhelmed or uncomfortable, when she stepped right up to his mother and extended her hand. "It's lovely to meet you both," she said. "I'm Mia. I'm a friend of Jesse's. Thank you for inviting me for dinner. It smells amazing in here."

Obviously, Mia was not feeling uncomfortable or overwhelmed. And she was right, it smelled like heaven in his mother's kitchen.

Gaelen had no idea Jesse was bringing Mia because he didn't want to deal with all the questions his mother would have bombarded him with, so he'd just brought her along. His mother always made enough food to feed a small army, so there would always be enough for everyone to eat.

"Thank you," his mother said. "And you're so welcome for inviting you." She flicked an instantaneous glance his way and he shifted his stance to feign ignorance. "I'm just glad you were able to make it." Gaelen took Mia's arm and ushered her closer to where she and Gretchen had been enjoying their snack. "Can I get you a glass of wine, Mia?"

"I would love that, thank you."

Gretchen reached into the cabinet to pull down an extra wine glass while Mia and his mother chatted over how much Mia loved their home. "She's cute," Gretchen mouthed at him.

"Yes, she is," he mouthed back, and Gretchen smiled mischievously.

All at once, the rest of the family bustled into the kitchen. His father, his brothers Shane and Owen, and Owen's two daughters congregated around the tall counter. The girls hopped up onto the bar stools so they could be part of the action too.

Mia turned to see a group of strangers filling up their plates with the various snacks Gaelen and Gretchen had prepared, all of whom were sneaking glances from Jesse to Mia.

Their father was the first to say anything as he crossed the kitchen. "Well, hello there," he said, extending his hand to Mia. "I'm Pat Murphy. It's nice to meet you."

"Mia," she said as her small hand was swallowed up in his father's giant one. "It's nice to meet you too."

The floodgates were opened. His brothers introduced themselves to Mia and his nieces glommed onto her like she was a shiny new toy. If he was worried that she wasn't comfortable with all that attention, he didn't need to be. Watching Mia field questions about all manner of things, from the people who knew him best, flooded his chest with pride. She was absolutely beaming in the midst of the chaos.

His mother insisted on getting her a plate of snacks, his brothers asked her questions about what she saw in a chucklehead like him, and his nieces asked her a million questions about anything and everything that popped into their wacky little heads.

"Thank you," she said to Gaelen. "He's an amazing man with a kind heart and a fierce protective streak," she said to Shane and Owen. "Polly Pocket was my absolute favorite," she said to Ava. And to Chloe, she said, "I've never had a dog, but I would really love to have one. I just need to wait until I have a house with a yard for a dog to run around."

"We can show you Grandma's dogs!" Chloe yelled. "Right, Grandma?"

His mother hadn't stopped smiling. "Absolutely, sweetheart. After dinner you girls can bring Mia out to meet the dogs, OK?"

His nieces jumped up and down, overwhelmed with the thought of having someone new to play with.

"All right," Jesse's dad said, pushing his family out of the kitchen. "Let's go. Give the girl some air." He looked at Mia and shook his head. "You'd think they'd never seen their brother bring home a girl before." Then he busted out a belly laugh as he turned to catch Jesse's eye. "Oh, wait. They've never seen their brother bring home a girl before."

"Oh, Pat, knock it off," Gaelen said.

"OK, guys, I'll bet your game is back from commercials," Gretchen said. "Maybe go watch it. And here, take this with you," she said, handing Owen the tray of nachos. We'll call you when dinner is on the table."

Mia looked at Jesse over the ridiculous group of people in the room, her eyes large and her smile devastating. She was in her element. Nothing they said bothered her or ruffled her in the slightest. Damn, he was a lucky man.

Mia had made herself comfortable with his mother and sister-in-law, while she had assured Jesse he was fine to go in and watch baseball with his father and brothers, By the time dinner was served, having her there felt as right as rain.

"So, J," Owen said, catching Jesse's eye from across the table. "Got any fights coming up?"

"I do," he said. He hadn't mentioned it to Mia yet and he felt her body stiffen slightly beside him. "First Saturday in July. You coming?"

"Damn straight. I had to miss the last one, but I'll be there. Just shoot me the details later."

"Me too," Shane said. "I'll tell Seth and I'm pretty sure we'll both be there."

His parents exchanged a look. His father shook his head slightly as if telling his mother not to say anything. That didn't stop her from putting her silverware down, plunking her elbows on the table and clasping her hands in front of her chin as she stared a hole through Jesse's skull.

"What do you mean you have another fight coming up? I thought you were done with that." The pitch of her voice went up with every sentence. "Isn't that what you said last time you were here? That you were looking to find something else to do and you weren't fighting anymore?"

Sensing his discomfort, Mia rested her hand on his leg and gave a gentle squeeze.

"I did say that," he said. "And I meant it. I really am looking for whatever comes next. But whatever that is will take some money to get started on." He looked at Mia, who just smiled at him, then looked back to his mother. "Everything I'm looking at requires some kind of education or training. And that all costs money."

Every eye at the table was fixed on him. "The payout for this fight, if I win it, will be enough to cover a decent chunk of that."

"And if you don't win?" his father asked quietly from his seat at the head of the table.

"Then it pays a smaller chunk," he said with a laugh. "But either way, that money gets put away for that purpose alone."

"Who's running your camp? Uncle Mark?" Owen asked.

"Him and Danny," Jesse said. "Like usual."

"So, you've got about seven or eight weeks from now to get ready," Shane said. "How're you feeling going into this one?"

Mia was still touching his leg and he reached down to hold her hand. "I feel fucking awesome." He winced and looked at his nieces, who'd started giggling. "Sorry," he said to the table at large. "But I really do feel good about this one. The guy I'm fighting is a little more of a ground fighter, so I'll have to up the time on my wrestling. Other than that, I'm leaving it in Uncle Mark's hands."

More than anything, he wanted this to be his last fight camp because he wanted this to be his last fight. But there was the obvious chance that he didn't win, in which case he might need to leave that door open to earn a few more bucks to bankroll his next move. Either which way, it also meant he needed to be more serious about this camp than any other he'd done in the past.

And, by necessity, that would mean less time with Mia.

L IFE HAD FALLEN INTO a steady rhythm. Mia worked during
the day, then spent her evenings reading, working on another
blanket, or otherwise trying to keep herself occupied until she could
see Jesse on Sunday afternoons. It was the only time they had together.

Work kept her busy, sometimes having to stay late to catch up on
paperwork that she didn't have time to do during the school day.

Working as a school nurse was entirely different than working in
the emergency room where she'd spent the earlier part of her career.
Before her spectacularly disastrous fallout with Brandon.

Needing to be as far away from the humiliation—not to mention
the pitying stares of everyone she knew—she'd given her two weeks'
notice at the hospital and signed on with a medical temp agency which
landed her the school gig in Oak Harbor.

It had taken a couple months to get used to the different pace and
the seemingly unending paperwork, but eventually she'd fallen into
the steady rhythm of the position.

Unlike working in an ER, life as an elementary school nurse meant
she worked regular hours, Monday through Friday, and had week-
ends and holidays off. Not to mention there was no such thing as an
overnight shift in this job.

Early June meant warm, sunny days and an explosion of new growth on all the plants, grasses, and trees. Another couple weeks would see the temperatures rapidly climbing, hearkening the arrival of summer.

With the warmer weather came the reality that the school year was winding down. Not only had she and Jesse made virtually no progress on his career change plans, but she'd also neglected her own job search.

Whether she was afraid of having to leave Oak Harbor or of having to go back to a hospital setting, she'd been closing her eyes to the inevitable: In four weeks she'd be out of a job. And people with no job had a tough time getting approved for mortgages. And people in apartments tended to have a tougher time being approved to adopt dogs.

The irony of the situation wasn't lost on Mia. When she'd left her old job and the apartment she'd been sharing with Brandon, the biggest draw to the Oak Harbor job was its finite nature. She'd been hired to fill in for the regular nurse who had gone out on maternity leave. It had looked like the perfect plan: get away from Brandon as fast as possible and go somewhere neutral where she wouldn't get attached to anything—or anyone—else.

Attachments only led to heartache.

A temporary gig in some little town up the Maine coast provided the perfect escape until she had the time and energy to figure out her next move.

Except her next move turned into a love of her new town, a genuine affection for the people she worked with and the children she cared for. And then, of course, there was Jesse Murphy, the wildest of wild cards life had seen fit to throw at her.

When she spent time with Jesse, her tidy, calm, orderly world had a habit of being turned on its head. While a night on the couch watching movies had always been good enough for Mia, he'd convince her in that inescapable way of his, to go outside and go for a walk with him.

When she would have been content to stay home and stream a show, he would take her hand and they'd walk the few blocks to the small theater to eat popcorn and watch a movie. He was always in motion and Mia had begun to finally feel comfortable with his always moving nature.

As she finished updating the allergy list for the upcoming third grade field trip to the zoo, she smiled as she recalled that first walk to the beach. They'd spent a cold but lovely evening sitting on the giant boulders at the edge of the surf. The chilly spring wind had whipped through her hair as every care she had in the world melted away while she sat tucked against Jesse, his strong arms wrapped around her, holding her close.

Looking back, she laughed. Why had she even bothered to try to keep herself away from him? It was obvious how he felt for her from very early on.

She glanced at her cell phone sitting beside her on the desk, picked it up to send Jesse a quick text to say hello, then put it back down, text unsent. As much as she wanted to say hello, a bigger part of her knew that it would only be a distraction for him.

The past few weeks, as well as the next four, were set aside for his training. It meant she would have very little time with him, especially as the fight drew closer. His training schedule basically took over his life. As hard as she tried to distance herself from them, familiar feelings of rejection poked through into her subconscious.

Between two workouts a day, with resting and eating in between, there wasn't much time for him to do anything else. Add to that an early bedtime that would put her Nana to shame, and it meant they usually had about twenty minutes of texting one another before he was asleep, and she was awake in front of the television working on her next blanket.

A gentle knock sounded at her office door. "Nurse Reed? May we come in?"

As the door opened, a young woman—one of the kindergarten teachers, Mia thought—walked through with her arm on the shoulder of a little girl with a long brown ponytail and big, blueberry blue eyes, rimmed with tears. The girl cradled one arm against her body.

"Come on in," Mia said, and pointed to the long cot where students sat. She approached the pair and knelt down to be eye-level with the little girl. "Can you tell me what happened?"

"Cecily hit me with a jump rope. By mistake," she said. Her voice wobbled as she held her arm out so Mia could see the big red welt that had formed across her forearm.

"OK," Mia said. "I can see that hurts, so I think it's a good idea to put some ice on it and see if we can get that swelling to go down, OK?" She smiled at the little girl before she stood to break a chemical ice pack. As she wrapped the pack in cloth, she turned to the girl. "I don't think I've seen you before. What's your name?"

"Rylee Murphy," she said with a sniff.

Internally, Mia laughed. Because, of course the girl was related to Jesse. What was that game she and her sister used to play with famous people? *Six Degrees of Separation?* It probably wouldn't be much fun to play in this town where it seemed six degrees would never be necessary.

Work *days* were easy. There was no end to the list of things that kept her distracted. The nights proved to be a little more challenging now that Jesse wasn't around to keep her company. Watching movies by herself didn't hold the same appeal that it used to. And with nobody to walk to the ocean with, rather than go by herself, she settled in to wallow in her re-found loneliness.

The only time Jesse was able to hang out with her in person was on Sundays. It wasn't ideal for a fledgling relationship, but it wasn't like she didn't have other things to worry about.

It was time to put some effort into her next steps. She had no idea what to do about work, though she still wanted to find a small house nearby where she could have the dog she always wanted.

Earlier in her life she would have called Lauren to talk things through, but that wasn't an option for her anymore. The hollow place behind her ribs doubled in size as she mourned the loss of her relationship with her sister all over again.

The last time Lexi had asked her to hang out with the group, she'd said no. But maybe it was time to start taking her up on her offers before she stopped extending them. With Lauren out of the picture, she couldn't depend on Jesse as her sole means of a social life. She'd done that once with Brandon and look how that turned out.

Already in her pajamas at eight o'clock on a Friday night, she sat wrapped up under a blanket and went back and forth between scrolling for new jobs and scrolling for open houses. Not having much luck on either front she decided to look through the local animal shelter's site for dogs that were available for adoption.

Her glass of chardonnay sat beside her, only two sips taken, when her phone rang. Her sister's name popped up as the incoming caller. Immediately, Mia went into panic mode. She and Lauren texted one another. They hardly ever called. The only reason for a call, especially the way things were between them, would be some sort of emergency.

"Lauren?" she said, accepting the call.

"Hey," Lauren said, her voice even, no hint of emotion of any kind. "Sorry to bother you but I figured you'd probably want to know."

Mia's heart lurched in her chest as her brain scrambled to fill in the blanks of why her sister was calling. Had Lauren and Brandon broken up? Was it something worse? Had something happened to one, or both, of their parents? Her fingers tingled as her adrenaline spiked.

"What happened? Is everyone OK?" Mia asked.

"It's Aunt Claire. She had a mild heart attack this morning." Lauren quickly added, "She's going to make a full recovery." Then, with a soft laugh, she said, "It's going to take a lot more than a heart attack to do in that old bird."

Mia didn't mean to laugh but she was so overcome with relief that nobody had died she couldn't hold it in. That, and it felt good to laugh with her sister again after only the harsh words they'd swapped for almost a year.

Unconsciously, her fingers drifted down to the rod of Asclepius tattoo on her ankle.

Their father's sister used to tell the most amazing stories when the girls were little. While Lauren used to block her ears and say things like, "That's *so* disgusting," Mia always found herself intrigued by the mystery of medicine and medical care.

But it was the other stories that truly brought Mia into the world of medicine: the stories of the babies named for ambulance drivers or other first responders, the elation of a family member making it to the hospital to see a loved one they thought they would never see again. It was the humanity in all its forms, good and bad, that intrigued her to no end. The blood and guts parts never swayed her interest and, by the time she was ready for college, she knew exactly what she would study.

"How long will she be in the hospital? I assume she's in the cardiac ICU right now." However long she was scheduled to stay in the hospital would give Mia the information she needed to know about how severe the heart attack was.

"Mom and Dad went to see her already. The docs told them it was a mild event and that with some new medication and a little more exercise she's expected to make a full recovery. They're going back tomorrow once she gets transferred to a regular room. I don't know how long she'll be there but I'm sure she'd like to see you if you have some time."

"Of course," Mia said. Lauren gave her the address of the hospital and after a few brief seconds of uncomfortable silence Mia said, "Well, thanks for calling."

"Sure."

Her first inclination was to send Jesse a text. She looked at the time on her phone and knew he'd already gone to sleep.

THE FOLLOWING AFTERNOON, MIA stood outside her aunt's hospital room, her hand poised to knock for a full thirty seconds before she finally rapped her knuckles on the heavy wooden door.

"Come on in," Aunt Claire called in a soft voice. "I promise I'm decent."

That was her aunt, always joking. Mia laughed as she poked her head inside the room. Her spitfire of an aunt looked small and fragile in the big hospital bed surrounded by blinking machines, IV lines, and an oxygen line. Mia's stomach dropped at the dawning realization that things change. Times change. People change.

Her eyes landed on Lauren and Brandon sitting side by side on the far side of Claire's bed, and Mia froze, her fingers clamped like a vice on the door.

"Oh," she said, looking from them to Claire. "I didn't realize you had company. I'll umm... I'll go grab a coffee or something and come back in a little while." Unclamping her hand from the door, she took a step back toward the hallway as Lauren and Brandon stood, letting their clasped hands drop away from one another.

"No, Mia, it's OK. You can stay. Brandon and I were just leaving."

Brandon made the briefest eye contact with Mia then had the common courtesy of being the first to look away and drop his gaze directly down at the floor as he shoved his hands into his back pockets.

Mia's belly flopped and tears pricked the backs of her eyes as she looked at the two of them, the betrayal of them both as raw and painful as it had been when the whole thing went down. She wasn't prepared for the assault of feelings to be as harsh and all-encompassing as it was proving to be, and she kicked herself for not waiting until the evening to visit her aunt.

She forced her feet to move out of the doorway, then stood completely still as she waited for Lauren and Brandon to leave before she went and stood by her aunt's bedside.

"Wow," Claire said, one gray eyebrow quirked in what looked like amusement. "That was awkward as shit, huh, kiddo?" From behind the tubes and IV lines that were helping her recuperate, she was obviously the same old Claire Mia loved so much.

She laughed at the older woman's frankness. "You're not kidding. That actually kind of sucked." She blew out a breath and rolled her eyes before she sat and took hold of her aunt's hand. "But I'm not here to talk about my traitorous sister. I'm here to check on my favorite auntie and see how you're doing and if there's anything I can do to help you."

Claire pulled a face. "Oh, you know me, honey. It's going to take a lot more than a bum ticker to knock me off. Old Zeus can't have me yet." She squeezed Mia's hand, trying to reassure herself as much as her niece, Mia was sure. They talked medical stuff for a few minutes so Mia could get a better understanding of the medications her aunt would be taking as well as the actual diagnosis and the recovery plan the doctors had put in place.

Once their medical conversation ended, Mia was confident that her aunt would make a full recovery... if she could manage to follow her care plan.

"Enough about me," her aunt said. "Talk to me about what I witnessed here between you and your sister. You two were always so close, I hate to see all that tension between you now."

Mia took a deep breath to steady herself. "We were close," she admitted. "But things change and now we're not."

"Cryptic," Claire said, cracking a typical Aunt Claire grin. "Can I assume it had something to do with Brandon? The way he shriveled like a goddamn prune when you opened the door would have been comical," she lifted her hand to touch Mia's cheek, "if *you* hadn't been so upset at seeing him."

Claire wasn't at the annual Fourth of July party at her parents' house to see the chaos and drama of Brandon dumping her for Lauren, but Mia had been sure someone must have told her about it between then and now.

"Mom never mentioned what happened between me and Brandon?" Mia asked.

Claire's head waggled back and forth, telling Mia her mother told her something, but she would rather hear the story from Mia directly. "Never been much for gossip, you know that."

Aunt Claire had more than enough to worry about with her own recovery for Mia to burden her with unnecessary stress, so she kept the story as bare bones as possible. Though, she didn't leave out what a horrible person Brandon turned out to be and what a traitorous harpy her sister was for falling for him...while he was still living with Mia.

"So, it turns out your mother had the story pretty spot-on," Claire said. "She was a little less harsh in her name calling, but otherwise..." Still holding Mia's hand, Claire looked at her with that same look of pity she'd seen on so many people and she couldn't take it from her too.

"Don't worry about me, Auntie, I'm totally fine. In fact, I'm better than fine. Who needs a guy with as much charm as a sweaty gym sock. Am I right?" Mia tried to laugh. "It was just a little uncomfortable seeing them together, that's all. But I'm fine."

Claire nodded, though looked entirely unconvinced.

"Speaking of gym socks," Mia said, eliciting a look of surprise from her aunt. "I've started seeing a new guy I met up in Oak Harbor." She nudged Claire's shoulder. "You'd like him, Auntie, he's an athlete and he's very handsome. And he has a smile that will knock your socks off."

A sly grin worked its way onto Claire's face. "Your socks, your clothes, your panties, whatever. Hmm?"

"Auntie!" Mia laughed, used to her aunt's lack of modesty. "But, yes, his smile is good for getting all those things off," she added in a low, quiet voice.

"That's my girl."

The women laughed together, and it felt good, therapeutic, like it used to be in the old days when Claire would pop in on family dinners every now and then. The two of them were known as the family troublemakers when they would get laughing and telling stories. Those were good times.

When Claire yawned, Mia knew it was time to go. Despite the excellent prognosis, her aunt was still lying in a hospital bed recovering from a heart attack. Having to leave her there hurt Mia in the deepest part of her heart. "I'm going to take off and let you get some rest. Mom and Dad are coming to take you home when you get discharged and I'll be sure to check in on you, make sure you're taking your meds and doing all the things." With a soft smile, she kissed her aunt gently on the cheek and held Claire's hand for an extra second before she headed toward the door.

"Hey, kiddo," Claire called.

Mia turned and looked back.

"Will I be seeing you at your parents' party this year?"

"Oh... I don't know. I'm guessing probably not, but like I said, I'll come by your house and check on you to make sure you're following the doctor's orders."

Her aunt smiled but was uncharacteristically quiet. Then she said in a small voice, "Maybe it's time to move on, hmm?"

Mia stilled, her hand on the door handle. "What do you mean?"

"I mean, your sister and Brandon seem happy enough together and, from the sound of it, you and your new man are doing all right too. Maybe it's time to leave the past where it is and move forward. You only have one sister and I'd hate to have you lose each other over something as stupid as Brandon."

Mia snort laughed.

"That didn't come out exactly how I meant it," Claire said with a slight shrug. "But you get the idea."

T HE WEATHER HAD WARMED up enough for Mia to have the
windows open while she waited for Jesse to show up. A cool
breeze blew the sheer curtains, billowing them out in the late afternoon sunshine. If only Mia's mood could match the carefree feel of
the day around her.

When the buzzer rang, anticipation ran laps through her body as
she waited for the elevator to reach the fourth floor. Opening the door,
she was bowled over when he grabbed hold of her, kicked the door
shut, and kissed her like he hadn't seen her in years. The scent of his
skin and the feel of his freshly shaved face in her hands melted into the
background of her thoughts as she turned up the heat on their kiss,
pressing her body into him as their tongues tangled and his fingers dug
into her bottom.

Eventually, she pulled away from him, breathless. "Hi," she said
with an amorous grin. "Did you miss me?"

He kept his hands around her waist, leaned his forehead against
hers. "I've spent my entire week with sweaty, smelly guys who are
trying their best to kill me. To say you look, feel, and smell good
enough to eat would be the fucking understatement of the year."

Inclining her head to place a gentle kiss on his lips, she said, "Well, that will have to wait until later because dinner is just about ready. I made baked chicken with roasted acorn squash and some brown rice."

When she tried to disentangle herself from his arms, he held her tightly and leaned down to kiss the soft spot beneath her ear. "That does sound good," he said between kisses. "But I still think I'd rather eat you first."

Normally it would have been a no-brainer to get naked with him as soon as he walked in the door, but the lingering emotional hangover of seeing Claire in a hospital bed, not to mention unexpectedly seeing Lauren and stupid-ass Brandon, she really just needed a good meal and maybe some snuggling on the couch before she was as ready to go as he was.

Trying to be as tactful as possible, she said, "Would you mind if we had dinner first? It's been kind of a hard couple of days, and I could go for a decent meal right about now."

Immediately he held her at arm's length. "Is everything OK?" he asked. "What happened?" His eyes scanned her face, and a look of worry creased his brow.

Sunday was the only time they had together, and she didn't want to waste it dumping all her problems on him, especially when doing so would point glaringly to the fact that she wasn't enough to keep her last boyfriend. Enough of what, she wasn't sure. But since he dropped her like a hot rock, most likely it meant she wasn't enough of anything.

"Nothing happened," she said. Needing to feel his arms around her, she pulled him closer for another hug. "I'm OK. Really. Just a little frustrated with my lack of job prospects."

"Come on," he said, taking her hand and leading her into the kitchen. He pulled out a chair. "Sit," he said. "Tell me what still needs to be done to get this dinner on the table." When she started to get out of the chair to help, he turned back to her, pressed her into the chair. "I said sit. If I have to tell you again, I'll spank that sweet ass of yours."

Heat blazed through her. "You wouldn't."

His eyebrows shot straight up his forehead, and she realized he most certainly would. "Try me," he said with a wink and then went back to taking the chicken and squash out of the oven.

"Can I at least get the plates to set the table?" she asked, feeling slightly uncomfortable watching someone else bustling around her kitchen doing something she was more than capable of doing on her own.

"What did I say would happen if you get out of that chair?" he asked over his shoulder as he opened one cabinet after another to find the drinking glasses.

Her ass tingled, wondering if he would truly follow through with his threat, thinking about how much she might like it if he did. "OK, fine," she said. "Glasses are in the top cabinet to the left of the sink."

"Thanks," he said. "How much squash do you want?"

Her discomfort melted away as Jesse moved around her space, his muscular arms on full display, his strong back filling out his shirt in a way that made her mouth water. And when he bent over to take the chicken out of the oven, she wished she had other things for him to take out of the oven, just to watch him bend over like that.

It felt nice to be taken care of, even in such a small way. Never mind that his body was a literal work of art, and she enjoyed watching it as he moved around her small kitchen.

His body was already different than it had been the last time they'd been together. The double workout days certainly had an effect on his physique. As beautiful as he was regularly, he was borderline intimidating and would only become more so as his fight camp wore on. Looking down on her own body, she felt softer than ever.

She wished she could shake that fear of him changing his mind about her. It was like, all of a sudden she was waiting for him to see who she really was and decide there was no way she could ever be enough for him. She wasn't even enough for Brandon, how the hell could she ever be enough for someone like Jesse Murphy?

During dinner she asked him about his week and what kinds of things he did for his training. It was the first time they'd really talked about the fight he'd taken. Being a fighter's girlfriend was a strange feeling, so she never brought it up.

Of course, she knew he might eventually have to fight, but at the same time, she didn't want him to fight and potentially get hurt. She saw what he looked like when that happened, and her heart ached thinking it would happen again.

Conversation flowed as naturally and easily as it always did with Jesse, her own bad mood temporarily forgotten as she got carried away in the excitement of his fight prep. He explained his training and what kinds of things he was working on to face the guy he was scheduled to fight. It all sounded exhausting to Mia, but Jesse became more and more animated and excited as the conversation continued.

"Can I at least help clear the dishes?" she asked once they finished eating. "I don't want to clean up and then get a spanking for my trouble."

He grinned. "No, you may not clean up. In fact, why don't you go change into something much more comfortable, then sit and put your feet up, look around to find something you want to watch tonight."

The idea of letting him clean up her kitchen was odd and yet comforting at the same time. Her emotions had gone back to teetering from her hospital visit, and pajamas and a movie sounded like the perfect way to spend an evening, especially once he came over to snuggle with her.

It took her longer to change her clothes than it did for him to clean up from dinner and by the time she made it back to the living room, Jesse was sitting on the couch, his feet on the table, looking very much like he'd already fallen asleep.

His eyes opened as she approached and he held one arm out, inviting her to sit next to him, but she had other plans.

While she was changing, she thought about how right her aunt had been; she and Jesse did have something good starting, and it would be stupid to focus on the things that went wrong instead of the things that were going right. And there was no time like the present to get started.

Rather than sit next to him, she walked around the couch to stand behind him, put her hands on his shoulders. Those beautiful, muscular shoulders that looked like they'd been sculpted to look that good. "Have you given any more thought to what you're going to do once you're done fighting?" she asked as she began massaging him.

His head dropped forward, giving her easier access to his neck and upper back. "Not really," he mumbled into his chest. "I've talked to a few people, but I've been busy training and haven't wanted to do the brain work once my days end. Too tired."

The hard muscles of his shoulders and back gave way to the pressure of her fingers as she squeezed, knuckled, and kneaded. They hadn't been together long enough for her to keep pushing him to think about things and make a decision one way or the other, but the indecision annoyed her; mostly because it was a mirror reflecting back her own lack of progress.

She pushed her own thoughts on the matter to the back of her mind and chose to focus on him and making him feel as good as he always made her feel. Leaning forward, she slid her hands down, on either side of his spine, over the large, solid muscles of his back.

"That feels fucking amazing, Mia. Thank you for doing this," he said in a low, gravelly voice that seemed to touch her physically in all the best places.

She looked at the faint line of scar tissue down the side of his face and marveled at how something so terrible could have led to something with so much possibility. Had he not reached up and made it bleed that night on the bus, she never would have jumped in to help him, and they never would have spoken to each other.

The fear she felt at seeing him at the bus stop that night seemed ridiculous against the reality of the kind of man he turned out to be.

Wrapping her arms around him she hugged him from behind, pressing her breasts against his back while she kissed the side of his neck.

Unsure if his deep exhale was exhaustion or simply comfort from being held, she said, "If you're that tired, you are more than welcome to just go to sleep. I'll wake you up when the movie's over." She said it hoping he wouldn't fall asleep but understanding if he needed to.

"Not happening," he said. "I haven't seen you in a week." He tipped his head up so they were cheek to cheek. "More to the point, I haven't had you in a week. Oh, and then there's this." He leaned forward and pulled a folded-up piece of paper from his back pocket, handed it to her without a word.

Unfolding the paper, she laughed as she quickly scanned it and realized what he was showing her.

He'd gone to one of the local clinics and had every STI test they offer, all of which came back negative. She refolded the paper and handed it back to him. Quietly, she moved to the front of the couch, removed one of his feet from the table, making room to kneel between his knees.

Jesse

H IS EYES FOLLOWED EVERY move she made, and his chest rose and fell on his deeper breaths as she scooted in closer, then unbuttoned and unzipped the fly of his jeans.

He lifted his hips from the couch and helped her pull the fabric down, leaving his hard cock directly in her line of sight. She licked her lips and he felt it throughout his entire body as he reached his hands out to stroke her cheeks.

"Are you sure you want to do this? You know you don't have to," he said, his voice breathy but calm. He loved a blowjob as much as the next guy, but he also understood that different women had different feelings on the subject, and he would never presume to expect one from Mia. But when she knelt down in front of him, a primal instinct kicked in and his need for it tore through his entire being.

Leaning forward she closed her eyes, licked him from base to tip, pressed a gentle kiss on the head then took the tip into her mouth. His head fell back, and he closed his eyes, focusing on the way she felt. He sucked in a hissing breath as she licked him from base to tip again, before taking the full length of him deep into her mouth.

Opening his eyes to watch her, he twined his fingers into her hair. Her head moved on him, licking, and sucking. Time stood still as he settled into the experience of her soft lips gliding over him and the intense sensations when she hollowed her cheeks near the tip.

"Holy shit, Beauty, I don't know how long I'll be able to last like this." Being away from her all week had been torture, but seeing her on her knees, with her mouth wrapped around him, was a whole different kind of torture. One that he welcomed with open arms.

She lifted her eyes to meet his as she continued to savor him, clearly enjoying the feeling of power she had over him at that moment. He'd never looked at any woman with such tenderness mixed with burning lust before. It was intoxicating.

She was intoxicating.

As she took him deeper, she snaked her arms behind his body, anchoring herself against him while she continued to bring him pleasure. Taking him as deep as she could, she started to moan. The vibrations spread through him, ramping him higher, winding him tighter.

His hips moved in perfect rhythm with her head as he kept up with her tempo. His fingers curled into her hair, pulling it, eliciting little moans and gasps from her. "You should stop now, Beauty, or I'm going to come in your mouth." His words came out in between gulps of air.

The thought of finishing that way became all consuming. As much as he wanted to have his hands on her body, he silently prayed she would finish what she'd started and make him come with nothing more than her lips and her tongue.

The force of his hips intensified as she increased her own speed. "Oh, God," he panted. "I'm going to come, Beauty. I need to come in your mouth right now." He fisted her hair, holding her head as he angled his hips, keeping his cock in her mouth while he let go with a deep growl that came from the depths of his fucking soul.

After she swallowed, he let go of her hair, and trailed his fingertips over her cheeks again. Staring down at her, he was transfixed by the stunning beauty and vulnerability in her eyes. He helped pull her back up onto the couch beside him then fixed his pants, adjusting himself.

Holding her against his side, he ran his fingers through her silky hair, letting the soft strands sift through his fingers. "That was... I don't know if I have words for that... Holy shit, that was awesome."

"I'm glad you liked it," she said, and ran her tongue along her bottom lip. "That was really fun for me too."

There was something off with her tone of voice. Disappointment? Sadness?

Turning toward the television, she laid down, pulled her legs up, and rested her head on his lap. He pulled the blanket from the back of the couch and draped it over her body, hoping like hell he wasn't to blame for whatever it was he'd just heard there.

"You never did tell me what happened this week that had you in such a bad mood when I got here." He brushed the hair back from her face and over her shoulder. "Anything you want to talk about?"

She curled the blanket under her chin while she thought about answering him. Finally, she said, "You know how I told you about my aunt?"

"The nurse? Yeah, of course."

Her shoulders slumped on a deep sigh, and he tensed, worried about what her next words would be. "I went to see her in the hospital yesterday," she said quietly. "She had a heart attack, so I went to visit her."

Jesse's fingers stilled on her hair, relieved that the woman hadn't died, but still a little hurt that he had to drag the information out of her. "Jesus, Mia, why didn't you lead with that? That's kind of a huge thing to hang onto by yourself."

She rolled from her side to her back and looked up at him. "It's not that big a deal. It was only a mild one, and she's going to make a full recovery." She shrugged. "It was just a little hard to see her with the IV line and the oxygen tubes and stuff. She looked so small and vulnerable, which is weird for her because she's always been sort of larger than life."

Her eyes drifted closed as he traced the edge of her jaw and let a handful of hair slip through his fingers. Getting mad wouldn't do anyone any good, so he tried to channel his frustration into something a little more helpful. "I know we haven't been together all that long, but you can call me anytime you need me, you know. I wish you hadn't had to do that by yourself."

She lifted her eyes to his briefly. "I wasn't entirely by myself," she said. "My sister was there."

That explained a lot about her bad mood. "Is that the sister you don't get along with?"

She nodded, pulling the blanket tighter under her chin.

"How did that go?"

"It was awkward. We didn't really say anything because her boyfriend was with her."

That was new information. "Do you not get along with her boyfriend either?" he asked.

"Not really, no," she said. "We have sort of a history."

"What kind of history?" She winced, and he had to dial back on his jealousy. His words had come out harsher than he intended as his protective instinct kicked in. Their relationship was still new, but that didn't mean he didn't already think of Mia as his—and only his. If that other guy had done anything to hurt her, Jesse would rip him to shreds if they ever came face to face.

She tried to roll onto to her side so she wouldn't have to look him in the eye anymore. As soon as she tried, he pulled her shoulder back, so she had nowhere else to look but at him.

"His name is Brandon," she said. "We met at the hospital where I used to work when I lived down in Ogunquit. I was an ER nurse," she held his gaze for a second before she looked away again, "just like my aunt. He came in with a suspected broken ankle." Her eyes refocused somewhere above his head. "It wasn't broken, only sprained. But he was really nice, and we talked a bunch. And then he ended up asking me out."

Her voice started to wobble as she held back tears. "We dated for over a year. We moved in together and everything." Already Jesse had decided that Brandon was a complete and utter waste of breath. Whatever he'd done to hurt Mia, made him irredeemable in Jesse's eyes.

After breathing out another deep sigh, she continued. "My parents have this big Fourth of July party every year and, stupid me, I thought it would be so great to tell him how much I love him at the party, you know, like some big, grand gesture." Frantically, she began to wipe tears away from her eyes and Jesse had to quell the urge to find out where this son of a bitch lived and go break his legs. And his arms. And anything else he could get his hands on that would break with a satisfying snap.

"It's funny, looking back on it now," she said. "The fact that we moved in together, yet neither of us had mentioned loving the other—not even in passing. That was weird, wasn't it?"

He handed her a tissue he'd plucked from the box on the table beside him. With a watery smile she accepted it and blew her nose. "Only my gesture wasn't all that grand because I told him how important he was to me and how I had fallen so deeply in love with him."

A small, sad laugh escaped her mouth and Jesse wanted to kiss those lips and remove all traces of that other guy's name from them. "I should have known something was wrong and just left it alone." She breathed out a deep sigh. "Instead of telling me he loved me too, he just said 'thank you.'"

Jesse's vision went black for a second and he had to pull himself back into the moment and let her finish her story.

"When I teased him about it and gave him a hard time, he was kind of harsh. Then he said, 'Mia, stop. Stop saying that. I don't feel the same about you. I'm sorry.' In front of everybody at the party, he told me he didn't love me back."

If he told her what that story was actually doing to him, he probably would have scared her away. But every nerve in his body was on standby, waiting to dismember that fucking prick. "I'm sorry," Jesse said, as gently as he could, and wiped away her tears with his thumb. "He sounds like a total dick."

"Wait," she said with a bitter laugh. "That's not the worst part. Not only did he tell me he didn't love me, but he told me he was in love with someone else. And had been for a long time." More tears fell.

He was quiet for a moment. "Your sister," he finally said, filling in the obvious blanks. Blowing out a breath to keep his anger in check, he said, "That's fucked up, Mia. Is that why you relocated here? Why you have your new job?"

She looked up at him and nodded. "Don't look at me like that," she said, averting her eyes.

"Like what?" Could she see the murderous rage that he'd been trying to contain?

"Like I'm some kind of injured animal that needs your pity."

"That's not pity you're seeing there, Beauty. I promise."

Sitting upright again, she wiped her eyes on the sleeve of her pajama top. "I'm sorry to dump all that on you," she said. "Obviously you're not interested in my broken heart sob story." She tried to laugh it off but was overcome with sobs.

"Hey," he said, pulling her into his lap. He snuggled her close and wrapped his arms around her. "Don't apologize for talking about things you need to talk about. Ever. I wish there was something I could do to take all that away from you." He kissed the top of her head. "Aside from folding that asshole up like a pretzel and choking the fucking life out of him, the best I can do is be here for you right now."

The tightness in his chest loosened instantly when she curled against him and started to laugh. "Thank you."

"For what? Listening? Or threatening your ex's wellbeing?"

"Both?" she said with a sniffling giggle.

"Trust me when I tell you both of those things would bring me nothing but pleasure," he said.

She sighed against him and snuggled her head beneath his chin.

Getting all of that off her chest seemed to make her feel better. But for him, it was as if someone lit a match in a room soaked with gasoline.

Rage burned beneath his skin while Mia settled in and fell asleep in his arms. He sat and held her for close to an hour before he finally scooped her into his arms and carried her to her room. After tucking her in, he laid down beside her and held her until her breaths came at the slow, even pace of a soundly sleeping person.

Mia

A S THE SCHOOL YEAR wound down, Mia had been putting in
the extra effort to make sure everything was up to date and in
good order for when the regular nurse came back in the fall. It turned
out it was a decent way to keep her mind occupied during the days,
which freed up her nights for the constant reminder of how alone she
was.

On Friday afternoon, she followed behind a group of her co-work-
ers on the way out of the building. "What time are we doing pool at
The Landing?" one of them said to the others.

"I think Joe said around seven," Lexi said.

Over the past couple weeks, Lexi had tried more than once to get
Mia to go out with the work crowd. But giving in to the melancholy
that had settled around her, Mia had declined each time.

"Yeah, he did," said Holly Burns, the PE teacher. "I think he said he
made a reservation for a couple tables around then. There's a few more
people meeting us there too. Don't know who, but I think there's like
eight of us going."

Mia hoped they would turn around and notice her, invite her to
play pool with them one more time. She knew where The Landing
was, she'd been there with Jesse—it was the first night they'd had sex.

Even if she wasn't sure whether she wanted to go, more than anything, she wanted to be asked. How many times would they ask her
when she always said no?

The small group continued talking as they pushed through the
front doors of the building. Mia slowed down so she wouldn't have to
wait behind them to get out. It would be humiliating if they invited
her only because they knew she'd heard their conversation. But it
would be even worse if they pretended they didn't know she heard
them and then they didn't invite her because they were tired of her
declining their invitations.

Mia's already fragile heart wobbled in her chest. She pivoted, feigning a forgotten item in her office, allowing them to leave without
acknowledging her presence.

Another night without Jesse gave Mia all the time she needed to live
inside her mind, imagining over and over again the humiliation she'd
endured at her parents' party, the looks on Brandon's and Lauren's
faces, the attempts by her parents to comfort her when her whole life
was falling apart. *No, she hadn't wanted to talk about it. She absolutely
hadn't wanted to get together with Lauren and Brandon and talk things
through.*

So, she'd done what she'd needed to do for her own well-being; she'd
quit her job and moved to a small oceanside town an hour up the coast.
Only, it turned out an hour away wasn't far enough.

Would any place be far enough to get away from those feelings of
disappointment and rejection and sorrow and shame? The gnawing

feeling of inadequacy lingered—she'd merely been a placeholder until Brandon mustered the courage to confess he'd found someone new, someone better.

Even the friends she thought she'd made at work had moved on without her, refreshing that burning sting of rejection. More than anything, all the days and nights without Jesse had her starting to wonder if being involved with him was just another inevitable heartbreak waiting to happen.

How long would she be a placeholder for Jesse? How long before he found out she wasn't as great as he thought she was and he sought a replacement—a shinier, more whole version? A guy like him didn't need an emotionally damaged girlfriend who still cried about being dumped a year after it happened. Especially when there were so many women in his orbit that would jump at the chance to be with him.

Once she'd told him the story, she glimpsed that familiar look in his eyes—the same pity reflected by everyone else. Of course, he claimed it wasn't, but she recognized it like an old friend, as familiar as each breath she took.

Worse than the pity in his eyes had been his unwillingness to connect physically with her on the only night they had together. She'd been so sad, so desperate to be loved and needed, and all he did was tuck her in and let her fall asleep. He couldn't even be bothered having sex with someone as broken as her.

The hurt intensified when she had awoken the next morning, only to find his side of the bed empty and cold—the empty space mirroring her own emptiness.

Despite the pity party she'd thrown for herself Friday night, Saturday dawned bright and warm, and she had an uneventful ride to visit Aunt Claire. After being discharged from the hospital, Claire had gone back to living by herself in her little house with the lovely flower garden in front of the porch.

Claire had always been a self-sufficient person, but even she needed a helping hand now and again. After taking her to the grocery store, Mia stayed for a few hours and prepped a bunch of meals for her; chicken soup, rice and beans, and her homemade black bean soup. Once the fridge and freezer were well stocked, she did a little cleaning, and then they took a short walk around the neighborhood together.

They mostly talked medical stuff about the doctor's orders. They talked about the home health aide who came by the house every morning to check on Claire and make sure she was taking her meds. The one thing they didn't talk about was the episode with Lauren and Brandon at the hospital.

"How's the sexy smile guy" Claire asked as they ambled down the next street.

"You mean aside from the fact that his body looks like it's been carved from marble and I'm this soft, doughy mess?" she said poking a finger into her belly.

"Stop," Claire drawled. "Don't talk about yourself that way. It's not healthy."

"Look who's talking about healthy," Mia teased.

Claire grinned and said, "Hey, I'm still kicking, aren't I?"

They walked in silence for a few more minutes before Claire spoke again. "Trust me," she said. "You're perfect exactly the way you are. Besides, he obviously likes you. And if he wanted some kind of hard body girlfriend, I'm pretty sure he'd have one." Then she looked at Mia with that 'just try and argue with' me expression she'd perfected over a lifetime of being her.

Sure, it was easy for her to say. Claire had lived her life happily single. She never had to compete against other women for the affection of a guy.

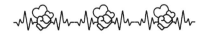

Jesse wouldn't be coming over until Sunday night, giving her the time to start getting her act together. She'd gotten irritated with him for not making any progress on his future and here she'd been guilty of the same damn thing.

Her first order of business was getting her resume updated and polished. There were openings for nurses at several major hospitals within a half hour of Oak Harbor. Most of them even offered decent sign-on bonuses. She applied to a few places and sent out a half dozen resumes, knowing that having a job was the key to everything else she wanted.

Once she had the job search actively moving, she looked up a few more open houses. Two of them were in Oak Harbor and one more was in Spring Hill, the next town over.

The Spring Hill house was probably the nicest house on the inside. But one of the Oak Harbor houses held the most promise from the inside and the outside. With a fenced-in backyard that would be perfect for a dog, as well as a fireplace in the living room, forty-four Birch Haven Road had sent Mia's imagination into overdrive.

After being tempted by Jesse's big soaking tub, she had added that to the list of must haves for her future home. And the Birch Haven Road house not only had a deep tub, but it was a two-person whirlpool tub where they could soak together.

She snapped a few pictures and sent them to Jesse, even though she knew he had things going on during the day. Part of her hoped he'd stop and chat with her just for a few minutes. It had been a long, emotional week, and the few hours before she saw him again were proving to be the hardest ones of her week so far.

A few minutes later her phone pinged with his reply.

Looks nice. Can't talk now.

Jesse

B ETWEEN THE BARKING DOGS, the giggling girls, and his father yelling down from upstairs looking for reading glasses, walking through the front door of the big purple house still felt like coming home.

"Oh, hi, honey," his mother said, dropping a quick kiss on his cheek as she hurried to the foot of the stairs. "Pat, your glasses are down here. Remember you left them in the office last night?"

"You're right!" His father's words were followed immediately by his heavy footsteps thudding down the stairs. He hugged Gaelen and kissed the top of her head. "What would I do without you, my love?" With a smile, Pat looked up at Jesse. "Hey, kid, how's the fight prep going?"

His mother hated listening to Jesse talk about fighting, not because she hated the sport, but because she hated that Jesse still participated in the sport. "Come on, girls," she said to Jesse's nieces, "these dogs aren't going to walk themselves."

His phone pinged in his back pocket, and he quickly pulled it out and saw that Mia had sent pictures from a house she was looking at. He had every intention of replying with something more than just,

'Looks nice. Can't talk now,' but got sidetracked when all three of his nieces bounded up and ran into the kitchen.

Rylee noticed him standing there, and with a smile as bright as the dawn, she bolted over and shoved up the arm of her sleeve. "Uncle J, look at what I got!"

From the other room, his mother grumbled something about "...another one..."

He looked down and saw a purple stripe across the top of Rylee's little forearm. It wasn't a fresh bruise, but fury still spiked through his brain as he wondered who had hurt his niece. His father made the briefest eye contact with him, the old man's eyes almost twinkling with contained laughter.

"Hey, Rylee Faye, what the heck happened to you?" he said, gently taking her arm in his hand and angling it to get a better look.

"I got a bruise," she said. "It looks like the ones you get!"

The kid was practically bouncing out of her shoes, but the dots weren't connecting in Jesse's brain. "What? What do you mean?"

Pat stepped closer and put a loving arm across his granddaughter's shoulders. "She means, she got hit—by accident—in gym class last week, and rather than be upset that she has a giant bruise on her arm, she is beside herself excited to look just like her Uncle J." His father's eyes betrayed the humor he saw in the situation but was obviously trying to hide for the benefit of Jesse's mom.

"Yeah!" Rylee said, shoving her arm at him again. "I look just like you!"

Jesse couldn't help but smile down at his adoring niece. The pride she felt in being like him brought a little pang of something to his heart that he couldn't quite name. She'd always adored him, and he her, but wanting to be like him was something entirely different. A small lump perched itself in his throat and he had to cough to clear it before he could talk.

"Ry, that is one badass bruise," he said. "But I don't want you thinking you've got to go and get hurt to be like me."

"I know," she said, suddenly quite serious. "That's what Daddy told me." Her eyes took on the same sparkle as her grandfather's and her grin was downright devilish. "I asked if I could do fighting like you do."

Pat's stoic face broke and a huge smile took over. In the other room his mother just mumbled, "For the love of God..."

Jesse could never imagine Seth letting her get into MMA but who knew how being a girl dad changed the way you looked at things. "Yeah?" he said, not wanting to contradict whatever decision his brother had made. "And what did he say about that?"

Her whole body practically vibrated as she said, "He said maybe."

"Rylee, honey," Gaelen called, "are you coming to walk the dogs with us?"

"OK, I'm coming," she called to her grandmother. "Bye," she said to Jesse as she took off to walk the dogs.

"Watch out, Conor McGregor, here comes Rylee Murphy," his dad joked, and both men laughed. "So, how is training coming along?"

Jesse hopped off the stool and grabbed a glass of water. "It's good," he said. "Uncle Mark can be a real ball buster, though."

"That's what you want, right? The whole point is to get in there and win, isn't it?"

"No, you're right. Nobody wants to step in there and get his ass beat, that's for sure."

Pat looked at him for a few seconds. "So, what's really going on with you?" He turned and pulled a bottle of iced tea from the fridge, twisted off the top, and took a big swig.

"You know that stuff'll kill you, don't you, old man?"

"Gonna die anyway," Pat joked. "Might as well enjoy the living part while I'm here."

There was no arguing against his dad's logic. He'd never win, anyhow.

"Now stop avoiding my question," Pat said, plunking his iced tea bottle on the counter.

"Never could get anything by you."

"Fucking right, you couldn't."

Jesse laughed. "If Mom hears you talking like that while the girl gang is here, she's liable to take you out before that sugary crap can."

His father shrugged. "Hell of a way to go, am I right? At the hands of the woman you love?" Damn, if his giant bear of a father didn't giggle when he said that. Another pang of something hit Jesse's heart. Longing? Jealousy? What was happening to him?

"How's things looking on the job front?" his father asked. "Like for after the fight, I mean. You give any more thought as to what comes next?"

That was the million-dollar question, wasn't it? "Plenty of thought when I'm not in the middle of training and shit, but no real decision one way or another."

"You know there's always a spot for you down with the rest of us."

Pat had always been a 'family first' kind of guy and Jesse appreciated that about him. But construction just wasn't in his future. "Thanks, Dad," he said. "I'll keep that in mind."

"Good enough," Pat said. "So, tell me about training. How's it going this time around?"

"It's actually going pretty well. I'm doing double workouts, and eating, showering, and sleeping every chance I get in between. Worked the explosive power movements this week. Next week we'll add in a little more speed work."

"How about the wrestling?"

"Oh yeah," he said. "Mark brought in a couple guys from another gym to kick my ass on the ground. One of them is a grappler and he just fucking kills me every time." If he was going to lose this fight it certainly wouldn't be for lack of preparation.

Pat nodded. "It's only going to make you stronger." He took another swig of tea and patted Jesse on the shoulder. "You staying for dinner tonight? Pretty sure all three of your brothers are coming."

"Nah, I've got so much shit to get done at home tonight. Then I'm supposed to go over to Mia's and hang out there for a little while before I start another week of camp."

"How's that going?"

"What? Mia and me? It's good. I think. It was good before fight camp started. Now I never see her. We can't text during the day because she works so we text a little bit at night but I'm usually half asleep and not much of a conversationalist."

His father's eyes narrowed. "Good thing this fight is happening soon. Not a lot of women would be willing to put up with being neglected like that."

Jesse was indignant. "I'm not neglecting her. I'm training for a fight so I don't get my skull busted in." In truth, he'd been having similar thoughts about Mia but didn't want to admit it to himself or his father. If he didn't say them out loud, somehow, they were less true. But now that they were out there, they hung heavy in the air.

There was a reason he'd never brought any of his girlfriends home for dinner. None of them had ever lasted long enough for Jesse to want to bring them home. Each and every one of them had decided they weren't willing to share him with his demanding training schedule.

The thought that Mia could be next in that chain struck his heart like an unexpected front kick.

There were still errands to run and food to prep and laundry to do before he went to Mia's. It was only two in the afternoon, and he was already exhausted just thinking about everything that had to be done before he promised to be to her place.

"All right," Jesse said, slapping a hand on the counter. "I just wanted to swing by and say hello because I haven't seen anyone in a couple weeks and because I won't be here tonight either."

"Your mother was hoping you'd be coming tonight, and she was really hoping you'd be bringing your girl with you."

"Sorry, Dad, not tonight. As soon as the fight's done I'll be back to a normal schedule and a normal routine, and I promise we'll be back."

Pat nodded again, his bushy gray beard resting on his thick chest. His blue eyes held Jesse in place like he was a ten-year-old kid about to get in trouble for something... again.

"What's that look, old man?"

With a shrug, Pat said, "Just don't want to see you screw things up with this woman. She seems nice, she had nothing but goo goo eyes for you, and the family already likes her."

"Goo goo eyes?" Jesse shook his head and laughed, then stood to leave. "I'll see you later," he said as he walked toward the front door. "And tell Seth to come by the gym and I'll show him around in case he decides to bring my girl down for some lessons."

"Will do, son. See you in a couple weeks."

After stopping at the grocery store and then a quick trip to the health food store down by the gym for another container of creatine, Jesse headed home to get his meal prep done before he had to jump into the shower.

With the fight coming up quickly, he was in full-on weight cut mode. Some of the other fighters he knew waited to the last minute and did all kinds of crazy shit to drop weight, but his philosophy has always been to lose some through diet before he switched over to dropping the water weight in the last day or two before the fight.

The hardest part right now was just being hungry as a bear coming out of hibernation—all day, every day.

Once he finished cooking up the chicken, his rice steamer had to finish its job, giving him about a half hour before he took off for Mia's. Plenty of time for a shower.

He dragged his body into the bathroom, stood beneath the hot spray for a good ten minutes and just soaked. After quickly washing himself, he stepped out and cinched a towel around his waist and shuffled into his room to get dressed. His bed sat there against the wall, nice and soft and cozy.

Needing just a minute to rest after stepping into his underwear, he sat down on the edge of the bed. He gave in to the yawn that hit him from nowhere and he laid back, just for a minute, to close his eyes.

JESSE'S BRUSQUE RESPONSE HAD been a bucket of cold water on what had been Mia's good mood.

Right then and there, she'd made the command decision to put in an offer on the house. She'd tell him about it when he showed up later.

Of course, it had nothing to do with spite. It was all about being an independent person who didn't owe anyone an explanation for the things she did.

Once she got back home, she decided to take advantage of the beautifully warm evening to burn off some steam. Slipping into shorts and one of Jesse's T-shirts, she strolled down to the ocean. The sun warmed her back and the sand tickled her toes as she walked barefoot down the beach that was dotted with early season sunbathers.

As the sun dipped to the west, it cast a shimmering gold path out over the water. Mia's heart mirrored the rhythm of the waves—sometimes crashing, sometimes retreating.

Jesse's absence weighed on her as she walked, an ever-growing ache. His demanding training schedule had become a silent rival; texts were becoming sparse, conversations virtually nonexistent. Loneliness burrowed deeper into her heart, adding an ever-present heaviness to her everyday life.

As she paced the shoreline, Mia wondered if being alone would be a better path forward. Perhaps it was time to cool things off with Jesse. Retreat into the safety of her own world. Focus on her future, and on herself.

The sun sank lower, painting the sky in hues of tangerine and rose. Maybe being alone was the answer.

By early evening, after a nice, long, soaking shower, she was feeling a little better as she pulled on a dark blue sun dress with a sweetheart neckline. It was long enough to be modest but short enough that there was no way Jesse would be able to resist the temptation to see what she was wearing beneath it.

Her fickle heart couldn't decide. When he wasn't around, it was easier to imagine a future without him in it. She could picture herself walking a dog around a new neighborhood. She could imagine making dinner for herself, then putting leftovers away in the refrigerator.

Those things were easy to imagine because she'd been on her own for close to a year already. How hard would it be to go back to that?

Yet, knowing he'd be at her door in a matter of minutes was enough for her heart to weave him back into her fantasy future life. *Walking back up to the front door of her imaginary house, it's Jesse who opens the door for her. After making dinner together, it's Jesse at the table across from her, no leftovers in sight.*

As she stood before the mirror, brushing out her hair and adding the finishing touches to her makeup, she took a good, long look at herself. She was a little softer than she'd like and a touch rounder in the hips than she used to be. But maybe Claire was right. If he wanted a hardbody girlfriend, he certainly could have his pick.

How many times had Jesse told her exactly how he felt about her body with his actions, by the way he caressed her and kissed her from head to toe, even more so than saying it with his words.

A buzz of anticipation raced through her as she imagined how he'd react when she opened the door for him. Looking down at her phone, she realized he'd be getting there any time in the next half hour or so.

Her nerves wouldn't let her relax enough to do any work on the blanket she'd started, so she spent the half hour straightening up the apartment, moving her books from the neat stack beside the couch back to the shelf, and giving the counter a third wipe down.

The half hour ticked by, and she still hadn't heard anything from Jesse. She scrolled through her phone to be sure she hadn't missed a text but there was nothing there.

Another half hour passed as Mia's frustration grew so she sent him a quick text asking what time he'd be coming over. There was no response. Her stomach growled as one hour turned into two and still no response. She texted one more time but when he still didn't reply, she gave up and ordered Chinese takeout.

While she waited for her dinner to be delivered, she whipped off her dress and tossed it to the floor, then threw on a pair of yoga pants and a baggy sweatshirt. She brushed out her hair and threw it up into a high ponytail then scrubbed off her makeup.

Her dinner was delivered, eaten, and cleaned up and Jesse still hadn't responded. After sitting in front of a silly romance movie, without actually watching it, she brushed her teeth and crawled into bed, overwhelmed by frustration and disappointment and her ever-present life mate, rejection.

Sleeping alone had never felt lonelier and the feelings of humiliation she'd learned firsthand with Lauren and Brandon smothered her again as she tried to fall asleep. She wondered if she should text Jesse one more time, or take his silence as his unsubtle way of telling her to back off.

Or worse, maybe he had found his replacement and being non-communicative was his cowardly way of breaking up with her.

Had she been replaced?

Or simply forgotten about?

She didn't know which made her feel worse.

M ONDAY WAS A SLOG. It started with a meeting with the school principal to touch base on a few things before the school year ended. Then a third grader came in with a stomach bug, but the kid couldn't go home because there was nobody to come get her.

The lowlight of her day was dealing with a kindergartener with a bloody nose that wouldn't stop bleeding. Mia ended up wearing almost as much of his blood as he did by the time it finally stopped.

She'd never been so glad for a day to end, even if she was going home to be by herself. She still hadn't heard from Jesse and had come to the painful realization that she'd been dumped.

Luckily for her, rejection was an old friend, and she knew exactly how to deal with it—Christmas movies, chardonnay, and microwave popcorn. And probably delivery pizza for dessert.

No, definitely a pizza for dessert.

Right as she settled in with her bowl of salty popcorn and clicked play on her movie, pounding on her door startled her. "Shit," she said, brushing off pieces of popcorn as she jumped up from the couch. "Hold on! I'm coming!"

"Mia?" Jesse's urgent voice yelled from the other side of the door.

Her hand hovered over the doorknob as she debated turning around and leaving him out in the hallway. She needed to talk to the landlord about putting up a sign asking residents not to let other people in while they had the exterior door open.

"Come on, Mia. I know you're in there. I heard you swear," he said. "Please open the door."

Eventually, she pulled it open and was met with the saddest puppy dog face she'd ever seen. At least he had the good sense to feel bad for crushing her heart.

"Oh my God, Beauty, I am so fucking sorry." He reached out to touch her arm, but she stepped backward to avoid his touch.

"Don't," she said.

"Don't what?"

"Don't call me that."

His face pulled into a grimace. "I know I was supposed to come over yesterday. I got so busy taking care of all the shit I didn't have time to do all week. Training for this fight has been brutal and time just got away from me and it completely slipped my mind. And then I ended up sitting down to catch my breath and I totally fell asleep." His words tumbled out with barely a breath in between.

Her heart had already broken and his explanation of forgetting about her and then falling asleep didn't make it any better.

"Oh," she said, struggling to keep her voice even. "Well, thanks for coming by. I'll see you later." She started to shut the door, but his foot jammed into the space and stopped it from closing.

"Thanks for coming by?" he repeated back to her. "See me later? What the fuck, Mia? I said I was sorry. Can't we talk about this?"

"I don't really want to talk about it, Jesse." Her hand still gripped the doorknob. "I accept your apology." She pulled up her courage and said, "Maybe this was a good thing—in a roundabout kind of way.

I've been thinking it might be best for us to just cool things off for a while." Every ounce of her energy, both physical and mental, went into keeping her voice even, her hands from shaking, and her heart from busting wide open.

"No, no, no, no," he said, pushing his way into her apartment. She stepped back, her brain on autopilot, and let him inside her space. "Absolutely fucking not, Mia." His beautiful eyes searched hers and she felt entirely exposed, like he knew everything she was thinking and feeling just by looking into her eyes.

"I'm not interested in cooling things off. Things are good between us," he said. "At least they were until I fucked it up yesterday." He reached his hands out to hold her, but she stepped away from him again. He took a step toward her, his features hardening. "Are you saying *that* was enough to end things?" The confusion on his face broke her heart further.

"No, that wasn't it," she finally said, a small quaver in her voice. "I've just had a lot of time to think about things the past couple weeks, and I don't know that I have it in me to be someone's girlfriend." Squaring her shoulders to summon a strength she didn't naturally feel, she said, "Remember, I told you that when this whole thing started. I told you I could only be friends with you."

His face was dark, angry. "Yeah," he said. "I remember. I also remember you being willing to give us a shot. And things were going great between us." Realization dawned in his eyes and he drew back from her. "Until you saw that fucking douche at the hospital. Isn't that what you just said? The past couple weeks? You saw him two weeks ago and now, all of a sudden, you're willing to just give up on us? Is that right? Is that what you're telling me?"

She didn't like the anger rising in his voice. It only added to her anxiety over what was happening. "Yes. I mean no." She was entirely too flustered as he held her pinned with that blazing look in his eyes. "Yes, it started when I ran into them, but that only started me thinking," she said. "Please don't think I still want him or anything. It's not like that. It's not about him. Not really."

"Then what's it about, Mia? Tell me." He folded his arms across his chest and suddenly took up twice the space he normally did. "If it's not about him, then what's it about?"

It was not OK with her to feel intimidated in her own home, temporary as it was, and anger and frustration and sadness overwhelmed her. "It's about me, Jesse! Did you ever think about that? That I have feelings and fears and experiences and goals and that I'm more than just a piece of ass you get to have once a week!"

His head snapped back, his eyes wide as if she had just slapped him across the face.

She wasn't being fair to him, and she knew it, but she wouldn't go back on what she said. She wanted him to be pissed off. She wanted him to tell her to go fuck herself and walk out the door. Then she wouldn't have to wait for it to happen naturally in its own time.

"I don't know what to say to that," he said, his voice unnervingly even. "Even though you know it's not fucking true." His mouth twisted to the side like he was chewing on his words before he said them. "And you know what? It pisses me off that you even had that thought, never mind said it out loud."

The proverbial first shoe had dropped.

His arms were still folded over his chest as he moved toward her, pushing her backward one agonizing step at a time. When she bumped into the wall and could go no further, he stopped, uncrossed his arms, and dropped them to his hips, forming a large human barrier between her and the open space of her apartment.

"Tell me what you want, Mia."

She couldn't take that look anymore, the one demanding something from her that she wasn't ready to give. She needed him to leave. Yet the thought of him leaving terrified her to her core. "I want to be friends with you. I want to know you, but I can't do whatever," she waved her hands in a haphazard circle between them, "this is."

She didn't want to admit that she couldn't face the risk of rejection and humiliation, not from Jesse, not from anyone, ever again. "I want to live my life and buy my house and get my dog and not have to worry about being hurt anymore!" An ugly sob broke free but she stuffed it back down and frantically wiped her eyes with her sleeves.

The mass of him closed in on her even further as he stepped directly into her personal space. "I told you I would never do anything to hurt you and I fucked that up yesterday. I was so fucking tired I just fell asleep." He reached out and touched her hair, letting his finger brush gently against her cheek. "And I'm really sorry about that, Mia. I am.

He shook his head, as if he couldn't believe they were having that conversation. "I have never felt about another woman the way I feel about you. Never once in my life. And, if you'll let me, I am willing to do everything in my power to prove that to you."

He waited for her to look him in the eye before he continued. "But what I am not willing to do is go back to being just your friend."

"But that's all I can offer you," she said, barely holding back the deluge of tears that sat behind her eyes. "That's all I have to give."

"You're lying. We've already had more than that. You've already given me more than that. Nothing's changed, Mia."

"Then maybe we didn't really have what you think we did."

Not only was he in her personal space, but he was also perilously close to kissing her. She closed her eyes, knowing it was coming and when his soft lips landed on hers, she tried to memorize the way they felt, the heat that rose up in her even as she actively worked to force it down. His mouth was hungry for her, but it was a controlled hunger, and that fiery part of her brain that wanted more was frustrated and disappointed when he pulled away.

"Are you seriously trying to convince me that what we have here isn't real? That we don't have something worth fighting for?" he asked, one hand on either side of her head, caging her against the wall.

Blinking her eyes to keep them from letting out the tears, she nodded and whispered, "Yes."

"Bullshit."

In a flash, his hands were gone from the wall, his body on his way out the door. Yanking the small duffel bag he'd brought with him from the floor, he stood in the doorway with his back to her. "I know you want to be friends with me, Beauty, but that can't happen. I can't spend time with someone I love, knowing it's a one-sided situation. I want all of you, but if that's not something you can give me, then I can't have any of you."

The door slammed behind him.

The second shoe had dropped.

Jesse

O NE THING JESSE COULD read was fear in the eyes of another person. Usually that other person was right to be afraid when he stood across from them, but seeing fear in Mia's eyes just about did him in.

She wasn't afraid *of him*, but she was afraid of being hurt again. He'd fucked up by falling asleep and missing their date. But he couldn't live without this woman. She was a light in his world, a sweet and gentle heart with a sex drive that could keep up with his.

There was only one thing he could have done; he had to let her break things off between them. She needed to get her head together and figure her shit out. He wished he could be the one to walk with her through it, but that's not what she wanted. He wasn't going to force himself into her life. It was a decision she needed to come to on her own and when she was ready to try again, he'd be waiting for her.

The sun was out later and later as spring rolled on toward summer and he watched the sun set as he walked down the block to his car. He kept a copy of the key to the gym on his keyring and he fingered the small piece of metal as he walked, needing the comfort of the physical outlet of exercise to help him clear his head, both to think and to not think.

With a fight scheduled for three weeks out, the last thing he needed to do was get sidetracked thinking of Mia. Maybe three weeks would be enough time for her to figure out what she wanted, and he could focus solely on his training without the distraction of another person to worry about.

If only she could be that easy to ignore.

The gym was still open when he got there. There was a Muay Thai class happening on the big part of the blue mat, so he changed into his workout clothes, strapped on a pair of gloves, and stayed in the back of the gym, where he took out his overwhelming frustration on an uncomplaining heavy bag.

There was no speed in any of his strikes. Every knee, punch, kick, and elbow landed with as much power as he had in his body. The sweat rained off him, landing in great drops all around the bag as he channeled every ounce of frustration, with himself and with the situation, through his limbs and straight into the bag.

"Hey, Coach," Eddie said as Jesse sat on the locker room bench after his post-workout shower.

"Hey, Eddie," he said. "You looked good out there tonight. That inside low kick's come a long way."

Eddie nodded. "Thanks, I've been working on it." Then he wiped his face and neck down with a small towel. "Everything OK with you?"

"Sure, I'm fine," Jesse said.

"Haven't seen you bring your new girl here in a while. You two still a thing?"

Jesse was not in the mood to talk, especially about Mia. He stood, grabbed his bag from the floor. "Good night, Ed. See you tomorrow."

"Night, Coach."

That was the good thing with guys. They knew when to stop talking. Grateful for that, Jesse took off, knowing he'd be back in the morning, because Mia or no Mia, this fight was getting closer by the day.

Jesse

"**F**OR FUCK'S SAKE, JESSE, wake up!" Mark's voice reverberated through the gym, a firestorm of frustration and fury. He pivoted away from the boxing ring, and with a roar, flung his stopwatch across the room. "If you walk into a fight like this, you're going to get your head kicked in!"

Mark looked at the group of guys he'd brought in to spar against Jesse, pointed to the one guy he hadn't used yet. "Ivan, get in there with him and see if you can get his head on right."

Jesse's mild-mannered uncle teetered on the brink of explosive frustration; a sight Jesse had rarely witnessed. Jesse understood he needed to get his act together before he was single-handedly responsible for giving the old guy a heart attack.

Ivan nodded, bit down on his mouth guard and slipped through the ropes to join Jesse in the middle of the ring. When Mark rang the bell, the two guys touched gloves. After spending the first ten seconds testing each other's distance and timing, Jesse made his first move and stepped in with a solid jab.

They circled a little more and Jesse's mind drifted back to Mia's comment about him only using her for sex, and his vision blurred. Ivan must've seen it because he stepped forward and landed a front kick to Jesse's sternum.

"Fuck!" Jesse yelled through his mouth guard, fury ripping through him as he tried to catch his breath. Even when they weren't together this woman threatened to be the death of him.

No more.

He was not losing this round of sparring and he was certainly not losing his last fight. He smacked his gloves together, settled into his stance, and squared up to put an end to Ivan in the four minutes left of the round.

The two men threw punches, each waiting and watching the other for the most opportune time to strike. Kicks landed, and Jesse had the advantage when he caught Ivan with a calf kick, hobbling his otherwise stellar opponent.

By the time the bell rang at the end of the round, Jesse had felt the fire in his veins. The spark that started in his belly quickly consumed him, allowing him to laser-focus on target after target on Ivan's body.

"That's what I'm talking about," Mark said as Jesse stepped through the ropes and hopped down to the floor.

Jesse held up his hand to Ivan as the other man followed him out of the ring. "Nice work in there," Jesse said, bumping gloves with him. "That was my hardest round so far."

"Thanks, man," Ivan said. "If you go into your fight with that look in your eye, it'll be over before it starts." He turned to Mark, "Thanks for letting me do this, Coach. I've gotta head out. See you next week?"

"Absolutely," Mark said, patting the tall man on the back. "Thanks again, Ivan. You did great in there." He turned back to Jesse and nodded his head to the side, telling Jesse to go take a rest.

Jesse's eyes were closed for most of the walk, knowing the place by heart, while he replayed his sparring session over in his mind. There were a few openings that Ivan had shown him and because he hesitated, Jesse had missed opportunities. They were mistakes he wouldn't make again.

"That was amazing," Seth said, his voice breaking into Jesse's world.

Jesse's head snapped up. "Hey, what are you doing here?" he said as he draped a towel around his shoulders and wiped the sweat dripping down the sides of his face.

"I'm on an errand to check this place out. I've got a five-year-old at home desperate to be like her uncle."

Jesse laughed. "Yeah, she showed me her bruise last time I was at Mom's."

Seth pulled out his phone, scrolled through and held it out for Jesse to see. "But have you seen this? She made me take this the day after it happened."

Jesse couldn't help but burst out laughing. His tiny niece stood with her bruised arm across her chest, both hands clenched in fists, and the meanest scowl she could muster across her face. "Oh, Jesus," he said once his laughter subsided. "I'm sorry about all this."

Seth slid the phone back into his pocket. "Nothing to be sorry about," he said. "Except maybe the tattoo part."

"The what now?"

"Mom didn't tell you about the tattoo?"

"Haven't been there in a couple weeks," Jesse said.

Seth's mouth quirked into a grin. "So, the other night, it's bedtime. Kid needs a bath. I poke my head into the bathroom to make sure she's all right and I see this black mess all over her stomach."

Jesse dipped his head, trying to hold back the laughter as he figured out where this story was headed.

"I'm like, 'Rylee, what's that all over your stomach?' and, I fucking kid you not, she's all attitude and she says, 'Daddy, it's my tattoo. It's just like Uncle J's.'" Seth's eyebrows were almost lost in his hairline as he fixed Jesse with a stare. "She took a fucking black permanent marker and drew her own mandala all over herself." He lifted one shoulder, let it drop. "I had to Google how to remove permanent marker from skin. Do you have any idea how many ways there are to do it? At least five, because I had to use that many to get it off."

His niece was one of the funniest people he knew, and he could easily imagine her drawing mandalas all over herself. "I guess you're just lucky she didn't draw one anywhere that other people could see it."

"Oh, fuck, don't even joke like that," Seth said with a laugh. "So, how does all this work if I really want to let her come in and try it out?"

Jesse spent the next few minutes giving his brother the rundown on how the classes worked at the gym and when the little kid classes were. "If you're serious about signing her up, that would be pretty cool. Mark and Danny are fantastic coaches. But it's Danny and Robby that teach the little ones."

His growling stomach was his constant companion in the final weeks before the fight, but Seth didn't even try to hide his astonishment at the sound Jesse's stomach made.

"I should let you get out of here," Seth said. "Let you go home and eat so you stop making that god-awful noise."

Jesse threw on a shirt, waved to Mark and told him he'd be back later in the day, then walked with Seth out to the parking lot.

"So, what's going on with you and your new girl?" Seth asked.

He'd finally gotten his mind off of Mia and his brother had to go and ask about her. "Nothing. She's not my girl." He opened the back door of his car and tossed his bag onto the back seat. "We broke up a couple weeks ago."

Seth nodded but didn't say anything.

"But you already knew that didn't you?" Jesse said, suddenly hating the way his whole family had the habit of being in each other's business. All. The. Time.

"Yeah, well, Lexi works with Mia and she's friends with Gretchen, so... I guess when one knows, they all know."

Jesse huffed out a huge sigh. "What do you want me to tell you? We gave it a shot and it didn't work. End of story." He leaned against his car, crossed his arms over his chest. "Does that really surprise any of you?"

"Surprise? Not really. Disappoint?" Seth grinned. "Nobody but Mom."

"I'm starving, man. I've gotta go eat something before I come back here and do this all over again." Jesse hopped behind the wheel and started up the engine. "Hey, you guys all planning to come to the fight? It's next Saturday down at Patriot Combat. Doors open at six-thirty."

"Yeah, me, Shane, Owen, and Dad'll be there. Pretty sure Gretchen has something going on with her friends and Mom's watching the kids so we can all go."

"Sweet," Jesse said. "I'll see you next week."

With a wave, Seth hopped into his truck and pulled out of the parking lot right before Jesse did. From inside his bag in the back seat, his cell phone pinged with an incoming voicemail. He played it through the car stereo.

"Hey, Jesse. It's Mia." His heart practically burst through his ribcage. "You left your sweatshirt here. I figured you'd want it back. I brought it down to your mom at the office and left it there." Her voice wrapped around him and threatened to choke the air from his lungs. "Hope you're doing well. Good luck with your fight."

LIFE WITHOUT JESSE PROVED to be harder than she thought it would be and that fact pissed her off. She was a perfectly capable woman who didn't need a man to give her purpose.

It was the other stuff she missed, though; having someone to talk to, to hang out with, and see movies with. It was the loss of a friend she felt more than anything.

Well, maybe not *anything*; the cool early summer nights were downright cold without him there.

She kept herself busy looking at open houses, expanding her search radius to include some of the towns around Oak Harbor, because the thought of running into Jesse around town terrified her.

Determined to keep her momentum moving forward, and aware that she'd be leaving her apartment as soon as the lease was up, she'd talked her reluctant landlord into giving her permission to adopt a small dog.

And then, fate showed up. Buttons, an Italian greyhound with soulful, deep brown, doe-like eyes, appeared on the shelter's website. Mia had to make Buttons hers. The little lovebug's unconditional affection promised to help mend the gaping hole in her heart that nothing else seemed to touch.

As quickly as she could, she filled out the online application and hit submit.

As the clock ticked, the silence settled in. There wouldn't be any kind of response from the shelter for at least a day or two, and the anxiety of having to wait pushed her up off the couch and out for a walk. She needed an onion and a potato for her dinner, giving her restless walk a purpose.

It was the same market Mia had been going to since she moved to Oak Harbor, so she was able to navigate to the produce section without having to make eye contact with anyone. She grabbed an onion and a potato and headed toward the checkout line, then picked up a small pack of chocolate chip cookies on her way by. Her heart skidded to a halt when she heard the deep, unmistakable timbre of Jesse's voice.

He stood at the counter, paying for his own groceries. Mia looked closer and saw that he was buying all the ingredients for the dinner she'd taught him to make. It was the first time she'd seen him since he walked out of her apartment almost two weeks ago and it felt as if the potato in her hand had suddenly lodged itself in her throat.

He looked thinner than he normally did, but she also knew he would still be cutting weight for his fight. He looked similar to the night they first met. The woman at the cash register seemed to think he looked just fine, though. She smiled at him with straight, white teeth, and a coy smile that made Mia's heart burn. Of course women flirted with him, he was a walking fantasy in jeans and a hoodie.

Mia's feet rooted to the ground as she watched their interactions.

"What kind of vegetable is this?" the woman asked.

"Parsnip."

"Are they good? I've never eaten one before," she said, searching through the produce codes to enter the parsnip.

"If you roast them with potatoes and stuff, they're pretty good," he said, his voice polite but not overly friendly.

"Maybe I'll have to give that a try. It sounds good."

The words of the conversation were boring, exactly the type of conversation she'd had with grocery store clerks a million times. It was the way the woman looked at Jesse every time she spoke, with those big eyes, and her flirty tone of voice that had Mia close to vomiting as she stood waiting for her turn. The other woman was practically feasting on him with her eyes and Mia's heart squeezed painfully in her chest.

Jesse tapped his card to pay, grabbed his bag of vegetables, and with a quick, "Have a good night," he took off out the door. The only thing that kept Mia from breaking down on the spot was Jesse's perceived lack of interest in the other woman. He was polite, but he didn't flirt back.

Her instinct on the trudging walk back to her apartment was to call and talk to her sister—the way they always used to do. Lauren would know the right things to say, she would understand the way Mia felt, and offer the next steps for Mia to take to move on with her life.

Holding her phone in her hand, she got as far as bringing up Lauren's contact information before she shut it off and shoved it back into her pocket.

The onion and potato she'd bought at the market sat unused on the counter while she laid down on the couch to lose herself in some mindless television. Grabbing the blanket from the back of the couch, she wrapped it around her curled up body, pulled it up under her chin, then closed her eyes. When the first sob broke free, she finally let it out and didn't try to stop it.

After the emotional roller coaster of the night before, and waking up bleary eyed on the couch, Mia dragged herself to work, her coffee mug full to the brim for the second time that morning.

"Hey, how's it going?" Lexi asked as she popped her head into Mia's office. "You ready for this year to be over or what?" Tomorrow would be the last day of the school year and aside from the upside of having the summer off to focus on her job, housing, and pet search, Mia secretly dreaded having to do all of that by herself.

"Oh, yeah," she said, halfheartedly. "Absolutely." Mia tried to smile but judging by the way Lexi looked at her, (damn the person who invented the look of pity) her smile wasn't entirely believable. "No, really. It's going to be a great summer. I've got a job to find first and foremost. Hopefully once I do that, I can narrow my house hunting circle, and then," she crossed her fingers for luck, "maybe I can finally get my dog."

Lexi stepped all the way into the office, closed the door behind her, and sighed softly. "Look," she said, "I know we don't know each other all that well, but I had a lot of fun going shopping together. And we do have a lot of people in common, I think."

Mia smiled because, although Lexi wasn't related to them, she knew the entire Murphy family.

"And if you want someone to go house hunting with or if you ever want to go out and grab a coffee or lunch some time," Lexi continued, "just text me. Or if you want to do some more shopping. We travel a little bit over the summer, but nothing crazy."

Emotion clogged Mia's throat, making it hard to reply, so she nodded instead. "Thank you," she finally squeaked out. "I appreciate that."

"Besides," Lexi said, "I freaking love open houses. I already have a house and I still love looking around at them. So, if you ever need a friend for that, you know where to find me."

Like a soft breeze, Lexi disappeared out the door and Mia was left alone to finish cleaning and disinfecting the surfaces in her office.

Her phone rang from its spot on her desk. Hoping it was Jesse, yet dreading it being Jesse, she snatched it from the desktop. Her heart kicked up as she saw the name of the animal shelter where she'd found Buttons. Her finger hovered, wondering if it was good news or bad, and whether to hit the green button or the red one.

You're overthinking this. Just answer the damn phone.

"Ms. Reed?" the man on the other end of the call said. "This is Bill March from the Whisper Woods Animal Shelter." His tone of voice was upbeat and Mia's heart beat double time; she knew what he was about to say. "I'm calling regarding your application to adopt Buttons."

Mia gripped the phone tighter. "Yes?"

"We spoke with the management office at your building, and they have given permission for you to move forward with the adoption process while you're still living there."

A little squeak escaped Mia's lips before she could stop it.

Bill March chuckled, most likely used to that reaction. "The next thing we need to do is schedule a time for you to come in and meet Buttons in person," he said. "Then we'll do a home visit, and pending a positive outcome there, you'll be on your way to becoming a dog mom."

Riding high over the news about Buttons, in between cleaning tasks, Mia jumped online to add a few things to her growing 'dog mom' wish list. A few seconds later, the phone on her wall started ringing.

"Hey, Mia," Lexi said when Mia picked up the receiver. "Principal Stone wanted me to see if you had a minute to come down to the main office."

"When?" Mia asked. "I have time right now if that works for her."

"That's perfect. I'll tell her."

Mia found herself a few minutes later, seated across the big wooden desk from Principal Stone. "We have truly enjoyed having you here this year, Mia," Principal Stone said.

The principal was the type of person who related as easily to the building full of children as she did to their parents when the situation called for it. She was good at her job and in the time they'd worked together, Mia had developed a respect for her capable leadership style.

"Before I continue, I would first like to apologize for waiting so long to talk to you about this." Mia's throat constricted and her hands got clammy as her mind struggled to figure out what she'd done wrong to warrant a call to the principal's office. The ridiculousness of the statement almost made her laugh from sheer nerves.

"Just a few minutes ago, I hung up from a conversation with Nurse Brown." Principal Stone leaned forward and folded her hands together on the desktop. "As it turns out, she has decided not to return from her maternity leave, and instead, stay home with her new baby girl." The woman's smile was kind as she spoke about the nurse Mia had only met a few times before she'd gone out on leave.

"Now, I know you had only signed on to work here through the end of this school year, and like I said, I understand how last-minute this is, but I would like to officially offer you the position of Parker Elementary School nurse if you're interested in returning in the fall."

Despite the roller coaster of emotion her life had been recently, Mia was still a professional. A professional who had no other job prospects for the fall.

"Wow," she said. "Thank you so much. I would love to come back next year."

"Excellent. Lexi will be in touch with you over the summer to get the official offer made and all the paperwork done," Principal Stone said.

They shook hands and Mia thanked the principal again before floating out the door. She gave an excited little wave to Lexi as she passed through the main office on the way back to the nurse's office. Now, her office.

She sucked in a deep breath and blew it out through a giant smile. For the first time in weeks Mia felt like crying—out of sheer happiness.

Sitting alone at her kitchen table eating dinner that night, she grasped desperately to hold onto the good feelings of the day. Again, she found herself reaching for her phone. Instead of her sister, this time her gut instinct was to text Jesse. She wanted to tell him about her job, about her dog, about how much she missed him and wanted to see him again. She wanted to see how his training was going. But most of all, she wanted to ask him one more time to be her friend.

Pathetic, she thought. Why was she willing to beg him to be her friend, when that was the one thing he told her he would not accept from her? At least not by itself.

He wanted her heart, only she was too scared to let him have it.

A little voice in her head (that sounded suspiciously like Aunt Claire) said, *"Did you ever pine over Brandon this way? Did your heart feel like it was going to rip out of your chest and follow him out the door, the way it did when you saw Jesse at the market? Were you jealous to the point of sickness when another woman spoke to Brandon?"*

She sat with those questions, one by one, for a long time, her dinner going cold on the plate.

"No," she finally admitted on a whisper. "I hated being made to feel like a fool, and I hated that he chose my sister over me. But I never missed him the way I miss Jesse. Never." Her voice was barely audible, but it was a truth she needed to hear from herself.

It was the permission she needed to start to move on from a past that was holding her captive.

The last time she'd seen her aunt, Claire had told her it was time to deal with that past. And for the first time, Mia knew deep in her bones she was right. And she was finally ready to do just that.

Swiping through her contacts, she found the one she was looking for, typed a message and hit send. Nerves shot through her, making her fingers and toes tingle from the little adrenaline hit. She hopped up from the table, dumped her uneaten dinner into a container and then tossed it into the fridge before she hightailed it to her room to get her things for a shower.

Coming out of the shower, her nerves had calmed somewhat, and she steadied herself to look at her phone, ready to deal with whatever she saw there, if anything.

Tears blurred her vision when she read the text:

I miss you too. I hate everything that's between us. I would love to have coffee with you.

Meet you at Starbucks on Route 1 in an hour?

Wiping her eyes so she could see the clock at the top of the phone, and realizing how little time she had to get there, she grabbed her backpack and yanked out her keys. She sent back a smiley face and a thumbs up, then ran out the door to meet her sister for coffee and some kind of resolution.

Jesse

H E DIDN'T WANT THE sweatshirt—not without her in it. But he couldn't just leave it at the office, a reminder to his entire family that he'd somehow managed to screw up his relationship with Mia the way he'd managed to screw up every relationship he'd ever been involved in. The only difference being this time he cared.

He cared about Mia. He cared about hurting her feelings, even after promising he wouldn't. He cared about that look in her eyes when he walked away from her.

Not only did he care about all those things, but he also wanted to atone for those things. He wanted to do right by her, to show her that even though he was a man with flaws, he was still a man she could trust.

A small sign sat on his mother's desk when Jesse walked into the Murphy Construction office, indicating that she was away from the office but would return within ten minutes.

Across from the desk, in one of the chairs along the wall, sat a woman Jesse didn't recognize. Her legs were uncrossed but her feet were together, her back was rod-straight, and her fingers clutched the strap of her purse as if she were holding onto it for dear life.

"Hi," he said, walking behind the desk. "Are you waiting for Gaelen?"

As if she just realized Jesse had walked into the office, her eyes snapped up and laser focused on him. "Hi," she said. "Yeah, I'm Phoebe Blake. I have an interview with Mrs. Murphy at eleven-fifteen."

Jesse flicked a glance at the wall clock: ten past eleven, so she wasn't late yet.

"Nice to meet you, Phoebe. I'm Jesse," he said. "I'm Gaelen's son. Don't worry, my mom will definitely be here on time. Most likely she ran down to the bakery to grab some muffins or something because you were coming in."

Phoebe's face brightened. "Oh," she said, fidgeting in her seat. "That really isn't necessary."

With a laugh, he said, "Maybe not, but that's just how she is."

Phoebe smiled. "She sounds nice."

"She is. Both my parents are pretty cool." He turned behind him and grabbed his hoodie from the top of the filing cabinet under the window that overlooked the parking lot. Ignoring the delicate scent of Mia that drifted up as he held it, he asked Phoebe, "What position are you interviewing for?"

"Mrs. Murphy's assistant," she said. "My friend Lexi told me about the job." Her fingers tightened around her pocketbook straps again. "I'm really hopeful about this," she said quietly, letting her eyes drift to the floor.

"Lexi Greeves?"

"That's her," Phoebe said. "She said she was talking to your mom and your mom mentioned this job. So, Lexi recommended me right away."

His mother's rapid footsteps sounded in the hallway. The clock had just ticked over to eleven-fourteen. "Told you she'd be here on time," he said to Phoebe as he hurried out from behind the desk to open the door for his mother.

"Oh," Gaelen said, as Jesse pulled the door open. "Hi, honey. What are you—" She stopped mid-question when her eyes landed on the sweatshirt in his hand. "Never mind," she said, and glanced over at Phoebe.

Gaelen bustled into the office and put a bakery box down on her desk before she turned and said, "Hello, you must be Phoebe Blake." She reached out and shook hands with Phoebe, who stood to return the greeting.

"Mom, thanks for holding onto this," Jesse said, holding up the sweatshirt and immediately regretting letting it get so close to his nose where he could smell Mia on it again. He dropped it to his side and looked at Phoebe. "It was nice meeting you, Phoebe," he said. "Good luck with your interview."

As he walked out the door, Gaelen called out to him, knowing full well he was cutting weight. "Jesse, honey, you want a muffin for the road?"

"Not funny," he said, and heard her giggling from the other side of the door.

His first instinct was to toss the hoodie into the trunk and forget about it entirely. His second instinct was to pull the heavy sweatshirt over his head and breathe in Mia.

Five seconds later, sitting in his car, wearing a hoodie that was entirely too warm for the weather, he thought about ways of getting her back. There had to be something he could say or do that would convince her they were right for each other.

Before he could send off a text to her, asking for just a few minutes of her time, another text came through, this one from his mother.

> I know you miss her. I think she just needs some time. Leave it be for now.

Christ, the woman was a friggin' psychic now.

> Fine

He wanted to hurl the phone through the window. Instead, he stuffed it into the hoodie pocket and sucked in a deep breath to steady his nerves.

THE GYM WAS CROWDED when she walked in the door. Jesse's cousin Danny stopped her to make sure she checked in. "Oh, hey, Mia," he said, when he realized who she was. "Haven't seen you in a while. Did you sign up for a membership finally?" His teasing smile was friendly and put Mia at ease.

"I'm not coming to work out," she said. "I'm actually here looking for Jesse."

"'Fraid he isn't here today," Danny said, a slight crease furrowing his brow. "Can I leave a message for him?"

She shook her head. "No," she said. "That's all right." Her nervous energy almost carried her right back out the door before she finally worked up the courage to go through with her plan. "You know what, can I just go leave something in his locker real quick?"

Clearly curious about her intentions, he didn't answer right away. His protectiveness of his cousin warmed her heart.

"I promise it's nothing bad." She made a little x over the left side of her chest. "Cross my heart."

Eventually Danny must have been won over by her elementary school promise because he relented and said, "All right. But be quick. You know which one is his?"

Her heart lifted. "I do," she said. "Thank you."

Hurrying along the long wall of the gym, she remembered the time they'd spent there and how much fun she'd had with him. She hoped she wasn't setting herself up to fail, but even if she was, it was a chance she had to take.

Jesse

T HE DAY OF THE fight was a non-training day, but he couldn't
sit around his place doing nothing, so he headed down to the
gym. He wouldn't exercise, but a good deep stretch and some light
shadowboxing would be a great way to burn off his nervous energy
and get his body warmed up for what was to come.

"Hey, Coach," Eddie yelled as Jesse crossed toward the locker room.
With a grin, he added, "How's your girl?"

"Shut the fuck up, Eddie."

Raucous laughter ripped through the gym, but Jesse ignored the
commotion and kept to his original destination. Opening his locker,
his eye caught on something that shouldn't have been there, and his
hand went slack. The bag he'd been holding dropped to the floor.

A square of paper with his name on it, written in Mia's handwrit-
ing, stared out at him from on top of what looked like a wallet. Her
wallet. He huffed out an uneasy laugh as he unfolded the paper.

Jesse –

*I'm sorry to bother you when you're getting ready for your fight. But
there are a few things I need to get off my chest and I was afraid I'd lose
the courage if I didn't do this right now.*

First off – I'm sorry. I know it probably doesn't count for much after being such a jerk about everything and telling you I could only be your friend. I hope you don't hate me and that maybe someday we can still be friends.

Second – I'm sorry. Holding the actions of a guy that I never really loved against you was both unfair and unkind. Once you were out of my life (all my fault) I cried more than I've ever cried in my life. I thought my heart had literally broken in half.

Third – I'm sorry. You've been preparing for a huge event, and I let my fear of what might happen get in the way of what was actually happening. I was not supportive of you and what you were going through the way you've been there for me.

There's so much more I'd love to tell you and maybe someday you'd be willing to talk to me again?

Good luck with your fight. I know you're going to be amazing because that's just who you are. If you don't get this until after your fight, know that I was cheering you on in my heart the whole time!

Always your friend – and so much more, if you'll have me,

— Mia

He folded the note and tucked it inside his gym bag, then grabbed out her wallet and flipped it open. Her driver's license and credit cards were not there, but in the small window she'd put a printout of one of the selfies she'd taken during their time together. It was the one of the two of them sitting on the rocks down by the ocean the first time they went there together.

It soothed his heart to know she was reaching out for him.

And it broke his heart that he'd have to keep her waiting for a few more days.

DRIVING DOWN TO HER parents' house, Mia felt as light as she'd felt in a long time. She hadn't heard from Jesse, and she wasn't sure she was going to, but she'd made peace with that.

After the hours-long conversation she'd had with Lauren, and the crying and laughing they'd done, the thoughts and feelings they'd shared, she knew nothing would hold her back from going after what she wanted ever again.

The way Lauren talked about Brandon was exactly the way Mia felt about Jesse, and it only reinforced the knowledge that Mia had never felt that way about Brandon to begin with. He'd always been safe and stable, a good match on paper, but without any of the passion she'd come to realize she needed in her life. Being with Jesse certainly provided her with that.

When Lauren had asked Mia to come to the big July Fourth party, she'd promised that Brandon wouldn't be there. And for the first time, Mia realized it would be OK if he was. "Bring him," Mia had said. "It's really OK."

For the first time in over a year the sisters had laughed together.

"Aunt Claire," Mia said when she saw her aunt in her parents' backyard. "You look fantastic. Looks like you've been taking care of yourself and following the doc's orders."

"Don't sound so surprised," Claire said with a shrug. "There's too much drama happening in this family. I didn't want to die and miss it all." She laughed and kissed Mia's cheek. "Oh, kiddo, I'm so glad you decided to come today." Then she crinkled her nose and looked around at the assembled crowd. "These people are so goddamn boring I need someone to talk to."

Mia laughed. "Auntie, these people are all very nice. And half of them are your family. Don't be mean."

"Oh," Claire said, looking past Mia with a look of pure shock. "I wonder what the hell happened to that poor sonofabitch." Her face pulled into a grimace and Mia turned to see the unfortunate soul that captured her aunt's attention.

Jesse's bruised but smiling face stared back at her. Holding her wallet in one hand and a bouquet of daisies in the other, he said, "Hey, you dropped this. I thought you might need it back." Holding out the flowers, he said, "And I thought these might make you smile."

Despite the pain that radiated so obviously from him, joy surged within her. She couldn't help herself; she sprinted toward him, arms outstretched, and enveloped him in a bear hug. The world blurred around them as she held him close. He winced, drawing in a ragged breath, and exhaled slowly.

In that moment, things felt right again.

"Look at you," she said, taking his face gently in her hands. She leaned forward and placed the gentlest kiss on his lips. "At least this time there's no stitches," she said with a chuckle.

"You should see the other guy," he teased. "Pretty sure he needed a few across his forehead from a well-placed elbow."

"You totally won, though, didn't you? I'm so sorry I wasn't there for your fight." She lowered her eyes to his feet. "I didn't know if you even wanted me there and I didn't want to distract you."

He wrapped an arm around her waist and pulled her closer. "I always want you around. Do you understand that? If you are a distraction, you are the best distraction that's ever happened to me." He kissed the top of her head. "But, yeah, I won." She felt him smile against her hair. "Submission by arm bar at two-thirty-nine of the third round. No biggie."

With her head tucked against his chest she was as safe and comfortable and at home as she was anywhere. The weeks between them dissipated into the heavy summer air like smoke.

"Clearly this is your fighter," Claire said from behind Mia. "He's very good looking. At least I think he is under all that bruising." She whacked Jesse on the arm. "You want me to get you some ice for your face?"

Mia felt Jesse's laugh against her cheek. "No, thank you. Ice was the last couple days. Now I just need to let them heal." He lifted one arm from Mia's back and held it out to her aunt. "You must be Aunt Claire? Mia told me nothing but great things about you. How're you feeling?"

Claire was never one to shy away from a conversation about herself, and she told Jesse all about her heart attack, from the care she received at the hospital to the home health worker who comes to check on her. To his credit, Jesse was a gracious listener and knew all the right questions to ask. If Mia hadn't been in love with him already, that moment would have sealed her fate.

"Phew, I'm tired," Claire finally said. "I think I'll head back inside and sit for a while." She patted Jesse's arm then whispered into Mia's ear, "I like him. Definitely think about keeping him. But let me know if you decide you don't want him anymore." With a chuckle, her aunt sauntered across the yard and into the house.

"Please tell me you'll keep me and not hand me over to her," Jesse teased. "I'm a little afraid of what she could do to me."

Mia laughed. "I've missed you so much. I'm so glad you came here." She looked up at him. "But how did you even know I'd show up here, and how did you know where my parents live?"

"Your sister invited me."

She spun around to find Lauren watching them from across the yard. "Lauren invited you? How?"

"Don't know. I just assumed she got my contact info off your phone. She sent me a text asking if I could come to the party." He tipped Mia's face and kissed her again. "And here I am," he said, pulling away from her. "So, if she was able to get my number from your phone, does that mean you spent time with her?"

Mia nodded. So much had happened since she'd seen him last. "I did," she said, snaking her arms around him just to feel him again. "We met up and had coffee the day before I left you the note."

While her relationship with her sister and Brandon was still a little shaky, they'd been able to make at least a little progress away from constant hostility. Hell, Brandon had even told her he was sorry for how he handled the whole situation. Said he panicked and felt like shit about it every day since. *Good*.

Jesse's expression was one of concern as he listened, but he didn't say anything.

"I told her how I'd been feeling about what happened and what it did to me. How hard it was for me over the last year. Believe it or not, she apologized for her part. She swore up and down that nothing happened between them—*physically anyway*—until after he and I had split."

"And you believe her?" Jesse asked, his tone completely incredulous.

She shrugged. "I don't know." Looking into his warm eyes and feeling the heat of his hands resting on her waist, she realized it didn't matter whether she believed Lauren or not. "I kinda think I do, but," she pulled tighter to him and rested her head against his solid chest, "I don't really need to waste any more brain space on it. I have you and that's so much more fun to think about."

"Damn straight it is," Jesse said, holding her as if he never wanted to let her go. "But that offer to fold him up like a fucking pretzel is still on the table."

Mia laughed, knowing full well if she asked him to, he would do it. That little flicker of vengeance that reared its head every now and then wanted to say yes. Wanted to see Brandon pay for what he'd done to her. She sighed. "What would be the point?" she finally said. "It's not like it'd prove anything."

Jesse huffed a laugh. "No, maybe not," he admitted. "But I bet it'd feel really good."

Mia stood on her tip toes and whispered into his ear. "Pretty sure we can think of other ways to feel really good." She placed a gentle kiss on his cheek. "Maybe better than good?"

"You're damn right it'll be better," he said and kissed the top of her head. "What do you say, Beauty. Want to introduce me to everyone? Then maybe you can tell me what changed between us to get you to leave a note like that in my locker."

Before long, Mia had introduced Jesse to her family, including her parents, and Lauren and Brandon. She waited for the interactions to be awkward or uncomfortable, but Jesse didn't let on that he knew anything about Mia's past with Brandon. He did, however, manage to keep his hands on Mia the entire time. Whether he was holding her hand, resting his palm on the small of her back, or straight up grabbing her ass, there could be no doubt in anyone's mind how Jesse felt about her.

Even her parents seemed to like Jesse, admittedly more so when he told them he'd fought his last fight and was looking to take his career in a different, though related, direction.

Every time she looked at him her heart thumped harder in her chest. She had no idea what she'd done to deserve the second chance he was giving her, but she promised herself she wouldn't mess it up. Watching him chat with people she'd known her whole life as if they were old friends was absolutely remarkable to her.

Jesse

T HE NIGHT WORE ON and the crowd grew as more friends and neighbors showed up to see the town's fireworks display from the sprawling backyard of Mia's childhood home. Mia had gone inside to wash her hands and was the only one in the house when Jesse found her in the kitchen.

"It's awfully quiet in here," he said. Walking up behind her, he wrapped his arms around her waist, pressing her hips into the counter. "Does that mean everyone else is outside?"

Her body melted against his and she nodded. "As far as I know."

He burrowed his nose into the hair by her ear. "Want to take me on a tour of the house? Maybe show me your old bedroom?" Reaching his hands up into her shirt, he stroked her nipples, knowing it would be almost impossible for her to resist.

She sucked in a breath, letting her head relax against his chest. "I don't think there's a bed in there anymore," she whispered.

"That's OK. We don't need a bed. There's plenty of things I can do to you up against a wall." His dick strained against his pants, desperate to be inside of her again.

When she whimpered, he took hold of her hand. "Lead the way."

Her parents' home was larger than he expected, and he followed her to the second floor then down a long hallway that made it feel more like an inn than an actual house. Not that it mattered as long as he was able to show Mia exactly how he felt about taking her back.

"This one," she said, opening a door on the left side of the hall. She stood in the doorway for a second, taking in her surroundings. "It's different," she said. "But still kind of the same."

"Kind of like you," he whispered as he closed the door behind them. Spinning her around, he pressed her back to the wall, lowered his mouth to hers. As he slid his hand down her abdomen and into the front of her shorts, he swallowed every whimper and every sound of longing he'd had to live without for weeks.

She stepped her feet apart, inviting him to stroke her. "Always so wet for me," he whispered against her lips and slipped his finger into her, capturing her moan.

His tongue pushed into her mouth, tasting her, twisting against her tongue as he slipped a second finger in with the first. His eyes closed and he leaned in to nuzzle his nose into her hair, breathing her in, feeling the excitement rising in her body. She gasped, sucking in panting breaths while he fingered her against the wall.

He couldn't let his fingers have all the fun and abruptly stopped to push her shorts down off her full hips, then dropped to his knees.

He ran his hands down the outside of her legs, then up the inside until his fingers met at her center. Running his hands back down to her ankles, he pressed against them, telling her without words to step her feet wider. Eyes closed, bottom lip bitten between her teeth, she obeyed.

Leaning in, with one slow lick, he tasted her, and he couldn't wait to fuck her with his tongue, his fingers again, and then his cock. Her chest heaved with rapid breaths as he pressed his mouth to her, his fingers teasing everywhere they touched. He kissed her clit, sucked on it then slid his fingers inside her. Her hips pressed forward, and she grasped for his head, gripping at his hair.

He was so fucking gone for this girl.

With his fingers still stroking, he pulled his face away and he looked up into her eyes. "Touch yourself for me, Beauty," he demanded. "Show me how you like to be touched."

Slowly she lowered one hand, floating it along her belly until her fingers were directly in front of his face. Letting her eyes flutter closed again, she used two fingers to stimulate herself while he kept fingering her.

"That's it, Beauty," he said as they worked together to bring her pleasure. "God, I've missed you. You are so fucking perfect," he said, encouraging her enjoyment of her own body. "I want to see you come like this."

Her eyes flew open, but she didn't stop. "I don't know if I can like this," she said on staggered breaths.

He grinned at her then leaned in and stopped her hand, kissed her fingers and then backed away again. "Sure you can. You keep doing that and I'll keep doing this—" He pumped his fingers into her, and her hand began to move to keep up with his pace. "That's it," he whispered. "Good girl. Let me see you let go before I bend you over and fuck you like you need to be fucked."

A trembling groan broke free from her as her legs quaked on either side of their hands. Her mouth fell open on a silent scream before she squeezed her legs tight and forced both of their movements to stop.

There was no way he was ever letting this woman out of his life again. "Fuck, Beauty, that was the hottest thing I've ever seen."

Her eyes found his, searched him, her emotions visibly close to overwhelming her.

"Turn around," he said with a gentle tug on her hips. "I need to be inside you now."

"Please," she whispered as she turned and placed her hands against the wall, pressing her exposed bottom half toward him.

"Please, what, Beauty?"

"Please fuck me, Jesse. Please," she begged.

He stood behind her and unbuttoned his fly, lowered his zipper, and pushed his pants and boxers down his thighs. With a mind of its own, his dick practically dragged him toward her. "I don't know," he whispered, holding himself back and trailing a finger over her ass, down between her legs. "Maybe you *haven't* been such a good girl. It really wasn't very nice of you to break up with me the way you did. To accuse me of using you but not caring about you." Her legs trembled as he continued to stroke her. "I'm thinking maybe a little punishment is in order."

Her head swiveled, eyes round as she tried to read his expression, the tiniest hint of fear there. "Punish me how?"

He dragged his hand up over her ass cheek and rubbed the soft skin. "This ass would look so fucking good a little bit pink." Before she could either agree or disagree, he landed the flat of his palm against one cheek.

She squeaked and jumped up, rubbing out the spot he just spanked.

"Did I say you could stand up?" he said, loving how she played along with him. "Bend over. Right now."

The pink showed up quickly and his dick was already slick at the top from want of her. Raising his hand, he brought it down with a sharp smack on her other cheek but this time she knew better than to stand up. She whimpered with her hands firmly against the wall.

He couldn't imagine being with anyone else. Thoughts of every other woman he'd ever been with had been completely obliterated by the reality of the life he was prepared to begin with the feisty, sexy, beautiful woman who willingly waited for him to have his way with her.

Who was he to disappoint someone as lovely as that?

"What do you say, Beauty? Are you going to trust me to take care of you from now on? To be there when you need me? To let me help you through the shit you're going through, so you don't have to do it alone?"

She whispered but didn't hesitate. "Yes."

Stepping closer to her, he brushed his fingertips over the slight pink of her ass cheeks. "Good."

With the front of his thighs pressed against the back of her legs, he stopped to run his fingers through her hair, continued down her back until he had her hips firmly gripped in his hands. With one hard thrust he was buried inside her. Using her hips for leverage he drove into her, pounded his body against hers, skin to skin.

His orgasm built quickly, his balls tightened and, in order to not inform the entire party what was happening in Mia's old bedroom, he leaned over her, buried his face in her hair and let go inside of her with a barely contained roar.

Mia

"**O**H, THERE YOU ARE, Sweetheart," her mother said as she and Jesse found seats outside with the rest of the party goers. "I thought you were going to miss the fireworks."

Claire snorted from off to Mia's right. "Pretty sure she already saw some fireworks."

Mia's mother laughed, a look of confusion on her face. Then as she looked from Jesse to Mia, realization dawned, and a furious blush colored her cheeks. "Oh!"

"Seriously, Auntie? You're killing me right now," Mia teased as she settled between Jesse's legs on the blanket they'd brought from the house. She felt his laughter as she leaned against his chest, then settled in to watch fireworks with the rest of her family.

As the pops and booms of the brightly colored explosions filled the inky night sky, Mia leaned her head back and placed a kiss on Jesse's chin.

"Thanks," he said, returning the kiss on her forehead.

"I love you so much," she said and watched the reflection of the bright red firework explosion in his eyes. Immediately, he shifted focus from the sky to her face.

"Are you being serious right now?"

"I couldn't be more serious," she said. "But if you don't feel the same, it's—"

She didn't have time to finish her thought as Jesse tipped her body and kissed her deeply in front of everyone she knew. She had no idea how many of them could see her but then her initial discomfort was quickly displaced by an overwhelming warmth that washed through her and over her. She could not have cared less who could see them kissing.

His arms cinched tighter and he held her fast to his body while he whispered in her ear. "I knew I was in trouble that night you invited me in for dinner," he said. "I looked like I got hit by a truck, and I know I scared the hell out of you, but you took a chance on me anyway." He kissed the side of her neck. "But I knew I was a goner when I got to see you dancing in your kitchen, like no one was watching. But I was, and it was like you were dancing just for me."

Her heart ached at the memory, and how silly she felt dancing in front of him, only to find out that was the moment he truly fell for her.

"It's been a long three weeks without you," she said. "Lots of big things happened and it killed me not to be able to share them with you."

The "ooohs" and "ahhhs" of the gathered crowd made it sound like they were responding to the quiet conversation between Mia and Jesse.

"Tell me now," he said.

"Really? Right here in the middle of a fireworks display?"

"Yep, I don't want to wait. I told you I want to be able to walk through things with you, so the sooner you tell me, the sooner I can do that for you."

Her rapid heartbeat kept time with the explosions in the sky, mimicking how she felt when she was with him. As she shared about her job offer, the offer she put in for the house, as well as the beginning of adoption proceedings for Buttons the Italian greyhound, the pride in her voice was reflected back in the look in his eyes.

"You are amazing, Beauty. I am so proud of you." He kissed her neck as she rested her head against his chest. "I can't wait to take you out to celebrate." One of his hands worked its way under her shirt and he rested it on the skin of her belly. He whispered against her ear, "Then take you back home to keep celebrating... until you can't walk right." His arms were tight around her and his breath warm against her cheek. "Then you get to show me what you've been hiding in that bottom drawer of yours."

Despite the darkness of the night, she was certain everyone could see her face flush beet red. But, held tight and safe in Jesse's arms, nobody else mattered. "Yes, please," she whispered.

The words were ones that sent feelings of exhilaration and anticipation tumbling through her. And in that moment, Mia realized that sometimes, the bravest acts were the quietest ones—the ones whispered in the dark, where hearts beat faster, and the future lay unwritten before them.

$\mathcal{M}ia$

One Year Later

"A M I RIGHT OR am I right?" Jesse asked as he and Mia sat with their feet hanging over the stone wall by the beach. The sun had just peeked over the horizon, blazing the sky in streaks of red and orange while it painted a brilliant gold stripe over the water toward them. "Best way to start the day, or what?"

In the year since they'd gotten back together, Jesse had brought Mia to watch the sunrise every Sunday morning. "Are you sure you're not going to miss this?" he asked, taking hold of her hand, and letting it rest on his leg, then interlacing their fingers.

"Who says we have to stop coming down here?" Her eyes gazed over the familiar stretch of beach.

The house Mia had set her heart on—the one that slipped through her fingers—was now someone else's dream home. But life had a way of working out, and in just three days, she and Jesse would close on a different house, a better house. A house they had chosen together.

The past year had been a whirlwind for both of them. Mia had settled into her role as a full-time school nurse, her days filled with scraped knees, bloody noses, and the occasional heart-to-heart with a worried student. Her social circle had expanded, fueled by shared lunches in the staff room and intentional connection with her coworkers. Even her relationship with her sister had taken a few baby steps forward.

Jesse's journey had taken unexpected turns too. Shadowing his brother Seth on construction sites had confirmed what he suspected: he wasn't cut out for the family business. Instead, he split his time between teaching classes, coaching the up and coming guys at the gym, and working toward an exercise science degree with an eye toward physical therapy. Occasionally, he would pick up shifts with his family doing manual labor on some of the job sites for extra money

And then there were their stolen moments. Friday nights still belonged to Jesse's training, but Mia had carved out her own tradition. Going with coworkers down to York's Landing, with its familiar pool tables and the chatter of a busy bar and restaurant, became one of the highlights of her week. She'd laugh with her friends, sip cold beer, and occasionally stay for dinner.

"Yeah? You won't mind having to get in the car to come watch the sunrise?" Jesse asked.

"Won't mind it a bit," she said, leaning over to kiss the scar on his cheek.

With a laugh, he said, "Why do you always do that?"

"Do what?"

"Kiss my scar."

The brilliance of the rising sun shone out in every direction and Mia's eyes were drawn to it like a moth to a flame. There was something primal about watching the sun coming up over the ocean while sitting next to Jesse. Everything was exactly how it was supposed to be.

The scar was a reminder of their beginning but it was also a testament to resilience and healing. "If it wasn't for that scar, I never would have met you. If you didn't need my help on the bus that night, none of this would have ever happened." She shivered at the thought of living her life without Jesse beside her.

"I don't believe that," he said, his voice quiet. "I think what we have was meant to be, no matter how it came about." He was quiet, thoughtful for a few seconds as he stared out over the water. "Even if we took a different route to get here, we still would have ended up right here, right now."

Jesse turned her hand over, letting the sunlight reflect off the blue sapphire in the center of her ring. "This right here," he said, lifting her hand to his lips and placing a soft kiss on her knuckles, "was absolutely meant to happen."

Sometimes, Jesse's softer side still surprised her. For a person with a hard body, even now that his professional training days had ended, his gentleness was one of her favorite things about him. At least, outside of the bedroom it was.

As she leaned into him, she whispered, "I love you, Jesse."

He turned to her, his eyes warm and sincere. "That may be true, Beauty," he said, "but not nearly as much as I love you."

Her heart swelled. Jesse's words were sweet, but there was no way on earth they were true. It wasn't that she doubted his love; it was just that her emotions for him were so big, they often bordered on overwhelming.

By the time they made it to Harbor View Café for breakfast, Mia's mind had turned back to wedding planning. She sipped her coffee to wash down a bite of scramble eggs. "Your mom added a few people to the invite list." Spinning her phone so he could see the email from Gaelen, she smiled from behind her coffee mug as Jesse's eyes bugged out.

"A few people?" he said as he scrolled through the list. "That's half the people that live in this town."

"Are you OK with all those people?" she asked.

He put her phone down, looked her in the eye, and said, "Beauty, as long as at the end of the day, you're my wife... I don't care if there's one person there or one million. Makes no difference to me. And as long as you're happy, I'm happy." He poached a fried potato from her plate. "Do all these people being there make you happy?"

She thought about the expanded guest list, some of whom she didn't know from Adam. But then people like their friend Lexi Greeves were on the list. And Sister Mary Ellen, whom she hadn't seen since the night she and Jesse met on the bus. Even Maggie Bowman, Gaelen's new Office Manager, and Phoebe Blake, Gaelen's assistant, were listed. And Mia wanted them all there to celebrate with her and Jesse.

Nodding, because her throat was clogged with emotion over the extended friends and family she could now call her own, she finally managed to squeak out, "Yes."

"Jesse, can you feed Buttons and Shamrock for me?" Mia yelled from the bedroom later that afternoon. "I just hopped out of the shower, and I realized I haven't fed them yet."

"Absolutely," he said, popping his head into the bedroom. "But I want to see you naked first."

With a laugh, she tried to shoo him out. "There's no time for that now," she said. "You still need to take a shower so we can get to The Landing on time."

Jesse dodged her hands as she tried to push him out the door. "Beauty, there is *always* time for this." Scooping her in his arms, he carried her to the bed where he laid her down, covered her naked body with his fully clothed one, and kissed her breathless.

Then, while Jesse went back to the kitchen to feed the dogs, she lay there, eyes closed, missing the warmth and weight of his body, wishing the Jack and Jill was another hour later, at least.

Luckily, her landlord had been gracious in letting Jesse move in with the dogs when the offer on the first house had fallen through, even though her adoption of Buttons went off without a hitch. As did the adoption of a scruffy little mutt Jesse fell in love with when they went to pick up the petite greyhound.

It helped that they'd finally found a house and would be moving out soon, but still she appreciated the understanding.

By the time Jesse showered and dressed for the party, she had finished doing her hair and makeup. He stood behind her and held her gaze in the mirror, a fresh bouquet of daisies on the bureau. "I'm a lucky man, Beauty" he murmured, his voice tender as it slid over her body. "How the hell did I ever get you to be mine?" He brushed her hair back over her shoulder, then trailed his hands down to rest gently on her belly.

They were stitching together a life—one that promised shared sunrises on the beach, laughter-filled celebrations with the people they loved, and nights wrapped in each other's arms.

She tilted her head, her expression playful. "Well, I made you fight for it," she teased, "and then I still cut you loose. Somehow, though, you were able to get past all my stuff and give us another try." Squeezing his arms tighter around her, she said, "So, I guess the real question is, how did I ever get you to take me back?"

His lips brushed against her ear, his breath warm. "That's easy," he said. "You let me bend you over and spank you, then take you against a wall."

Her laughter bubbled up, filling the room. She turned in his arms, hugging him tightly. "That's all it took?"

He leaned down, capturing her lips in a kiss that spoke of promises kept and futures intertwined. "Well," he said, pulling away just enough to meet her eyes, "it was partly that, and partly the fact that you still dance in front of me and don't stop when you know I'm watching."

In that moment of shared laughter, their hearts swayed to an unspoken rhythm; a rhythm of sparks that had ignited the instant their eyes met on a cold spring night. It was more than attraction; it was an unavoidable collision of souls.

But their story was more than chance encounters and fleeting sparks. It was about the deliberate choice to weave their lives together, stitch by stitch, creating something enduring—a love that would weather storms and light up even the darkest nights.

The End

I hope you enjoyed Jesse and Mia's story and your introduction to the Murphy Family and the town and residents of Oak Harbor.

As an indie author, reader reviews are so important. If you liked this book, would you mind taking a minute and leaving a rating and/or review on your favorite site? It would mean the world to me!

I would love to have you come along on the ride with me, staying up to date on my writing, release dates, and other assorted writerly things. Join the *Whispers and Works in Progress* mailing list and hang out with me every couple weeks. (Link is available at eabradyauthor.com)

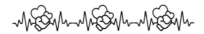

Get ready to meet Maggie and Sean in ***Barstools and Beginnings***, coming fall, 2024

When single mom Maggie Bowman accepted the position as the new Office Manager for Murphy Construction Company, she had no idea how her life was about to change.

Working for Gaelen Murphy means being included in all things Murphy-family-related, including the upcoming wedding of Gaelen's youngest son, Jesse.

Little does Maggie know, everybody knows everybody in Oak Harbor. And the sexy bar owner she meets at Jesse and Mia's Jack and

Jill party shows up when she least expects it, throwing her completely off-kilter.

But can Maggie keep her heart safe from Sean's charms? Will she give him the chance to prove that they could be something truly special?

Barstools and Beginnings is a blend of romance, family dynamics, and unexpected connections. Fall in love with Maggie and Sean as they navigate the twists and turns of life, love, and the Murphy family. Mark your calendars for this sexy tale—it's a story you won't want to miss!

Acknowledgements

Like any creative endeavor, a story comes from a place of inspiration. While I often gain inspiration from beautiful places, more often, I find it in the people all around me on the daily.

To Steve – You are an amazing husband and the biggest cheerleader I have. Because of how hard you work for us, I can do what I do—spend my days writing stories about made-up people doing all kinds of things! Thank you for being willing to take random road trips to scout out possible locations for my books!

To my kids – Thank you for keeping me young, while constantly reminding me that I'm not! I'm so proud of you both and being your mom is the best job and greatest adventure I've ever had.

To Devin – Thank you for introducing me to the art of eight limbs, turning every class I've taken since into my own personal Muay Thai class. Without you, the fighting details of this story would be mere fiction. You unraveled the mysterious world of combat sports for me by teaching me the language, the skills, and the mental side of what you do. (You also taught me how to not fall down after taking a liver kick—lol!) I am forever grateful.

To my Girls – Thank you for supporting me and believing in me and encouraging me to do this. We've known each other for a long time and having friends like you is a treasure and a gift. I love each of you!

To Meghan – Oh my goodness – how do I even thank you?! Your input into this story made it exponentially better and gave Mia the steps toward closure that she needed. Thank you, thank you, thank you!

About the Author

Despite spending my first few years in New York, I consider myself a New Englander, through and through. My stories are set in fictionalized versions of several of my favorite New England locations and my characters are "real" people who are trying their hardest to make it through to their very own happily ever after.

When I'm not working on new stories, I spend my time working on my Muay Thai round kicks and trying to perfect my left hook. I live in a 130-year-old (haunted?) house with my husband, two amazing kids, and two spoiled tabby cats. I wouldn't have it any other way.

Find out more at eabradyauthor.com

Also by E.A. Brady

Berkshire Romance Series

One Week at the Faraway Inn
Picture Me Yours
Christmas at Whispering Hills

9 798990 479708